SO-BDO-101

Gift of Truth

Fiction
Fleming, Robert, 1950-
Gift of truth
[02/14]

Gift of Truth

Robert Fleming

www.urbanchristianonline.com

Urban Books, LLC
97 N18th Street
Wyandanch, NY 11798

Gift of Truth Copyright © 2014 Robert Fleming

All rights reserved. No part of this book may be re-
produced in any form or by any means without prior
consent of the Publisher, excepting brief quotes used
in reviews.

ISBN 13: 978-1-60162-711-7
ISBN 10: 1-60162-711-4

First Printing February 2014
Printed in the United States of America

10 9 8 7 6 5 4 3 2 1

*This is a work of fiction. Any references or similarities
to actual events, real people, living or dead, or to real
locales are intended to give the novel a sense of reality. Any similarity in other names, characters, places,
and incidents is entirely coincidental.*

Distributed by Kensington Corp.
Submit Wholesale Orders to:
Kensington Publishing Corp.
C/O Penguin Group (USA) Inc.
Attention: Order Processing
405 Murray Hill Parkway
East Rutherford, NJ 07073-2316
Phone: 1-800-526-0275
Fax: 1-800-227-9604

Gift of Truth

Robert Fleming

"And when he putteth forth his own sheep, he goeth before then, and the sheep follow him; for they know his voice."

– John 10:4

In appreciation of my father, Robert Fleming Sr., whose valiant life in the Deep South is reflected in these pages.

ACKNOWLEDGMENTS

This book was made possible by the support and guidance of Joylynn M. Ross of Urban Christian. She has proven to be a good friend and an effective editor.

To Donna Johnson, who keeps me going when I falter. Her love and courage are exceptional.

To the nation's black farmers, who are struggling to maintain control of their rich, fertile land against all odds.

To my readers, who support me while keeping me on my toes.

To Elissa Gabrielle, the Queen of the Beloveds and CEO at Peace in the Storm Publishing.

Thanks to Thea and the folks at Black Christian Book Promo for their fine promotional help.

And to God, whose blessings in my life are beyond measure.

1

GIVE OF YOURSELF

For dust thou art, and unto dust shall thou return.

That was what the Bible said. But I wondered that maybe there was no beginning or end. Maybe it was this thing where a person started breathing in the middle of his days, in the middle of his life journey to the grave. Hopefully, all these hours, days, weeks, months, and years were helping me know myself better. All I realized about my life thus far was that it was about compromise, loss, and persistence.

What life meant, what time meant, what destiny meant, I didn't know anything about any of it. But then, nobody knew.

A few months before my wife killed herself and the kids, she pressed a gun to my head and smiled like she knew a secret. I didn't know there were two bullets in the chamber when she laughed and pulled the trigger twice. I peed on myself from the fear.

"Just fooling, baby. Just fooling." She giggled.

Any person who comes close to mortality, close to dying, changes drastically. That *day* I made a deal with the Creator that if I survived this crazy woman, I would do something to make my life worthy of Him saving it. I meant that. I meant to keep my end of the bargain. I would cut all the fat and the waste out of my life, and trim my existence to the bare essentials.

"Why are you such a Goody Two-shoes?" my wife once asked. "Did you ever consider that you might be doing all this good stuff and die and find out it was all a waste? How would you deal with that?"

I had no answer for her. I had no answer for her until after she had committed her crime. I kept my dead wife and children in my heart, in a stainless-steel lockbox of memories in my soul, so they were alive still. There was no human death, much like Christ and his crucifixion.

After this last epiphany, I wanted to go into hiding, but something wouldn't let me. I knew I had done the right thing. Nobody had to tell me that. It was important for me to cut myself off from all the church folks, remove myself from the rituals and practices that would trap me in the comfort of the holy community. The ruckus with the Dr. Smart scandal sparked up for a moment, blazed in the local media, and then it died when some loony tune tried to drive a car loaded with explosives into a college cafeteria.

Nobody could forgive Dr. Smart for stealing church funds to aid his family. Nobody, myself included, could excuse him for betraying the members of his congregation. He was a liar and a thief. However, I couldn't bear a grudge against him for what he tried to make me do, to use my charms to get the rich widow to pour cash into his pockets.

Far from New York City, I rented a cottage that fall and attempted to wrap myself in a warm jacket of a sunnier outlook. Gratitude was not lost on me. I felt grateful for so many things. I counted my blessings as if I were a man on my last days. Terminally ill. I kept a diary during this time, a lesson that I learned from the Christian sage Thomas Merton, and reviewed its entries periodically. Rather than thinking about what was going wrong with my life, I realized there was more going right than I ever knew.

I learned not to rush about so much, to relax. One of the things I did was to walk into town, taking my time, going at a leisurely pace, with no deadline. On afternoons, I would fish or read or just sit in the high grass and nibble sandwiches and wash them down with ginger ale. It was a good life. There was something to be said about making time for yourself.

One of my cousins called me up there and asked me what I was doing. Was I getting bored with myself?

"No, I just cut everything off and vegetate," I replied.

He told me Reverend Peck was trying to find me. "He sounded very hectic, real nervous," my cousin said. "I didn't tell him where you were. I haven't told anybody. They were trying to pry it out of me, but I refused to tell them."

"Good for you," I said. "Wonder what he wanted."

"Didn't say."

I stared at the flame, blue and mysterious, in the fireplace, in the dark, and said he could give him my number. "But nobody else. Understand me?"

"I got it. Nobody else." His voice was firm. I knew he wouldn't tell. My secret was safe with him.

"Did anybody else ask about me?" I asked him.

My cousin sighed. "If you mean that woman you were running around with, I think she's forgotten you and gone on to somebody else. Women sometimes have very short attention spans."

I was a little miffed. "I don't believe you."

"I saw her at church with some other fella, well dressed, hair all done up, really spiffy professional guy," he said. "I don't think she's worried about you anymore. I imagine this guy has moved you right out of the picture."

A painful moment of silence. I cleared my throat before talking again about the importance of Reverend Peck's call to me at my hideaway.

After hanging up the phone, I wondered whether I had any more dreams or desires. When I was a young boy, I remembered, an old woman, a Creole seer, snatched my little hand and told me I possessed an old soul. Furthermore, I was probably a pagan, a heathen in another life. I had sinned against the elders, disobeyed the ancestors, and that taint, that curse, was still with me.

That didn't make sense to me then. And it didn't make sense now.

"Did God tell you how to see the future?" I asked her loudly as a crowd surrounded us. "Did you go to school for your magic?"

She waved her hand like she was shooing a fly. "Go on now."

"Where did you get your training, ma'am?" I asked her at the top of my voice. Some of the people laughed at my question.

"I'm finished with you," the old woman replied harshly. "You got all the answers I can give you. Go on now and let somebody else come forward."

I was eight and very stubborn. "I just want to know how you know all these things. Did God teach you?"

Now the crowd was roaring with laughter and pointing at her like she was the faker they knew she was. The old woman offered me a handful of coins, and when I didn't take them, she shoved me to the floor. A couple of spectators picked me up, brushed me off, and led me from the tent.

A woman put her hand on my shoulder and smiled. "Boy, you had her pegged. She couldn't fool you. You're a smart little guy."

I grinned. I didn't know if I was all that smart.

"Little fella, you saw right through her," the man with her said, walking with me across the carnival grounds. "Are you here with your parents? They must be worried about you."

I thanked them. "I live near here. I know my way home."

Home. One thing Dr. Smart told me that was true. And he'd added that everyone wanted to find their home in this life. His version of home was a place of comfort, belonging, and purpose. Everybody arrived in this life with a purpose. That purpose gave meaning to our life.

"That's a crock." That was what my cousin said when I told him Dr. Smart's beliefs about preordained purpose. My cousin didn't believe any of this stuff. He didn't believe in the afterlife. He didn't believe in Christ. He didn't believe in God or heaven. He didn't believe in a meaning to this life.

"I think that's why you drink," I'd told him. "You must believe in *something.* Everything is here to serve a purpose. Everything."

As I was thinking of my cousin's worthless nature, the meaning and purpose of life, and Dr. Smart's comment long ago on the significance of the Four Horsemen of the Apocalypse, the phone rang in the hallway.

I stood there, looking out the window, while it continued to ring. The answering machine picked up the message. It was the urgent voice of Reverend Peck. Something was really getting under his skin.

2

AND YET SUBTLE

As I watched the afternoon news on the ancient black-and-white Admiral television, the image on the screen was of two Filipino fishermen holding a long net between them, wading into foamy water with hundreds and hundreds of dead fish surrounding them.

I thought of a conversation I had with the postman, a gaunt white man who delivered mail. He had talked about our choice to deplete the earth and how we were reaping the consequences of our decisions. Greed and profits.

"You never saw the rich farmland in the country bake like it is now," he'd said, handing me a bunch of letters. "We're screwing things up. We got everything out of balance."

I had taken the mail from him and smiled. "I guess so."

"Look at how the oil companies messed up the water in the Gulf, down there off Louisiana and Florida," he'd hollered over his shoulder. "That place'll never be the same again."

My steps took me right onto the porch and then back into the house just as the phone rang. I knew who it was right away. If Reverend Hickory Peck possessed any of the exceptional qualities of a man of God, he was quite punctual and prompt. My cousin's call had triggered a quick response from him, and no doubt, he'd lay out the nature of the emergency. What was going on? Why did he need my help so urgently?

It was his voice, worn-out and quite stressed, that worried me. "Thank God I found you. I thought you had vanished from civilization. Nobody knew where you were. Literally nobody."

My laugh carried less drama than his words. "Reverend Peck, I'm in the witness protection program. I'm hiding out."

"Are you really?" He pretended to believe me.

"No, not really. What's happening with you?"

I could hear his sharp intake of air into his tired lungs. He was thinking about how he would put the problem to me in such a way that I would not bolt or panic. I had no tendency to do either. The reverend had been a true, loyal friend throughout the Dr. Smart crisis, and I owed him big-time.

"I'm in trouble with the church and the congregation," the reverend began. "While I was going around, trying to make spiritual connections to benefit the church, a snake slithered into our midst and is poisoning the members against me and the spiritual community that I've built."

"Those are some serious charges, Reverend," I said.

"Well, it's true. Something is wrong with our tabernacle," he replied. "We worked so hard to get this church strong and powerful in our tradition of faith. Now, with this new assistant, everything is going bad. The church is turning its back on God, turning its back on the holy scripture."

"Are you sure?" I asked. He seemed very worked up about all of this.

His words came in a long string of emotion, desperate and needy. "My son, God was always in this place, a very holy place, a very blessed place, and that has all changed. The congregation has hardened their hearts. He has taken over their minds with this crazy talk."

"Like what?" I was curious about what could scare him like this.

"God and a strong sense of faith were all our elders had when they built our church," he said proudly. "They were God-sent people who worked hard, who worshipped hard, who praised the Lord hard. That community there in Alabama was one big family. Going to church and praising the Lord was in their blood. In fact, going to worship was sometimes the only time we all got together. Everything was tied up with the church."

"A lot of places used to be like that in our communities," I suggested. "Now some of that is going away, fading."

I heard the memories wash over him as he recalled the golden ole-timey moments when the neighbors were neighborly and didn't act like the way they did now. Now the folks acted real cold and apart from everything, remote from the warm feeling of community. The community of yesterday could be counted on to do the right thing. He gave a chuckle like he was reliving it right that instant.

"I used to give supplies to poor families there in the area, cheese, cornmeal, rice, flour, and sugar," he said, remembering. "Big bags, huge bags of it. Yes sir, we'd ride through the fields, through the neighboring towns and villages in flatbed trucks and give the stuff out. The folks were grateful to get it. I'd be right out there, with my overalls and big-brim hat and work gloves. Hot as heck out in the sun. Sweating like a field hand, tossing bags off the truck."

There was a fly in the ointment. Who was he? I asked him about the snake who slithered into the church, among the pews.

"This is what is troublesome," he said, deepening his voice to add emphasis. "We hired this Negro from up North, around Boston way. Somebody said he went to school at Union Theological Seminary in New York City, worked as a counselor for the city's corrections department, taking on some of the hardest cases on Rikers Island, and was a spokesman for the state representative. Good credentials."

"What is the problem, Reverend?"

"The guy, this Lamar Wilks, has got an agenda that is counter to the traditional ways of our church," he said with a snarl. "The deacon board hired him as an interim pastor because I was going off in all directions, trying to get funding and contacts to make our church stronger. He's got them all hoodwinked."

"Do you still have the support of most of the members?" I asked.

He swallowed again. "Some are for me. Some are not. But most people are supporting me, but that's dwindling. The young man's power is growing. He talks about everything but the Bible itself. He talks a lot about certain political and social issues to uneducated members, who really don't understand him. This junk has nothing to do with the saving of souls."

"And you say his influence is growing?"

The reverend snorted harshly. "He uses big, ten-dollar words. That sways the young folks every time. But you can see most of them are puzzled by him."

"Oh, really?" I was stunned he was so threatened by this Wilks.

"We wrote a blueprint for the church, where it was going, where it was leading the community," he said.

"He's got white folks involved with the church for the first time. One of his teams got some crackers with money from Atlanta, Charlotte, Winston-Salem, and Raleigh. White money is just pouring into the place."

I wanted a cigarette so bad. "It sounds like the boy has juice."

The reverend wasn't buying it. "A lot of the old-timers are nervous about getting all these white folks mixed into our business. They think these crackers gon' to turn on this Wilks fella. They think some of his trickeration gon' to put poor white folks and poor black folks at each other's throats."

"What do you think he's up to?" I quizzed him.

"Heck if I know," he said, adamant. "But I know he's up to no good. There's something evil about him. The devil is in him, sho' 'nuff."

The American South. Dixie. I'd always got scared when I thought too much about it. We, as a family, had taken two trips down there, one to Memphis and another to Biloxi, Mississippi. The Biloxi trip was the one that had frightened me. Any colored boy knew what Mississippi represented: race hate, lynching, the Klan, the eyes lowered when a white person passed, and stupid Jim Crow laws. It was a little better now.

He laughed slightly. "One of the Northern newspapers interviewed him when he first came down here, and the members thought he was a big shot. I always thought he paid for the publicity. There was something about him belonging to some committee that spearheaded the rebuilding campaign of fifty black churches that had been burned during the mid-1990s. You'd have thought he was a Rockefeller or a Roosevelt or somebody with the way he carried on. He was an instant celebrity."

"So he has a big head, Reverend?"

He laughed again, a mocking laugh. "The biggest."

I scratched my head. "I don't know what he's up to."

"Something no-good."

I made my voice pleasant. "How are you holding up?"

"Clint, I feel all right. But I'm on my knees every night concerning him, carrying his name to the Lord. If Mr. Wilks is up to devilment, I want to be ready for it. Prayer can prepare you for anything."

Yes, prayer could make a big difference. There was no situation that existed in life that wasn't covered in the Good Book.

The reverend was turning the pages in his Bible, preparing to read me some of the verses with which he was arming himself. Something in the Holy Word about wickedness, something in there about evil.

"When I get a chill running along my spine, I read a part of Psalm thirty-seven, and it subdues the dark forces," he revealed. "Do you know the passage that I'm talking about?"

I told him yes. It was written by David, the same David who hurled a rock at the temple of the mighty Goliath. The Psalms were some of the finest poetry in the Bible, capable of soothing a troubled spirit.

He started reading the first verse. "Fret not thyself because of evildoers, neither be thou envious against the workers of iniquity."

His voice was perfect for reading scripture, mellow and easy on the ears. He sounded like one of those silky-voiced announcers on an R & B radio station.

"For they shall soon be cut down like the grass, and wither as the green herb," the reverend continued. "The wicked plotteth against the just, and gnasheth upon him with his teeth." The reverend was starting to get revved up.

"Amen, brother."

Reverend Peck went on. "The Lord laughs at him, for He sees his day is coming."

"Teach, brother. Teach!" I was egging him on. He needed to get it out of his system. The nasty taste of insult and humiliation.

He was reaching his crescendo, his apex of emotion. "Fret not thyself because of him who prospereth in his way, because of the man who bringeth wicked devices to pass."

"I love the Psalms," I commented to him.

"But this is the kicker in the scripture," Reverend Peck said in an exulted voice. "This is where God gives a remedy. This is where He teaches wisdom to the faithful."

"What is that?" I knew that part of the Psalms well. I just wanted him to read it. I wanted him to get emotional relief from the passage.

The reverend made his speech quiet and important. "Cease from anger, and forsake wrath: fret not thyself in any wise to do evil."

We both laughed on that solemn note.

He waited for me to finish sniggering, and then he asked the question I knew was in his heart. It was a question, a request that I knew I must obey.

"So, my son, when are you coming here?" he asked very seriously. "I need your help. I cannot do this by myself."

3
DEVOTION

Solitude. A flock of starlings and crows circled above the grove of elm, oak, and sycamore trees surrounding the small house. Needing a break from the all-consuming silence, I walked into the woods, feeling the brisk breeze, my steps crushing the dried leaves of red, copper, and gold. That crunching sound temporarily drowned out my romance with silence and solitude, a welcome moment away from reading from my Bible, dipping into my favorite articles from a stacks of books and magazines.

As I strolled through the beauty of nature, I whispered my prayers to let the Lord guide me through my return to the city. When I came here, I was suffering from nervous exhaustion, worn out from the betrayal of the Smart scandal and the smashing of everything I knew.

Once I had my fill of the wilderness, I returned home and thought about how cold and snowy this place would be with the onset of winter, the roads frozen and icy. I had to make up my mind about whether I would stay here when the frost arrived or risk the madness of city life and get back in the rut of the religious routine.

The phone rang as I saw a deer run across the field near my window. Do I really need to answer the reverend's call? Do I want anything to jar me out of my serenity?

"Hello, hello," I said before the person spoke up.

It was Orville, my cousin, the only link to civilization. "Hey, Clint. Did he call? I told him what you said. Did he call you?"

"Yes, he did, but what he was asking me . . . well . . ." I was thinking about Reverend Peck's request and the urgency of his plea to come down there and sort things out.

"What did the reverend ask you?" my cousin asked.

I sighed. "He wants me to come to Alabama. He's got some trouble with his church, and he wants to get to the bottom of it. It sounded like he was desperate, as if something was gnawing away at him."

"Are you going to go down there?" He was prying.

"I don't know." That was the truth. I still hadn't decided yet.

"Well, this isn't the reason for my call," my cousin said with that curious tone he sometimes reserved for serious business. "I didn't want to call you with this bad news. You've got enough going on without worrying about something else."

"What is it?" I could take anything.

"Clint, I know how much you love Aunt Spivey," he began with a slow rhythm. "The folks at the senior center say she wandered away from the place and got herself into a bit of a fight. They don't know whether she was beaten or robbed or what."

"Was she hurt? Was she hurt badly?" I didn't want to hear this.

My cousin took his time telling me the sad tale about how my aunt vanished from the center late Thursday night and was not found until early Monday morning. A truck driver delivering the *New York Times* newspapers to neighborhood stores discovered her standing in a parking lot, battered and bruised.

"We were looking for her everywhere," he said. "Her daughter called the police, and an alert was sent out. She was nowhere to be found. Then I got the call that she was over at the hospital, and when I saw her, I broke down and cried. It was like somebody had just teed off on her face and pounded the crap out of her. She looked like she had been in the ring with Ali in his prime."

I swallowed bitterly while I pictured the little, frail brown-skinned woman, with her face smashed to a pulp, in a hospital bed. It was an insensitive world that would pummel an old woman just for the fun of it. Her daughter had suddenly appeared out of nowhere, but I was glad to have her there .

"Did she have any money on her?" I asked him.

"When I talked to her, she couldn't remember any of it, the wandering off or the beating," my cousin said sadly. "I kept after the center officials about how she could just walk off without them knowing it. She was supposed to have twenty-four-hour supervision. You cannot let a woman who is in poor health go off without anybody knowing where she is."

"How long has she been acting like this?" She was always so alert, so thoughtful. This was not like her.

"Her social worker said Aunt Spivey refused to eat or take her medications," he replied. "She was becoming unruly. I talked to her daughter, and she said they wanted to push her out. They wanted her to leave the center because she was becoming a problem. They can't control her."

"Aunt Spivey never causes problems," I said, surprised.

My cousin was reliving the nights she was missing. "When she, her daughter, that is, called me and said she was missing from the center, we spent hours and hours trying to figure out where she could have gone. We called the center, but all they said was our relative has not been located yet. I called a detective who I knew back in the day, and he said they had spotted her on a security camera leaving the grounds."

"Where did they search when they found out she was gone?"

"They scoured the neighborhood around the center and the shops near the train station," he said. "The detective vowed they would find her, and he sent me good wishes for her safe return. I was hoping they wouldn't find her dead in a vacant lot."

He heard my agonizing exhale, for she was one of the people I loved the most in this life. Why did she run away? What bad news had she received from her doctors? Also, why hadn't her family kept closer tabs on her well-being?

"What did the center tell you after they found her?" I asked him sourly. "Did they apologize? Did her daughter say they said they were sorry for her disappearance?"

"No, they didn't," my cousin insisted. "These people in these places are out only for the money. If you can pay, they do everything for you. But if anything goes awry, they treat you like you're nothing. That's how they treated our aunt Spivey."

Without thinking, I said I was going down there. I needed to see Aunt Spivey. I needed to show her that I had not forgotten how much she meant to me. I told my cousin that I would drive down there tomorrow. Maybe we could get together for dinner after I saw how she was.

***

Driving down to the city, I always thought about how traffic was heaviest in the evening, cars and trucks and buses lined up in a slow-motion parade into the tunnels. I resisted leaning on my horn. A driver's patience was sorely tested when he took to New York highways, enduring the stop-and-go pace, the sudden aggressiveness of speeders, and the manic cell phone crazies.

At the parking lot of the senior center, I checked to see how tight security was near the entrance. I noticed two groups of uniformed guards on patrol near the fence and among the cars. There was a checkpoint with a person monitoring the comings and goings of cars from the facility, communicating with the office on the whereabouts of patients and personnel. I couldn't imagine how Aunt Spivey could just walk away.

I talked to security about the mystery of my aunt, inquiring whether the alarm about her disappearance had been sounded in a timely manner, whether everything had been done to search for her.

"Sometimes people don't want to be found," one of the security guys said confidentially. "We don't usually lose many of them. But sometimes one or two of them slip past us."

"When did you get the call to search for her?" I asked.

"I wasn't here," the security man replied. "That's not my shift."

"I see," I answered, starting to walk away.

"Come back tomorrow and you'll get all the facts you want," he said. "My partner will be in, and he knows more about the case than I do. Tell him Emory said to cooperate. He'll be forthcoming about everything, probably more than you'd get from the front office."

I got in my car and went to my Harlem apartment. Nobody knew I was there, so I had a restful night's sleep. After brewing myself a cup of peppermint tea, I listened to Ella and Basie perform a couple old Broadway tunes on the CD player. Then I conked out.

That next morning, I showered, shaved, and brushed my teeth. My routine was to get a cup of black coffee, two pieces of wheat toast, read the newspaper, and go out for a walk. That was not the case today. I headed to the hospital to see Aunt Spivey. Waiting for visiting hours to begin, I checked in with the receptionist and sat for the few minutes, until it was time.

Aunt Spivey was sitting up on the edge of the bed when I walked in the door. A nurse, a pretty little Latina, dabbed make-up on her busted nose. Both of her eyes were blackened, and she had scratches on her left cheek and a busted lip. A square had been cut in her hair in the middle of her head, where a long scabbed wound sat.

"She's also got bruised ribs and a fractured wrist," the nurse whispered to me. "It looks like somebody wanted to hurt her real bad. She doesn't remember any of the ordeal. Maybe that's best."

My aunt tried to rise but couldn't make it. "I thought the front desk was going to announce you. I'm a mess. I look the worst for wear."

"No, you don't," I said, leaning over to kiss her cheek.

I motioned to the nurse, letting her know I wanted to talk to her in the hallway, and she pulled a pink robe on my frail aunt before joining me outside the door. She shook her head sadly before speaking.

"What happened to her?" I couldn't believe it.

"All we know is somebody, a newspaper truck driver, found your aunt wandering in a parking lot," the nurse said in a hushed tone. "He found her in the same battered condition that she was in when she was brought to the hospital. She doesn't know what happened. She doesn't know who beat her. We think she suffered traumatic memory loss as a result of this incident."

"Will she get that part of her memory back?" The news was getting worse. I didn't want to hear any of this.

"Did you know about her receiving a recent diagnosis of dementia?"

I knew my aunt had been undergoing some kind of medical treatment, such as blood work and pills, but that was it. My aunt was not the kind to share any weakness. If you asked her about her health, she was always hale and hearty.

"No, I didn't," I replied.

"That's not all," the nurse went on. "I guess her daughter told you that she has cancer, a serious case but not life threatening. They're giving her chemo. That's why her hair is falling out."

I had noticed how short her hair was. I had concluded it was stress, nerves.

"How often does her daughter visit her?" I wanted to find out whether she was genuinely concerned, and not just waiting to cash in on the insurance and the old lady's property.

"Oh, yes, Natalie has been here every day since she's been in the hospital," she answered. "I think she cares a great deal for your aunt."

I thanked her, smiling, and went back into the room. Aunt Spivey was propped up, watching one of her game shows, *The Price Is Right,* which the guy from Cleveland was hosting. A couple was hopping up and down, screaming over a brand-new car with the sound off.

I crossed the room and lovingly squeezed her shoulder. "I missed my favorite aunt. You've got to take care of yourself. I mean it."

She giggled. "It took a butt whupping for you to come to see me. I thought you liked me."

"You know I love you," I said, pulling up a chair.

"Funny thing, I don't remember none of it too clearly," my aunt sighed. "All I know is I was in a parking lot and my face felt like it was on fire. Some nice man in a truck called the police, and then I landed up in here."

"Do you know how you got in the parking lot?"

She shrugged a shoulder, like it was hurt or something. "Not really. They'll tell you I ran away from the center. I wanted to get out of that place. See, they want to say something is wrong with my head. I don't believe them when they say I'm suffering from dementia. Nothing is wrong with my mind."

"I can see that," I agreed. "But they say you've got cancer too."

"That's what the docs say, but they don't know anything," she said defiantly. "I got tired of the chemo and the other pills. I wasn't hungry, and they couldn't make me eat. I just wanted to get out."

"You sound like you're throwing in the towel," I said. "That's not like you. You've always been a fighter. That's what I have always loved about you."

She turned the sound higher on the TV, making it a little louder, so I could barely make out what she was saying. "I made out my will last year."

"What is all this talk about dying?" I didn't like it.

"I always wanted to die quickly and quietly, like in a sudden car crash or with something falling on my head." She spoke slowly with her eyes closed. "But this slow, lingering death is horrible. Sometimes I see death standing at the foot of the bed."

"Don't talk like that, please." I was almost pleading with her.

"I'm tired of doctors poking and prodding me," she whined. "I'm tired of medicines, doctors, nurses, and hospital rooms. Eat this. Eat that. I'm tired of getting up one step to health and then sliding to another setback. I can't do anything for myself anymore. I can't even dress myself. I'm all thumbs. It's horrible."

"Stop this talk. Please stop." I wished I could shut her up.

She laughed a low, dry laugh. "I remember something my mother scribbled in a book about death, a little note. 'Death is a sleep and a forgetting. You will never know that you are dead.'"

"Where did all of this morbid chatter come from?" I asked.

"I've been thinking about things," she said, keeping her eyes closed. "I've been thinking about life. It's a sacred gift. We haven't done anything to deserve it. Such a glorious gift."

"I know, Auntie," I said. "I think about my wife and my kids out there in the ground. I know it's precious."

Her eyes opened, and she stared at me. "Do you think about heaven? Whether or not it exists?"

"I think about it sometimes," I replied. "But I try to follow the righteous path so I can deserve it. Temptations are many and so powerful. I have to keep on the straight and the narrow."

"So you should as a man of God," she said, rubbing her cheek. "But you should think about the big questions too. Heaven, I can't imagine it. As much as I try, I can't see heaven. My sweet mama used to say that heaven is where you would see everybody you knew and loved, where angels would be lounging, where the Almighty would be a constant visitor. I can't see it. Can you, Clint?"

"I don't know." This was getting heavy for me.

"I mean, really. Heaven as a divine reward?" she asked.

I chuckled. "I really don't know. I know nobody has ever come back from there and given us a report. But as a Christian, I just have to take it as a part of my faith. I can't question it."

The old woman sat up. "Do you believe in God?"

"Yes," I quickly replied. "God got me through some very difficult times. You know what I mean. We prayed together through part of the hard times."

"I know. But all this stuff is driving me crazy."

I understood what she meant. When my wife killed the kids and herself, I thought about death. I said, "Death, come on. What do I care? I want to take my last breath and be finished with all this mess." Life had taken away everything I had. I wanted to die.

It was as if my aunt was a different person. She straightened up and flashed her warm smile at me. "Clint, we've got to think about you. You need to think about what you're going to do with your life. Yes, that chapter has closed, but what now?"

I crossed my legs, wishing I had a cigarette. "That's what I'm trying to figure out. Any suggestions?"

"You've got to let all that mess go," she said firmly. "You know that."

"You're not telling me anything new."

"Clint, I don't want to hear about how you're frustrated or insecure," she continued. "You're not self-destructive. I've never known you to be any of those things. You're a strong black man, Clint. And you should act like it."

"That's why I went off alone, out into the country," I said, wanting to explain the isolated life with its benefit of contemplation. "I needed to get my head clear. The bottom had fallen out of my life, and I'd lost my place in the world and my purpose."

"I can understand that," my aunt said. "Everybody must take a break and be quiet. Everything is noise. We rush around and need noise and sound to fill our days. But sometimes we need to be quiet."

"So you know what I'm talking about, Auntie." I smiled broadly.

"Maybe you need to get out of the way of yourself, Clint," she suggested. "If you only think of yourself, you'll live a sorry life. Get involved. Volunteer. This was what I was trying to tell you the last time. Leave your past behind by replacing it with something more positive and nourishing to your soul."

"I know. I know." That was the key.

Her face took on an almost angelic quality. "I'm telling you this from the bottom of my soul. Get comfortable in your own heart. Don't become narrow. Don't be afraid to risk. Take a chance on life. Become free of fear and attachment. Don't cling to grudges and slights. If you do this, you can change your life from the ground up."

"I know." I sat there, with my troubled head in my hands.

"Now, do I sound like I'm crazy?" Shortly after she said that, the nurse interrupted us and told me visiting hours were over. I kissed Aunt Spivey on the cheek, and she held my hand in both of hers. She looked lovingly into my face and grinned like we had a dear, sweet secret between us.

The following day, she died of a massive heart attack. I locked myself in the bathroom for hours and cried and cried until my eyes hurt.

4

SETTING THE TABLE

Joanne Orne Spivey's funeral was an event, held in Harlem's Mount of Olives Pentecostal Assembly on the second Tuesday of the month. As one of her Baptist friends later said, it was equal parts funeral, James Brown Apollo concert, Thanksgiving dinner reunion, and Shriners gala shindig. I never knew my aunt Spivey had touched so many lives and influenced whole legions of admirers and fans.

Ever thoughtful, Natalie, her daughter, sent a limousine to take me to the church. I was seated in a place of honor near the church people, eight pastors of regional tabernacles, two rabbis, four priests, three imams, and one stranger, who whispered that my aunt had paid people to smuggle his son out of Iran.

"Thanks for coming, Reverend Clint," her daughter said, hugging me. "You know, you were one of her favorite people. Remind me to give you an envelope I have at home. She wants you to have it."

I took a quick look at the program, which listed the order of the service. It began with the call to worship, which was followed by the First Baptist Choir singing the hymn "When We All Get to Heaven"; two readings of scripture, Ephesians 6:12–14 and Luke 19:10–14; the Calvary Methodist Church Choir singing another hymn, "Take My Hand, Precious Lord"; and a unison reading of the Twenty-third Psalm.

The surprise of the funeral service was a group of young ladies from one of the poorest parts of Uganda, whom my aunt had mentored, converted to Christianity, and educated sufficiently so that they would be accepted at a private school. The young women, now adults, sang the hymn "The Lord's Prayer" with a soloist whose passionate voice filled the rotunda and brought the gathering to tears.

Next came the remembrances of Joanne Spivey's remarkable life, with Andrew Young speaking on her civil rights efforts, Kofi Annan detailing her work with refugee camps in Africa, a UN aid official discussing her tireless energy in fundraising campaigns on behalf of Haitian earthquake victims, and two poor white widows of West Virginia miners describing her bankrolling of a clinic in Appalachia.

One of the sisters of the movement, a wig-wearing woman in her Sunday best, talked about Aunt Spivey's love of smoke-cured Virginia ham, baked yams, and fried okra. She recalled Dr. King's reliance on her with the ladies among the common folk on the bloody battlefields of Selma, Birmingham, Jackson, and even Memphis. She was not far from his side or that of A. Philip Randolph, a man she revered, during the 1963 March on Washington.

"She wanted something more for the country than a cosmetic overhaul," the woman said. "She wanted a kinder, gentler nation, rather than the divided blue and red states of the political parties. Jim Crow was not her friend. She considered the Klan a disease and wondered if America had the cure. Miss Spivey believed in equal rights and democracy."

Another of the faithful boasted about her humanitarian work with the various groups of Delta Sigma Theta Sorority, whose members sat in the favored areas in the front of the church. She had loved the sisters of the sorority and had tutored the poor young mothers, fought for the girl scholars in the projects, and given pep talks to the roughneck female gang members behind bars. The woman had been into everything, and that why was I loved her.

A group of followers of Marcus Garvey was not permitted to speak but remained, talking loudly over some of the praise of her good works. Garveyism seized my aunt's imagination in her teen years. The glorious Back to Africa movement. Later, one of them tugged at my sleeve and protested about having been silenced, for my aunt was one of the determined young members who signed up people for petitions to prevent the Black Messiah's exile.

In keeping with the wishes of the church and the funeral directors, the obituary was read silently and a moment of contemplation was quietly observed throughout the church. I thought I knew about her life, but I actually learned quite a bit today. Everybody had pleasant secrets and things they would rather not boast about.

I was surprised to see the usual minister of her church, Reverend Allen Underwood, remain seated, while Reverend Ruth Palmer, a visiting pastor from another church, one of the AME variety, stood behind the pulpit.

"We called her Aunt Spivey, like all her friends and family did," said the tiny minister, who had toiled beside her in Haiti. "Aunt Spivey hated sin. Aunt Spivey was a sin eater, but not in the Catholic sense. Aunt Spivey never made excuses for sin. She never considered sin a mistake in judgment. She knew how much temptation contributed to sin. She also knew sin and its results were disillusionment, despair, depression, depravity, disease, and death."

"Amen!" someone shouted.

"Testify, sister!" another parishioner said heartily.

"Aunt Spivey realized that sin and all humanity went hand in hand," Reverend Palmer said, leaning over the pulpit. "Some people sin because they know our time is short, that we are on borrowed time. She knew the cure to sin is to embrace the spirit of God. She knew there is no limit to God. His wisdom has no limits. His power knows no limits. She knew all of this. She knew there is no limit to His mercy."

"Talk about it!" Some in the congregation were getting worked up.

Her voice lowered an octave for dramatic effect. "However, Aunt Spivey knew that all of us have total freedom to choose, to reject, to denounce sin. Each person is given the freedom to choose between two paths. Some of us choose sin, but Aunt Spivey chose salvation and redemption. In her life, Aunt Spivey chose the divine love of God."

"Bless your name, Jesus!"

Reverend Palmer placed her hands across her heart, and the gathering heard her speech crack with emotion. "She saved me, blessed me with her wisdom, rescued me from confusion. I loved Aunt Spivey with all my soul. She was a warrior for Christ!"

That was true. My aunt gave me my first Bible, a cherished possession, while I was in my teens. One day, she came to my apartment and noticed God's book had marks all over it: I'd underlined critical verses and circled significant passages of healing and recovery. I was so grateful for her gift of scripture.

"Let the Lord lead your life," she would say. "I know your pain is real pain. I know you think this wound will never heal. I know you think, 'I cannot do this alone.' Rely on the Lord, and He will bring you over the river Jordan."

After the minister finished, the same soloist sang the hymn "Peace Be Still" with incredible sensitivity and great feeling. I'd never heard such a rendition of that song, delivered with that husky timbre of the late African singer Miriam Makeba. It made your hair stand up on your head.

Natalie, Aunt Spivey's daughter, was introduced after the song. With the weight of her grief showing on her face, she stood and acknowledged the somber greeting from the congregation before adjusting the microphone. She cleared her throat a couple times before starting to read from the paper that she held with trembling hands.

"I love my mother, and I will miss her very badly," she began carefully. "Being a single mother requires courage and nerve. She never questioned the amount of love and support she was willing to give. A loving mother and a responsible parent, she always found time for me, to listen to me and advise me. She was a good listener. But you never wanted to get on her bad side. That was not pretty to see. Sometimes she would stare at me, and when I asked what was wrong, she'd reply, 'Nothing.' I think she loved the role of parent so that she could see the values and skills she taught me."

"Amen!" came a shout.

"Let me close with this," Natalie said solemnly. "My mother taught me that everything we do has consequences. She'd tell me that even doing nothing had results. She would say, 'Don't postpone life. Live fully in the present.' That's what I learned from my mother. I love you, Mom. God bless her soul."

She motioned for me to get up and say something. I hesitated, but I took the steps to the raised platform where she stood. We hugged, and then she left my side.

"I loved my aunt Spivey, really loved her like a mother," I said. "She was my counsel, my conscience, my teacher. There are so many things I learned from her. I learned we should never think we are less than anybody else. I learned we should never accept less, because we are worth much, much more. She'd say, 'You are the best. You deserve the best. You should never be treated with disrespect. You are not inferior to anyone.'"

"Teach, Reverend!"

Another voice boomed. "Praise His holy name!"

"When I had the lowest, most painful experience of my life, my aunt Spivey lifted me up and set me straight," I continued. "She was a woman of God. She was an original, a rebel, a saint. And I'll miss her so badly." After I said my remarks, I quietly returned to my seat.

Reverend Underwood rose to his feet, stretched out his long arms, and delivered the benediction before the pallbearers lined up around the closed casket. At a signal, they lifted the casket and carried it down the steep stairs to the hearse.

My mind was abuzz with memories of Aunt Spivey and her guidance. *Pray. Quiet your mind. Silence, serenity. Pray. God will listen and speak. God will listen and decide. God will listen and choose. He may not grant you the thing you ask. Still, you will know that He has chosen wisely, for He is God.*

Listen, Clint, I always say God compels a person to that sacred place where you can discover truth, where you can discover the soul of yourself. The real issue is to submit to His will and obey.

When I spotted Natalie in the crowd near the hearse, I noticed her red, swollen eyes and the pinched expression on her face. I knew exactly what she was feeling. I felt that sharp, overwhelming pain of loss when I saw the pallbearers load the coffins of my wife and children in the hearses. The brief memory of that final moment left me sick to my stomach. Walking up to her, pushing my way through the mourners, I hugged Natalie and told her that I was not going to accompany the coffin to the cemetery. She said she understood my decision. I walked off down the street, thinking of my departed relative.

5
BACK AND FORTH

There were two tense days until I heard from Reverend Peck again. His voice didn't have much life to it, almost choked by nerves and stress. We talked about my aunt's funeral, the home-going ceremony her loved ones and associates had given her out of respect and adoration. I really didn't want to talk about her that much. I turned the conversation to him, the crisis occurring at his church, the mutiny shown by some of the young deacons and the mother board, the situation of strained leadership between Reverend Wilks and himself.

"When are you going to come down here, Clint?" he asked. "You don't have anything holding you there. I don't know if the church will take you back after the struggle you had with Dr. Smart and his cronies. There's nothing holding you there. I'm sure Dr. Smart poisoned the congregation of your church against you when you didn't do as he asked. He talked badly about you before you decided to leave the church. Plenty of bad, ugly rumors."

"I don't know, sir," I replied. "I know I promised, but there is so much to be done here. I want to get my life corrected before I start running around. I need balance."

He chose his words carefully. "I think I know what Wilks is doing here. He's trying to steal my church right out from under me. Now I've got proof, and I didn't have it before. Also, I have some people I want you to talk to, people who will back up some of my worst fears."

"You have this evidence?" I asked him.

"Sure I do."

Maybe he had the evidence, maybe not, but he wasn't going to reveal anything over the phone. I had a feeling I had to go there to get it. I had to see him face-to-face, listen to his proof, and then make a decision.

"I can have you here in a matter of hours," the reverend added, trying to lure me into his web. "Once here, you'll see that everything I said is true. No lies, no deception. If you come here and it sounds like I've just been talking through my hat, then you can go right back to New York."

I must admit that I was curious. "How will you get me down there? I don't want to waste a lot of time on this. Don't get me wrong. I want to help you, but I don't want to be a part of a wild-goose chase."

"It's not a waste of time," he assured me.

"How am I getting there?" I asked again.

"By plane. I know a guy who can fly you down here. There's a private airstrip in New Jersey. Teterboro or some such thing. Somebody can pick you up from the city and drive you out there. The flight is about three hours or something. Then we can talk, and if you don't like what you hear, you go home. Simple as that."

"Simple as that?" I repeated.

"Yes, simple as that."

"Are you sure you can't give me the proof over the phone?"

The reverend stuck to his guns. "No, I can't."

"I don't understand that." I was not convinced.

"I'm rounding up some people I want you to talk to ." He was pulling out all the stops. "Their words are important. They know things. They've seen things. They know things that I don't know."

"Is what they're saying criminal?" I asked. "Is Reverend Wilks involved in some criminal activity? Is he going to do some great wrongdoing?"

He was stubborn and firm. "Yes, I think so."

"Then why don't you go to the police?"

"No. I don't want to get the police involved in this. I don't want to tip my hand. I want to uncover everything so I can just lay it out on the table before them and make sure that he goes away for a long time. He's smart and very clever. Very devious."

"I don't know, Reverend."

Impatient, he was getting to the end of his rope. "Clint, are you going to come or not? I need to know, because if you're not, I need to make other arrangements."

"Other arrangements?"

"Yes, I've got to protect my butt," he replied. "Who knows what this man will do? Wilks has got a lot at stake, and he'll stop at nothing to get control of the church. *My* blasted church! I've got to make sure that doesn't happen."

I sat down and scratched my head. "I think you need to go to the police if you think he's got some kind of scheme up his sleeve. You've been there far longer than he has. You've got influence with these people."

"Wilks has turned them against me, my congregation, my friends, even some of my own family," he said, snorting. "He's got a silver tongue. He can convince anybody of anything. He's a con man."

"I really don't understand any of this," I said.

He had an alternative plan for me. "Clint, don't make up your mind now. Give it a couple of days. Let it percolate in your mind and then give me your decision. Is that all right with you?"

I answered him slowly . "Yes. That's fair."

"Promise me that when you decide whatever, you will call me," he said quietly. "Don't think too long. It's either you do or you don't."

"I promise, Reverend—" He hung up before I got finished speaking.

In that moment, I recalled Aunt Spivey talking to me in that tiny senior center room, sipping her peppermint tea as she spat out her words. "Clint, don't let this life or the church cut your balls off. Don't let them geld you, boy. You know what my papa used to say. 'A man good for excuses ain't good for nothing.' Think about that. Make a choice, right or wrong, and stand by it. No matter what."

She was right. I had to commit myself. I had to choose.

As I put a CD in my machine, I watched out the window as the cars pulled in and out of the parking lot of the motel. The music was James Newton's *The African Flower,* with an all-star lineup performing some of the classics of Duke Ellington and Billy Strayhorn. I loved the supporting cast backing the flutist: Arthur Blythe on alto sax, Olu Dara on cornet, Roland Hanna on piano, Jay Hoggard on vibes, Billy Hart on drums, and Rick Rozie plucking the bass.

The phone rang one time, then stopped. Suddenly, the phone sounded again.

It was Orville, my cousin. He had got the information on Mr. Wilks. I was all ears, trying to get something so that I could justify the trip down to Reverend Peck's neighborhood.

"Mr. Lamar Wilks is an incredible con man," my cousin said excitedly. "He's a third- generation scam artist. His grandfather was a traveling minister who worked the frontier towns and farm regions. The old guy was shot to death while trying to make out with the wife of an undertaker in this town where he set up his tent."

"Some bloodline, eh?" For some reason, I was not surprised, but I still needed to find something that could convince me to fly down there.

"By the way, his grandfather's name was Richard Campbell. The guy went around the South, taking advantage of rich widows and gullible girls who had a fella away during the World War," my cousin added. "And that was before he found religion and the Holy Ghost."

"All right, that takes care of the grandpa. What about Mr. Wilks's daddy?" I asked him.

"Now, this is where it gets really interesting," he said. "The father was a mean mother. He didn't let anything or anybody get in his way. He was a cook in the navy during the Korean War, and after he left the service, he hooked up with Father Divine's outfit, where he quickly proved his worth to the man who claimed to be God."

"What did he do for him, Orville?"

My cousin laughed out loud. "Joe Craig Campbell, one of the key advisers to Father Divine, had the gift of gab. He had the holy man's ear. Joe could talk up a storm. Father Divine admired him and kept him close. The Messenger, as he was called by the followers, wanted to keep ahead of the other Black messiahs of the time, such as Daddy Grace, Noble Drew Ali, and Charles Harrison Mason. Father Divine was not easily fooled. He'd gone through a number of close advisers and henchmen who wanted to earn his trust, but many of them came up short."

"What do you mean?"

My cousin couldn't wait to tell me. "Well, Father Divine's early trouble with the law got him in a struggle with local Southern pastors in nineteen thirteen, and they set him up. They had him sentenced to sixty days in a Georgia chain gang. That following year a group of his followers paid off the authorities, and they still arrested Father Divine for lunacy. No, The Messenger didn't trust easily."

"Joe conned the con man, right?" I asked him.

"Joe was slick and stressed that the Messenger should fly under the radar since there were still problems with his white wife," my cousin noted. "White men didn't like the fact that this five-foot-two black man was topping this elegant pale white gal. This was during the civil rights days of the nineteen fifties. Although Father Divine said he didn't have sex with her, the resentment was still there."

"Was she from money?"

"I don't know," he replied. "Father Divine had a hilltop mansion outside of Philadelphia, where the followers came after everything started to go badly. He wanted the white folk to pay blacks for their time as slaves. He thought whites and blacks should live together. A lot of people didn't share that view, especially after the lynching of the young black boy Emmitt Till."

"What happened to Joe?" I asked him.

"Joe left Father Divine to set up his own church in New York, but one of the local politicians started to investigate where the new minister was getting his money," my cousin said with a giggle. "The law wondered how Joe was financing his big house, fancy cars, and a private jet on the backs of the poor folk."

"Now, where does Mr. Wilks come into this?"

"After a couple of strokes, Joe sent the young Whit-ley Campbell away to live with his mother," he said. "First, Whitley and his mother lived in the Bahamas with his younger brother. When he was around fifteen or sixteen, Whitley came back to New York and Har-lem, trying to team up with Reverend Ike up there in Washington Heights. The Reverend Ike ministry had their church in a fancy former Loews movie house, which was the perfect showcase for the gaudy pastor, who loved money. They say Reverend Ike didn't ap-preciate Whitley trying to muscle in on his racket and chased him away."

"Then where did he go?"

My cousin sighed. "Whitley Campbell disappeared off the face of the earth, and then he reappeared as Reverend Lamar Wilks, the heir to Creflo Dollar. He admires and worships Reverend Dollar and his wife, Taffi. I think he has searched around for a church to control and has his eyes on Reverend Peck's congrega-tion."

I fished around for a cigarette, lighting it nervously. "That's what Reverend Peck is afraid of. He knows a virus when he sees one. He told me he thinks Wilks is the devil's messenger. He's probably right."

"Clint, I've got some feelers out in New York law enforcement, trying to get more on this character," my cousin added. "Believe me, you never know what they'll turn up."

"How dangerous is this guy, Wilks?" I wanted to know.

"Very." The word was spoken harshly.

I needed to know why Wilks was so dangerous. How could he hurt my friend and destroy his church? What plans did he have for this congregation in the middle of nowhere?

"What makes him so dangerous, Orville?"

"Whitley Campbell, or whatever his name is now, is a snake, but it's the first-class gang of rats he surrounds himself with," my cousin explained. "From what I understand, these folks do not play. They take no prisoners, and your preacher friend might be out of his depth going against these people."

"Get more on these people, okay?"

"Sure will," my cousin assured me. "I'll tell you all about them in no time, and how best to avoid tangling with them head-on. I'll have something for you the next time we talk. Is that good enough for you?"

"Great, Orville." I laughed. "You're turning into a real Sherlock Holmes. Sleuthing suits you."

He chuckled and joked, "I think I get it pretty earnestly. Remember, my mother knew everything about everybody. She had her spies. She had a mental file on friends and foes alike, and didn't mind using it if she got into a pinch."

I smiled because I knew that was so true. "Ah, Aunt Tenille."

When we said our farewells, I went back to listening to James Newton blowing some of the sweetest flute imaginable for the Ellington song "Fleurette Africaine." I also thought about what I would say when I talked to Reverend Peck. I dreaded flying on a noncommercial plane, especially given that it was supposed to rain heavily all the rest of the week.

It took a couple of days before everything came together. The pilot, an old pal of the reverend, was given a down payment so I could join fifteen other passengers on this converted DC-8 plane, making one stop in Atlanta and then flying on to my destination.

In preparation for my mercy mission, I dressed appropriately for the damp weather, packed a traveling bag, since I didn't intend to stay long, and a large umbrella. The car picked me up shortly after nine in the morning. The rain was coming down like it was in the tropics. It was dark and dreary.

The pastor had said there would be people going along on the flight, a group of customers with improper ID who didn't want to be searched closely at the airport. Sometimes the pilot made mail runs to out-of-the way places.

In no time, we were loaded onto the plane, we strapped ourselves in, and the ancient plane taxied up to the runway, shuddered twice, and began its climb over a cluster of trees and gray factories, turning south into the storm and the dark clouds.

6

THE DEVIL MAN

When the plane landed at some remote airport in rural Alabama, there was a car waiting for me. Everything was so hush-hush. Top secret. The driver was very polite, quiet, and quite helpful in giving me the instructions from Reverend Peck. He couldn't be there to meet me, but a meeting would happen late that evening. There was some business that had to be addressed.

The little motel, located by the highway, was so out of the way that nobody would think of looking for me there. I settled in my small room, complete with a hard bed, a small icebox, a hot plate, and a miniature plywood table with two old chairs. The hot plate smelled of bug spray, air fresheners, and Clorox bleach.

I wondered what I was doing here. The driver had given me the phone number of a safe house where church members sympathetic to my friend's cause could always reach him. I walked out into the parking lot, looked at the vintage autos rusting on the asphalt, and made my way to the office. There were loud sounds of lovemaking coming from one of the shuttered rooms, a woman's shrieks and a man's husky moans, and the radio had been turned up to drown out the noise.

This was farm country, all right. I glanced up and saw a large truck pull in, loaded with fat hogs packed in close quarters. Their grunts and squeals made this a very surreal sight. The farmer behind the wheel waved at me, and I waved back.

Upon my return to the office, I told the guy behind the counter that I was expecting a call. Ignoring me, he didn't look up. Instead, he worked on a crossword puzzle from a newspaper. My phone was not working in my room.

"No worries. I'll send somebody to get you," the counter guy assured me in an aggravated voice. "If I finish my shift, I'll pass along the message to the morning girl. Anything else you need, sir?"

"No, I'm good." I didn't like his attitude.

As the hours passed into the night, I sprawled out on the bed, drank a cold root beer, and read the speeches of one of my idols, the singer-actor-activist Paul Robeson. The book was titled *Paul Robeson Speaks,* edited by a noted scholar, Philip S. Foner. For a man of his time, Robeson possessed a keen perception of the political and cultural world, an uncanny insight into the points at which capitalism and racism were intertwined.

Paper clipped inside the book was a local magazine written by the prophet Lamar Wilks, the silver-tongued shaman of the Kingdom of the Faithful. The magazine chronicled a speech he delivered before a gathering of eight thousand three months ago, a speech in which he promised them everlasting celestial life and called for his flock, which he called the "Beloveds," to gather those in need of salvation. The media had been invited to the spiritual lovefest.

"We need to be like the disciples with the Lord, to become fishers of men, bringing sinners to God," the article quoted the alleged holy man as saying. "We need to show them a glorious example as the Beloveds of Christ, to show them the way."

The article went on to quote Wilks as saying he was a major prophet of the Messiah, greater than Paul or Peter or even John the Baptist. Nowhere was there any mention of his doctrine of prosperity or profit. And there was no mention of Reverend Peck, the official leader of the church that the prophet was representing.

Collecting facts for the piece, the reporter was amazed at how Reverend Wilks waded among the people, his Beloveds, hugging them warmly and stroking their faces tenderly. His staff, which controlled all media exposure, allowed a photographer to take a shot over Reverend Wilks's shoulder to show the size of the crowd, and they permitted the printing of a small portrait of the prophet, from the side, in shadow. I wondered what Wilks was planning. He looked like a cat who had swallowed a canary and was about to cough up a feather.

Maybe I dozed off, but when I heard a faint knock at my door, I awoke, startled. I walked toward the sound, and a wee child's voice shouted from the other side of the door. As I opened the door, the kid was running down the walkway. I cut the lights off, no easy target.

"The man in the office say you got a call," the boy yelled over his shoulder. "He say to come there. He say to hurry and come there!"

When I turned to shut the door partway, the boy was gone, had vanished into thin air. I walked briskly to the office, listened to the bell announce my arrival, and the man came out.

"The boy said I had a phone call," I told him.

The guy behind the counter said it was a man's voice, plain and soft-spoken. Sounded like a businessman or a lawyer. "He hung up," the guy said, frowning. "Maybe it was a wrong number. Maybe he didn't want you, after all."

I asked him if the man on the phone had left a number, a callback number, but he said no. His words rang in my ears. *Maybe he didn't want you, after all.*

The walk back to the room was disappointing. I was tired of waiting for the reverend to make his appearance or to give me some information about where we could meet. I needed my rest.

When I entered the room and turned on the light, there were three people awaiting me. One was Reverend Peck, who promptly hugged me, and two girls were sitting on the bed. I could tell the pastor was happy to see me. He was smiling from ear to ear. I looked at the girls, teenagers, who were dressed in long white dresses. Both of them wore their hair up in a tight bun.

"I'm sorry to crash in on you like this," Reverend Peck said. "We had to move fast. Everything is hitting the fan. I'm so glad you could come."

I looked closer at the girls. There was a lot of blood on the bed. One of the girls was hemorrhaging and needed care. I didn't know what to make of this.

"Why didn't you go to the hospital?" I asked the pastor.

"Can we use your bathroom?" he asked. "Ruth will clean her up. This is Ruth, and the other girl is Sarah. While they're in there, we'll talk and figure out a plan."

The girls stepped into the bathroom, and I removed the bloody blanket from the bed, folded it up, and put it in a corner. Looking worried, Reverend Peck pulled up a chair and watched me, finally telling me how he'd smuggled the girls out of the church compound in a car. The frightened girls had ducked down in the backseat to get past security on the church property.

"I didn't know where to take them, so I came here," he said with an alarmed expression. "I had to take them away from there. Sarah's mother asked me to get her girl away from there. She thinks the girl's pregnant, but she doesn't know who the father is. The girl's mother was worried that Wilks would do something to her."

"Like what?"

"I don't know," he replied. "Things have been crazy around here. Mr. Wilks and his gang have almost taken over. I've got a few faithful members, but their number is dwindling. We can no longer meet at the church, because there are spies everywhere. They watch every move I make."

I heard water running and splashing from the bathroom. "Where do you meet? Is it that bad? I can't believe this."

Reverend Peck shook his head in amazement. "It's that bad. We have to meet secretly in the homes of the members. I don't know who to trust. I don't know what Wilks is going to do next."

"How did this Wilks get such a foothold in your church?"

We both pivoted toward the bathroom when we heard the water stop. He listened as the girls talked low among themselves behind the closed door, and then he continued on about the rise of the alleged prophet.

"Bit by bit, Wilks gained influence in our community," he said. "He just took over. He started speaking on behalf of one of our ailing deacons at our council of the elders. From the first, I thought there was something creepy about him. I didn't like his manner. I didn't like how he mistreated folks who had been here in the church for years and years, and he treated them like dirt. He was a nobody when I hired him, but everybody had to admit he had a certain kind of charisma."

"Charisma?" You would have thought he was talking about that fictional religious con man Elmer Gantry.

The reverend was getting angrier by the minute. "Wilks tries to put himself up like some sort of God. He says he has this inspired plan, that he has been prompted by the Messiah, that only he knows the way to become a true follower of the Lord. One Sunday, we squared off during the service, and he accused me of having lost faith."

I made a joke, and maybe it was a bad one. "In the beginning was the Word, and the Word was Mr. Wilks." The reverend didn't laugh.

"Are you girls all right in there?" Reverend Peck called out. "You're taking quite a while. Do you need help?"

The reply sounded strong. "No, sir. We're okay."

"Did you know he sells tapes of his sermons?" the reverend said. "This is my church. And he sells sermons to my congregation. He's a real con man."

I thought he had balls. "Maybe you need to fight fire with fire. Let the people see what a charlatan he is. He's a faker. Let your congregation see him for who he is."

His hands made weird gestures, as if he were going to fly. "Wilks is a spiritual bully. An outsider. What he does is exploit the weakness that lies in our hearts and souls, in each and every one of us. He has no problem with using it against us. He has totally brainwashed the members of my church, totally."

Almost on cue, the girls came out of the bathroom and took a seat on the bed. Both of them looked at us as if we had all the answers, but unfortunately, we had none. I could see they were terrified.

"The bleeding has stopped," Ruth informed us. "But I think she needs to go to a hospital or a doctor. Or something."

Reverend Peck got up off the chair and approached the sick girl. "How do you feel? Other than the bleeding, is there anything else off-kilter with your body? Any pains or anything?"

She shook her head no. I was very glad.

"Still, I think she needs to be seen at a hospital," Ruth said again. "Something's not right. Maybe it's the pregnancy, but something is not right."

I noticed both girls wore a golden acorn pendant with a Gothic cross on their lapel. That made me curious. "What is that on your lapel?" I asked.

Before Reverend Peck could reply, Ruth answered that the pendant signified a member of the church in good standing, one who exhibited the traits of loyalty, faithfulness, moral responsibility, fidelity, service, and commitment. Wilks had designed the jewelry of the Beloveds himself.

"Show your back to the minister," Reverend Peck instructed them. "I think he'd like to see who we're dealing with. Wilks is a cruel, coldhearted man who demands obedience."

Ruth pulled down her dress, exposing her bare back, which was covered with savage red welts, some crusted, but others still raw. She lowered her head, as if she was ashamed. The other girl, Sarah, did not strip. Instead, she sobbed, the tears coming from a place deep within her. I could tell she had been hurt and humiliated as well.

"She has them too, only much worse," Ruth said quietly.

"Why would he do such a thing?" I asked them.

Sarah finally spoke up between tortured sobs. "Mr. Wilks is the prophet. Mr. Wilks is the Messiah. Mr. Wilks is God. He is the daddy of us all. He is the Divine Father of us all."

"Huh?" I couldn't believe what I was hearing. *Daddy?*

"Daddy Wilks says He is like Christ before the crucifixion, at his spiritual peak," Ruth explained. "Daddy Wilks believes we are all sinners. He believes we are all godless, but we have a chance at redemption and salvation because we are in His presence."

"Is this why he beat you?" I asked the girls.

"Partly," Sarah said with remorse. "He beats us so we will obey and submit. He beats us so we can know the Lord and know Him as the Divine Father."

I turned to Reverend Peck, astonished. "Did you know about this? Did you know how he was mistreating your congregation?"

The reverend slumped. "No, not all of this."

Well, I was here in this godforsaken place, committed to helping my friend with his burden. First, we had to get Sarah to the hospital, then we had to put the girls in a safe place, and finally, we had to confront this monster. I had dealt with some demons before, some people with a great amount of darkness in their souls, yet this one took the cake. I hoped we were not too late to save my friend or his precious church.

7
WASH ME CLEAN

As the people of Jubilee, Alabama, streamed into the Patrick Henry High School gymnasium, we sat in the reverend's car near the building and calculated the audience for Daddy Wilks at about twelve thousand. In Jubilee, in the heart of rural Alabama, a group of dedicated farmers and growers worked the fertile land under ideal conditions. We had delivered the battered girls to a relative of Reverend Peck in a neighboring town, about fifty miles away from the church. He had concluded they would be safe there after being attended by a local doctor who was a friend of a deacon. A lot had happened to me since my arrival in Alabama only eight days ago.

"Do you think this is a good idea?" I asked him.

The reverend laughed. "Wilks already knows you're here. He knows everything. Probably the guy at the motel called him as soon as you checked in."

I shrugged. "Then let's do this. I want to see this guy in action."

He had shown me a poster proclaiming that Daddy Wilks's spiritual crusade was coming to the school, under the banner of my friend's church but with no mention of him. However, the poster featured a large photo of Daddy Wilks, standing like the Redeemer in a long white robe, with his arms outstretched. All in color, the poster must have cost a pretty penny. Across the bottom of the poster was the message: Come. See. Be Healed.

We walked in with the throng, some of the people pushing and shoving, and took refuge in a concealed place on the second floor, near the fire exit. One of the church members had recognized the pastor, waved us on, and permitted us to go upstairs.

"It's a shame that the prophet didn't invite you, since he's representing your church and all," the church member had said sorrowfully. "I don't think that's good manners. Not at all."

I was proud of the reverend's fine behavior, since he had the right to go off and make all kinds of nasty remarks, but he had pushed right through the crowd, saying nothing. However, I saw the full scope of Wilks's treachery in the church and in the community at large.

Now the show was starting. Some members of the choir took their place onstage as the organist traversed it with a little zip in his step and the staff checked the microphone and the sound. A group of local pastors, council members, politicians, teachers, and esteemed officials of the neighboring tabernacles sat several feet behind the makeshift pulpit.

Prophet Wilks, as he was now called by the media and the church members, walked quickly across the stage, his long arms uplifted, as if he were a representative from the Vatican, in a theatrical flourish. He knew how to make a dramatic and energetic entrance. There was a brief hush from the crowd. The photographs didn't do him justice. He was over six-feet-three, tall, but he seemed even taller.

"He cuts a striking figure, huh?" I said to the reverend.

"I hate how he has them fooled," Reverend Peck said bitterly.

The prophet didn't slouch, holding his long, tall body rigid in his luminous white suit. Somebody had pinned a bright red rose to his lapel. He looked out over the throng with piercing, hypnotic eyes, occasionally smiling. His hair was slicked and combed straight back above his caramel-colored features.

He nodded to the group gathered onstage, shaking the hands of some of the bigwigs while giving a curt grin to others.

The organist hit the first chord of "How Great Thou Art," which Reverend Peck said was the prophet's theme song, and the crowd joined in singing the uplifting lyrics. Prophet Wilks didn't sing; he let the others sing for him. The choir and the crowd sang on until he tapped a finger on the mic and nodded to the organist to end the song. Very smoothly.

He stood quiet for a few seconds, grinning like the snake oil salesman he was, then stepped closer to the microphone.

"Praise be, let us all say amen!"

Those in attendance shouted out as if in one voice. "Amen, Amen."

I could tell this was not the first audience he'd addressed by his speaking style, which was so practiced and so polished, honed over decades of selling things to people who didn't need them.

"Hallelujah to the Almighty!" The prophet was polite in his demands. "Say hallelujah!"

"Hallelujah!"

"We love you, Prophet Wilks!" cried one girlish voice.

He grinned again. "I love you too, all of you."

A few people laughed at his reply, but you could tell this man was used to adoration and affection. He didn't blink an eye. Instead, he took the microphone in one hand and started to stroll across the stage.

"It's a great pleasure to be here today with Christians, those of you who have discovered the joy of serving the Lord, and with you sinners, who are starving for salvation," the prophet said in his statement of welcome.

"Amen. Teach, sir!"

He reared back and let his voice fill the room. "Behold, the Word of the Lord came unto me, a sinner, saying, 'I knew thee before I formed thee in the womb, and I sanctified thee to act as my prophet, to bear witness among the fallen and the wicked.'"

"Praise His holy name!"

He walked on and stopped. "Then I ran from the Lord, crying, 'I cannot speak for the divine, for I am just a sinner, a lowly, wretched sinner. But the Lord said unto me, 'Say not that you are a lowly sinner, because I have made thee whole, I have made thee pure, and I have made thee cleansed.' The Lord put forth his hand, and a glow radiated all through my body, causing me to shudder in its power, its transcendent power. And the Lord said unto me, 'I have put my words in thy mouth.' You know that verse, Jeremiah one, nine. I know the Lord never lies. He never tells untruths, for He has lifted up a people and He has raised up a prophet. I am that prophet! I am that prophet!"

The faithful cried out, "Praise His holy name!"

"Yes, Beloveds, I am that prophet, because the Lord said to the master, 'There's a man you can use, God.' And you know, my Beloveds, that man is me!"

"Amen!"

"Preach the Word!"

He leaned over with the microphone and made a face, the weary expression of a soul crooner. "Let's go back a ways. Some say God turned His back on us when

Adam and Eve acted out in the Garden of Eden. No, he didn't turn his back. He put us to the test. He is always testing us, just like Satan is always tempting us. You know what I mean, don't you, my Beloveds?"

"Teach, teach the Gospel!"

"Amen. Talk about the Word!"

The prophet strolled around and put his hand on the shoulder of the high school principal, startling the man. "You see, we as sinners are tired of hate, malice, sickness, sin, bloodshed, envy, jealousy, pain, loneliness, confusion, and torment. Aren't we?"

"Oh, yes, Prophet!"

He grinned widely. "And taxes too."

That brought a round of chuckles.

He moved around behind the assembled officials and local celebs and walked to the center of the stage. "My Beloveds, we have let the evil one come into our midst," he shouted. "It's time to drive him out into the wilderness. We don't want him. We don't need him."

"You got that right, brother!"

The prophet kneeled quickly and held the microphone in a way that suggested he was praying to the Almighty. "We pray and we pray and we pray. Don't you pray? What do you pray for? Don't you pray?"

"Bless God, we pray!"

He was still on the floor, his voice all tortured and pained. "We pray and we pray and we pray. But sometimes God doesn't answer. And sometimes He does. When He does, His voice is loud and clear. He says that these are the final days, the end of times, that we are nearing the day of judgment. And you know, my Beloveds, He is coming back, coming back. Will He find you ready when He calls your name?"

"I'm ready!" one of the mother board members yelled.

"Do you know what the chapter of Second Peter say about all of this? Do you know what the apostle says?" He remained kneeling. "And what does the Lord say? The Lord says this. 'When you see all these signs, you know that the end draweth nigh. When you see earthquakes in many places, all over the world, wars and rumors of wars, famine, all these dark things, and the armies of the world threatening Jerusalem, then you know the end draweth nigh.'"

One of the young boys hollered that they were protected by the prophet, that no harm could befall them, no danger could strike them.

Finally, the man stood up and whirled around. "God is punishing us for our lust, greed, and wickedness. God is punishing this evil world. But I am one of God's true servants. I am one of the chosen. I have his ear, and He listens to me."

"Hallelujah!"

The prophet made a shriek of joy, and the crowd stirred in response. "How do I know? How do I know what the Lord thinks? Because He tells me so. He says I have some duties as a man of God, to spread the Gospel and redeem sinners, to heal the sick, to cast out demons. I have to proclaim the coming of the Messiah. Say amen!"

"Amen!"

He lifted one arm and started prancing around in a circle while the organist played some ditty that sounded like an old Jackie Wilson tune. "Yes, the Kingdom of God is coming! And this is the true church of God. He says I should heal the sick. But when you get sick, who do you turn to? Not to God, but to a doctor."

"Now, you're preaching, Prophet!"

The prophet pointed out into the audience accusingly. "God is punishing us with super-germs. The doctors and the hospitals cannot heal us. All the medicines they create cannot heal us. You say I'm making this up, my Beloveds. Hear the facts. Look at all the AIDS, the cancers, the Ebola virus, the mad cow disease, SARS, and all the illness in our world. Can somebody say amen?"

"Amen!"

"Teach the Holy Word!"

He strolled to the edge of the stage as the crowd was shouting its praises. The organist was working a hip-wiggling bottom underneath his rhythmic, popping words.

"In these last days, will God heal you?" the prophet asked. "Does God heal any of the sick and the shut-in today?"

"God heals. God heals. God heals!"

The prophet began bouncing up and down, up and down. "Yes, God does heal. All these fake healers in these tents and mega-churches, all this hollering and whooping, that is not divine healing. I can show you some divine healing. Please say hallelujah!"

"Hallelujah!"

He lifted up his hands in dramatic fashion. "Only God can prolong life. Say amen! Can somebody say amen?"

"Amen!" came the collective reply.

"The faithful call God 'the divine physician,'" he shouted over the microphone. "God promises to heal us of all our ills. Did you know He used Paul and the other apostles to heal others? Yes, He did. God knows that divine healing is the only natural means of repairing the body and the soul. My Beloveds, do you believe that?"

"Yes. Praise His name!"

"My Beloveds, do you believe that?" he repeated in a calm voice.

"Yes! Praise His holy name!"

"What did I say before? You'd rather run to the doctor for treatment than get on your knees," the prophet exhorted them. "The medicines they give you are evil, man-made poisons that defile and corrupt the body. The body, which the Bible says, is the holiest of temples. Do you believe in divine healing? Do you believe in Him?"

"Amen!"

"Hallelujah!"

The prophet whispered, "Do you believe in me?"

With that question, the crowd went crazy, shouting, clapping, whooping, and hollering. I turned to Reverend Peck and told him that I had never seen anything like it. He had them eating out of the palm of his hand. He possessed total control of the crowd.

"This man is evil," Reverend Peck warned. "He is a false prophet, and the people who follow him will suffer. He was sent by Satan."

I laughed, startling a group of people standing near us. "I'll tell you what. He puts on a good show. I've not seen this kind of thing since I used to go to the carnivals and tent revivals."

Two of the mothers brought a small girl who was maybe seven onto the stage and told the prophet that she stuttered really badly. All the other kids made fun of her. The little girl was called a fool in her classes because she refused to read or speak.

"What is your name, darling?" the prophet asked her.

"Bernice, sir," the girl said. "I c-can't . . . t-talk . . . good. P-people m-make . . . m-make fun . . . of me."

The holy man rubbed his hands together very fast, producing heat of some sort, and then he held his palm over the girl's mouth. I thought he was going to suffocate her. Finally, she fainted like a heroine in one of the silent movies. Gently, going down softly.

One of the mothers, who were dressed in all white, helped her up and braced her for support. The crowd was on the edge of their seats, waiting to see this miracle.

The girl's eyes fluttered open. She didn't seem to know where she was. One of the mothers talked to her, informed her that she was onstage at a holy service.

"Welcome back, Bernice. Can I get you to read me something?" the prophet said, handing her a sheet of paper. "Remember, my Beloveds, I told you that God heals. Do you believe in His power? Do you believe in His goodness?"

"Praise His holy name!"

"Now this girl is cured by God, and He has made her whole," the prophet said excitedly. "Do you believe God can heal? Bernice, read what the paper says. It's from First John, fifth chapter and third verse. Read it, darling."

The girl took the paper and read smoothly like a radio announcer. "I love them who fear me, saith the Lord. I love them who fear me and keep my commandments."

"Did you hear any stuttering, my Beloveds? Did she trip over words or speak in a halting voice?" The prophet was full of himself. "Read it again, darling, so the people cannot say it was trickery."

"I love them who fear me, saith the Lord. I love them who fear me and keep my commandments," said the girl, who smiled a gap-toothed smile at the audience and bowed.

"Oh, my Beloveds, you want to know whether God is still on the throne," the prophet said, patting the girl on the shoulder as she was led off into the wings. "God is not a liar. God does not speak falsehoods. God doesn't mislead or betray our faith in Him."

Two of the brothers, dressed in all white, came with a young couple onstage, the withered husband in a wheelchair, his skin covered with scabby red lesions, completely engulfing his face, neck, and hands.

"Welcome to God's house, and what can we do for you?" the prophet said while one of the brothers read how badly the young man was afflicted with this horrible skin disease and other symptoms of an overall wasting ailment infecting his body. All the while, the man's wife was crying and looking pitifully at the prophet. Curious, the crowd was again clamoring to see what the holy man would do.

"What is your name, young man?" the prophet asked him.

The man was having a hard time holding up his mottled head to address the prophet and was shaking and trembling. "Glen, sir. Can you help me? The doctors have given up on me."

"The Lord never gives up on us, never," the holy man said, touching him first on the hand, then on the forehead. "Heal, Almighty Father. Heal! Cast out this sickness of the flesh. Heal!"

Suddenly the man fell to the side of the wheelchair, then pitched forward. The prophet placed his hands on both sides of the man's head, causing the afflicted soul's legs to shoot out and shudder.

"Will you brothers help the man remove his shirt and stand up?" the prophet asked. "Do you believe God can heal? Do you believe?"

The man stood on shaking legs, and the shirt was removed, with the red lesions drying up and disappearing. A brother rolled away the wheelchair so the man could stagger across the stage, feebly but on his own power.

"Do you believe now?" the prophet asked. "Do you believe the power of Him who must be obeyed? Do you believe God does heal? Say amen, somebody! Say amen!"

"Amen!" The crowd went into a frenzy, wildly screaming the name of the prophet, who smiled and watched the frail man depart.

After the man walked slowly off the stage, a brother assisting him, two brothers carried out a young woman, probably in her thirties, on a gurney, strapped down. Her agonizing shrieks filled the hall. Her arms and legs twitched and thrashed in a spasm, and her eyes rolled back in her head.

"I love this guy. This is better than vaudeville," I said to the reverend. "He is surely a showman. I hope they are filming this."

"You're not funny," Reverend Peck shot back. "This false prophet must be exposed. Everybody must see him for what he is."

The prophet walked over to the organist and talked to him, and the choir started to sing another song, "I Believe." He moved back to the flailing woman, caught up in her agony, and listened to one of the mothers read into the microphone about how the woman had caught a plague of demons from messing around with a Ouija board. Her family said she had been like this for three weeks, and nobody could help her, even though she had been in a hospital ward.

The prophet grinned and joked with the crowd. "This is an easy job. God says to cast out demons wherever they may be. The devil is a liar and a coward. He runs off whenever he is confronted by truth and righteousness. Do you believe, my Beloveds?"

"Yes, yes, yes!"

"Do you believe God can chase away demons?" the holy man asked them. "Do you believe, my Beloveds?"

"Amen!"

"Praise Him for whom all blessings flow!" One of the crowd yelled the praise at the top of her voice, again and again.

The prophet put his healing hand on the woman's throat, lifting it and then stroking it down the length of her neck. One reporter later wrote that people in the front row could see sparks, like electricity, pass through the holy man's hand and into the woman's skin.

"Go, son of mammon! Go!" the prophet shouted. "Release her. Release her to the power of God. Flee, evil. Flee!"

Shortly, the woman started to become calm, her arms and legs ceased their erratic movements, and her body went into a slumber of sorts. The prophet walked away from her as some of the people onstage moved forward to see the miracle.

"God heals," the prophet yelled into the microphone. "He can heal you if you let him. Evil cannot stand before God. God heals! Say amen!"

Security—eight burly men—was stationed in the aisles to keep the crowd at bay. They returned the frantic faithful to their seats, sometimes roughing up those who didn't go willingly.

Now the prophet was on his knees again as the brothers carted off the woman, who was still strapped down but was as limp as a dishrag. The holy man was talking slowly and solemnly into the microphone, in a jagged, pained voice.

"My Lord, have mercy on us, on us sinners," he said, making his words cry. "I believe Jesus Christ is the Son of the Living God. I believe He died on the cross and shed His precious blood for our sins. I believe God raised Jesus from the grave by the might of the Holy Spirit, and he sits on the right hand of God at this moment. Say amen!"

"Amen!"

He seemed to be on the verge of an emotional breakdown. "My Lord, I invite you into my heart. You see what I've done here, and I hope you find it worthy. I hope you find it pleasing. Please wash away all my filthy sins in the blood you shed on the cross. Wash us clean. Please forgive our sins and save our souls."

"Praise His holy name!"

"My Lord, your Word says you accept everyone and will take no one away," the prophet moaned. "Please include me in that number, you most humble servant. I know you have heard me. I know you have heard our prayers. As sinners, we will show our thankfulness by doing as you command and sinning no more."

One of the brothers helped him up while the choir sang his theme song at full throat. He collapsed once more, still shouting praises. "Praise the Lord. May God bless you and reward you abundantly." His face was covered with sweat, and his shirt was drenched with it.

For a moment, there was complete silence while the crowd collectively held its breath. This was Sinatra at the Paramount. This was James Brown at the Apollo. This was better than Barnum & Bailey or the Great Houdini. They had witnessed the work of a master showman.

It was as if the hearts of those in the gathering were pounding as one. Then the roar of the applause sounded, like one rippling wave after another, gaining in power and force. The prophet smiled and strutted across the stage in the glare of the spinning colored lights. The crowd applauded and applauded while the loudspeakers played his theme song, "How Great Thou Art." They continued clapping with an energetic zeal I'd never seen.

The prophet purred like a satisfied tomcat, waved at his Beloveds, pointed at them in divine recognition, and eventually held up his hand for them to stop. But they kept on clapping wildly. He grinned, bowed, holding up both hands for them to cease, for silence.

They clapped on and on and on, until the palms of their hands burned. I'd never seen anything like it.

"I've seen enough," Reverend Peck snorted as he started for the stairs.

Once we were both inside the car, the reverend confessed that his wife had an ulcer in her stomach, and it had been getting worse and worse until she went to see the prophet. Supposedly, he put his hands in the infection in her gut and removed it, and she immediately started to get better. No scar.

8

FOR HEAVEN'S SAKE

On the next day, after the Wilks revival, I returned from an afternoon of grocery shopping to find a large manila envelope marked: private. There was no doubt who it was from. Reverend Peck. I made a glass of iced tea, settled myself on the bed, and started reading the interview transcript. Who could have guessed the reverend had such good connections?

Exclusive Interview with Prophet Lamar Wilks
ITT News Exclusive with Rev. Dr. Lamar Wilks
Interviewed by ITT Correspondent Jeff Hahn
Transcript created October 15, 2010

Hahn: Prophet Wilks, I want to thank you so much for joining us today. Your schedule is a very busy one. Our many listeners will appreciate that you are will-ing to take part in this candid interview.
Wilks: You're very welcome, Jeff. Everything is in the open. I have nothing to hide.
Hahn: It's puzzling that you say you have nothing to hide. Some say you have wrestled control of the church of your former friend Reverend Hickory Peck right under his nose. Can you answer that charge?
Wilks: Everybody asks me if I betrayed a friend, a good friend. No, I didn't. Reverend Hickory Peck is a

man of God who I totally respect. The church members came to me and asked me to assume the leadership of an esteemed spiritual institution when they saw that it was not meeting their religious needs. There is some resistance, especially from the former pastor and the old guard. But the inspiration to keep going comes from God.

Hahn: Why is there some resistance?

Wilks: Like I said before, I have nothing to hide. As a man of God, I am a servant of the Lord, and He is the only one I answer to. The resistance comes from some of the members, those who don't want to change. They want the status quo. See, God gives man free will and lets us decide for ourselves. Sometimes God steps in, and sometimes He does not. Believe me, I don't understand many things that happen.

Hahn: What do you think is the role of the minister and the church in the black community? Do you think those roles need significant overhauls?

Wilks: No, I don't think so. The minister and the church in the black community play a very important role. Historically, we had Richard Allen, Absalom Jones, Henry M. Turner, Adam Clayton Powell, Martin Luther King, Ralph Abernathy, and Jesse Jackson. These were all fine men who led our community out of the darkness. The Baptist and Methodist churches placed themselves between us and slavery, between us and Jim Crow, between us and evil.

Hahn: What about the role of the minister in the church? Does that need to be changed?

Wilks: All I know is that I was called. I answered that call from the higher power. I was chosen. What I try to do is teach the life lessons of the Bible and to translate those teachings of a spiritual life for the real *world. I believe in the Word of God, that it doesn't teach hate, greed, or intolerance. The Word teaches us love, compassion, patience, forgiveness, serenity, a sense of moral responsibility, and a sense of balance. Loving God and believing in His Holy Word should make us happy, not bitter or close-minded.*

Hahn: Do you believe in religion serving as a political force? Do you believe in the separation of church and state?

Wilks: I have many friends who are elected officials, but I believe the church has no part in politics. That is, until the politicians try to ram things through that are not pleasing in the sight of the Almighty.

Hahn: And what are those things?

Wilks: I'm not a Tea Party member, but I do agree with some of their platform. However, I believe the government should leave us alone and let us do the business of serving the Lord. I'm not concerned about abortion, gay rights, affirmative action, or the black vote, except when it goes against the tenets of the Good Book. I'm concerned about spreading the Gospel, saving the souls of sinners, and casting out demons. That's the role of a man of God.

Hahn: Some say that your ministry is a selfish one, that it's a religious mission that is all about you.

Wilks: What is your question, Jeff?

Hahn: Are you exploiting the poor and the needy for your own profit?

Wilks: How can you ask me that? This is the age of neuroses. My community needs me. I am their beacon. Some say my ministry is solely about my needs, my desires, my wants. Not true. I'm here in this life to rid souls trapped in sin of their shame and dehumanization. The Bible teaches there should be no shame. Sal-

vation and shame cannot coexist. Shame has broken the spirit of so many people. What I say to society is to give those people with that shame to me, and I'll give them hope and salvation.

Hahn: And how will you do that? Give me some specifics.

Wilks: One way is through prayer. I see prayer as an art form. It is not a one-way conversation, because not only does God listen, but He also answers back.

Hahn: Some say that you charge a great deal for membership in your church and that your ministry is nothing but a theatrical performance. Do you charge money to heal in the name of the Lord?

Wilks: That's nonsense. When there are people who are sick and desperate, they turn to God and want some relief. Our church's financial concerns are nobody's business. God's money isn't supposed to be scrutinized by men.

Hahn: What are you saying? If there is something criminal about the church's financial dealings, it's nobody's business. Is that what you're saying?

Wilks: Something like that. You could look at it like that.

Hahn: At your last church, the state attorney general wanted you to disclose all financial information, and you declined. In fact, you passed along your ministry to another and disappeared. Law enforcement officials there still want to question you.

Wilks: I don't know about any of that. If you want further information, I'd say please get in touch with my attorneys.

Hahn: Do you have many aliases? They say you have many names and identities. Can you address that?

Wilks: There are some things I don't discuss about my past. Just know that God's anointed should be treated differently, and the chosen do not ask questions when they are blessed by the Lord. I don't question God's ways. I choose to trust Him, even if I don't understand Him all the time.

Hahn: At your last appearance, at a local high school, there was standing-room-only attendance. You healed some of the people there and cast out demons in another. Are you qualified to cast out demons?

Wilks: There are two Bible passages that pertain to the casting out of demons. Matthew 12:31–32 says, "Wherefore I say unto you, All manner of sin and blasphemy shall be forgiven unto men: but the blasphemy against the Holy Ghost shall not be forgiven unto men. And whosoever speaketh a word against the Son of Man, it shall be forgiven him: but whosoever speaketh against the Holy Ghost, it shall not be forgiven him, neither in this world, neither in the world to come."

Hahn: What does this passage mean? And what does that have to do with the casting out of demons?

Wilks: Maybe this other verse will do. It's Luke 11:19–20. "And if I by Beelzebub cast out devils, by whom do your sons cast them out? Therefore shall they be your judges. But if I with the finger of God cast out demons, no doubt the Kingdom of God is come upon you." That should explain what I'm doing.

Hahn: It sounds like you're a false prophet, such as described in the Bible.

Wilks: Jeff, you have no idea about anointing. I am the chosen. I am a servant of God on earth. I have a duty to heal, spread the Word, and cast out demons. And that's what I do. I don't ask questions of God. I accept what He has in store for me.

Hahn: What about your purchase of a 5.7-million-dollar mansion, a new private jet, and a Rolls-Royce car? What do your members think about that?

Wilks: They don't ask questions of a true servant of God. Neither do I. If God commands me to buy these things, I buy them.

Hahn: I don't understand. So nobody can question your motives or agenda? You don't find that all this excess contradicts the true purpose of being a Christian or a man of God?

Wilks: What do you find contradictory? Tell me what.

Hahn: All this excess, the false theatrics, the arrogance of your religious status. Nobody calls you on it.

Wilks: Because nobody sees anything wrong with it except you and some of the politicians. I'm just doing what God tells me. He doesn't want any of his servants to be poor and raggedy. Remember Father Divine or Daddy Grace? No, this was before your time.

Hahn: I've heard of them. They were con men as well.

Wilks: They were healers and spread the Good Word. They were men ahead of their time. I'm a healer. At the last service, I healed a young woman and cast the demons out of her body. My whole body was tingling, full of the divine power. I could feel it surging right down to my toes, and when I touched her, the demons fled from her body.

Hahn: There are so many false healing ministries today. Everybody's a seer, a prophet, a guru. What I would say to these people, these unfortunates, is that they should be wary of you guys. Buyer beware!

Wilks: Everybody loved Kathryn Kuhlman and Aimee Semple McPherson, and A. A. Allen, even Benny Hinn. I have to throw Jimmy Swaggart in there too.

These were beloved servants of the Lord. I don't know why you people think you can criticize God's anointed.

Hahn: How did you get into the prophet business?

Wilks: God first appeared to me when I was six. I was being bullied by some bigger fellows, and I heard a booming voice. There were four of them. The voice said for me to pick up a rock and ball it up in my hand and smite these boys.

Hahn: The voice said "smite." Is that true?

Wilks: Yes, it is. And I did what the voice said, and victory was mine. God has been appearing to me ever since. When I found myself out of work years later, I heard the voice again, but this time there was also an incredibly bright yellow light in my room. It showed me things, visions, such as speaking before large audiences, traveling all over the world to spread the Gospel, making a pilgrimage to the Holy Land.

Hahn: Have you been to the Holy Land?

Wilks: Yes, I have. Twice.

Hahn: What else did God show you?

Wilks: The Almighty showed me that I would be a true servant of Him, performing all kinds of miracles, signs, wonders, and healings that would defy explanation.

Hahn: Do you really believe this? I can't believe that you do.

Wilks: I remember being on TV, on Pat Robertson's The 700 Club, and he never questioned my commitment to the Lord. He knew the power of being a man of God. You would be smart not to question God's will or my anointing.

Hahn: Some would say you're a wolf in sheep's clothing. Some would say that your commitment is bankrupt, that you're peddling a false God and a false Gospel. Some would curse you for tainting a positive faith, a loving and caring God, and a life-affirming message that could help thousands and thousands of people.

Wilks: Watch out! You're committing blasphemy.

Hahn: Just think of someone thinking you're representing God, when really you are not doing that. You're a faker, a phony.

Wilks: I ask you, can God raise the dead? Can God heal the sick?

Hahn: I'm a religious man.

Wilks: But do you believe in God's power? Yes or no?

Hahn: Yes, I'm a Christian. But I don't believe in you. I don't believe that you represent God and His church. I smell a rat.

Wilks: Maybe I have a head cold, because I don't smell anything. Let me say this. I came on here so I could get some things clear. I do not do the Lord's work for money or expensive things. I make no excuses for God. He chose me.

Hahn: Do you truly think you've been honest with me and our viewers?

Wilks: Yes, I do. All I'm saying is that if you want to judge the prophet, I warn you to be careful. Be sure that it is not out of jealousy.

Hahn: All I want to do is to get to the truth. I want to expose you for the fake that you are.

Wilks: (Grabs Hahn's arm.) I bless your life with God's awesome power. I bless your wife and children with long life and with divine protection. This is the voice of the Holy Ghost speaking through me. May every satanic attack fail against you and yours. Amen, amen, amen.

Hahn: Is this some kind of a reverse curse against me and my family? What are you doing? Are you threatening me? Are you threatening my family? I'll have you escorted from the building by security. This interview is over.

Wilks: (Standing.) *Our blessed Lord will look over you. Don't worry.*

9

THE HYMN IS YOU

The ancient Ford Fairlane sedan followed me out to the old schoolhouse near the highway over in Carterville, a rickety beaverboard structure with a tin roof that served as an elementary school for the poor kids of the farmers in the area. I had seen the car parked out in front of my motel, then near the grocery store, and finally at the drugstore where I got some allergy medicine. The guy wasn't hiding the fact that he was shadowing me. He wanted me to know it.

I pulled up to the schoolhouse and saw that the reverend's car was not around. I watched a lanky black woman, dressed in a plain powder-blue dress, shepherd a group of energetic, spry kids out into the field near the building.

"Don't you do that," the teacher called to them as two boys chased a girl in a circle, trying to snatch her ponytail. "Behave yourselves."

The driver of the Ford parked off on the side of the dirt road, where he could keep an eye on me. The sun was hot and bright. There was a breeze, light and very passive, in the air.

In a cloud of dust, Reverend Peck's shiny blue Oldsmobile came down the road and backed into the parking area beside the school. He leaped from the automobile, obviously in a hurry, saw the Ford, and waved to me. I started to get out of the car, but he walked over.

"Hey, Clint. How long have you been here?" he asked. He was dressed very casually, no suit and tie today. A pair of sunglasses covered his eyes, so I couldn't see his expression.

"Just got here," I replied. "Did you see our friend there?"

He leaned down at the window on the driver's side. "I saw him. I've got one too. He goes with me wherever I go. Sometimes I can shake him, sometimes not. I don't mind a shadow as long as nobody gets unlawful. You know what I mean?"

I nodded. "I do. Why are they tailing us?"

"Mr. Wilks wants to keep tabs on us, to make sure we don't rock the boat," he answered. "He's afraid of us. He thinks we'll do something to mess up his plans."

The reverend opened the door and let me step out. We walked back over to his car, and he unlocked the trunk. He lifted a box of slightly used clothes into my arms; then he picked up another box, this one full of books. A smile spread across his face, and he closed the trunk and walked to the schoolhouse.

"The kids'll love all of this," Reverend Peck said, grinning. "Their parents don't make enough to properly provide the things they so desperately need. Clothes are always welcome, and the books will go to the school's library. I got some dictionaries and a set of old encyclopedias. They can look things up with them."

Almost on cue, we could hear the children singing, shouting, and laughing in the field behind us. They were the future for this economically depressed region of rural Alabama. I knew Reverend Peck's total commitment to them and their education, which would enable them to leave this place.

"Did you meet their teacher, Miss Addie James?" he asked.

I shook my head. "I didn't go inside. I didn't want to miss you, and I also wanted to keep an eye on my pal in the Ford there."

We went inside the schoolhouse, into the first of three rooms, where the classes were held. The doors were in need of repair: they didn't shut, possibly because of the warping of the wood. There were two windows covered with cardboard to keep out the cold wintertime air, as well as an old wood-burning heater.

We put the boxes down on a desk and sat down. He wasted no time in getting down to business: the abduction of his church by a false messiah, the low morale of his congregation under siege, and the transformation of his place of true worship into a slick theatrical-show palace of phony healing and insincere religious practices.

"What did you think of Mr. Wilks?" the reverend asked.

"I've got to give it to him. He knows how to entertain a crowd," I said. "He's a great showman. I watched him at that school, holding the crowd almost under a hypnotic spell. He's good, real good."

I was fidgety, wanting to do something with my hands, possibly smoke a cigarette. Through the remaining windows, I could see the gravel field that served as a parking lot and, beyond that, rows and rows of yellow corn on a nearby farmer's land. The joyous notes of the small black faces in the orchard near the edge of the field were still loud and were a welcome sound to my ears.

Something was eating away at the reverend's resolve. "Clint, have you ever been so desperate that you'd do anything just to breathe? Probably not."

"What do you mean, Reverend?" I knew by the tone of his voice that there was more to this than Prophet Wilks's stealing his church.

His back stiffened. "I know the Baptist doctrine. My whole family has served the Lord and has served Him well. But I know once Wilks gets ahold of my congregation, really gets ahold of them, they'll follow him to the grave."

There was not much to understand; this was a man of God who had just had his church stolen right from under his nose. He felt betrayed by the church members. They knew his life, knew his preacher father, and the heavy sacrifices his family had endured for that place of worship. And now this faker was taking it all away from him. He had a right to be ticked off.

"Do you have another vision you can offer your congregation?" I asked, not wanting to show him up or anything. "It seems Wilks has dazzled them and has made them lose their senses."

He drummed his fingers on the desk in front of him. "I know, I know. I'm not a dummy. I'm not a country hick. He thinks he can con the council of elders to go along with his schemes. He stands up there, spewing some garbage, some get-rich-quick hokum, and performs some foolish vaudeville healing stunts, and they're ready to accept him as the new Messiah."

"Tell me about this council of elders. This is the first I've heard of them. How do they figure in all of this?"

Reverend Peck stared up at one of the walls, at the framed portraits of the Kennedy brothers, Dr. Martin Luther King, Rosa Parks, and President Obama. I saw the flood of pride and warmth wash over his face. The Peck family had been warriors in the civil rights movement, beginning with the Montgomery bus boycott, then on to the bloody Selma march—they had grieved during the funeral of the three little girls in Birming-ham—to the March on Washington, and to Reverend King's final days and his slaying in Memphis. They had been there during the whole ordeal.

"The council of elders meets once a month, deciding the future of the church by committee," the reverend began quietly. "We chose the council from church people in this community, four men and three women, all experienced, with the wisdom of age, in the purpose of faithful spiritual worship. I trusted them before this stranger came into our midst. Now I'm not so sure."

"What has stirred up so much doubt?"

He rubbed his eyes with a weary motion. "The council of elders thinks Wilks is a man ahead of his time. They have drunk the Kool-Aid and have opened all doors to him. I don't distrust my religious brethren, but I wonder about their judgment. He's turned our church into a circus, complete with carnival sideshows, and all we lack is a bearded lady and a sword swallower."

"Do you really think it's that bad?"

The reverend wrinkled his nose. "Yes, I do. He's filled the church with a bunch of sinners, agnostics, and atheists disguised as believers. I believe the Lord will make us pay for his misdeeds."

"He is a kind and loving God," I reassured him. "I don't think He jumps to conclusions or makes snap judgments. When you're dealing with the Lord, there are no mistakes. Everything has a purpose."

"Maybe so." The reverend smiled, toyed with his mustache. "Still, it's easy to get caught up in the whirl-wind of change and forget the bedrock of tradition. I know that if the church doesn't change and increase its outreach, we're going to lose so many precious souls to sin. However, I don't think this is the way we should do it."

"What changes has Wilks put into place?" I watched his face, his eyes, for further signs of panic or anxiety.

The reverend threw up his hands in frustration. "That creep Wilks has changed the entire agenda of the church. Everything is focused on his extravagant weekend services, the large gatherings in workshops about how to get rich using Biblical prophecies, and big healing sessions. He loves a dollar. He wants to get rich."

I thought about Dr. Smart and his greedy scheme and why I left his church in a hurry. "What else, Reverend?"

"No more Bible study, no more youth counseling sessions, no Tuesday prayer service or Men's Fellowship Fridays," he said sadly. "He even cut out the Sistas' Social Saturdays, where the girls and women could discuss issues pertaining to females. Now he has private counseling at his house. Some of the church members are real suspicious about these meetings, especially with the young girls."

That made me think about the pitiful girls Reverend Peck had brought to my motel room at the beginning of my Alabama trip, over a month ago. "Whatever happened to those girls you drove to see me? Are they okay?"

"Yes, praise the Lord. They're safe and sound, where Wilks cannot get his hands on them. When it's time, I plan to produce them so I can make my case. Maybe I can convince the church of Wilks's evil plan."

"Are there other changes to the church?" I asked, satisfied that everything was all right with the battered girls.

He waved his arm around the ill-equipped schoolroom, pointing out the lack of functioning desks, the broken windows, and the cracked blackboard. "Clint, you can tell this is one of the poorest areas in the South.

Around here, there are a lot of people living without the basic essentials. Just barely getting by. That's why we have a regular food pantry. We used to bring boxes of food, clothing, and books to the poor families in this area and to neighboring communities near the church."

"That's admirable," I said, grinning. "That's what a church should do in a community like this one. We must help the poor and needy."

"No. Wilks says it's a waste of money," the reverend said, sneering. "He wants to discontinue the food pantry and the charity outreach to the families and put more funds toward building up the healing shows. He wants to make them more theatrical and gaudy. All the council of elders can see is the added revenue, fistfuls of money to buy fancy clothes and big cars. Wilks has replaced their faith with images of greed and lust. He could give a hoot about prayer or worship. All he wants is to make a buck."

"Holy cow," I said, stunned by how fast Wilks had worked his magic. "And that's why he sees you as such a threat."

The reverend's eyes narrowed. "Wilks knows I see right through him. He knows I'll not tolerate seeing all the work my family did in building this church go right down the drain. In two weeks Wilks is going to present an entire list of his proposals to the council of elders, and I've got to stop him."

"Wilks is a smooth operator. That's for sure," I said, shaking my head. "I don't know if you can stop him. He seems to have the council and the congregation completely fooled."

The reverend blew out a loud breath of worry and fatigue. "Boy, I'll say this. He's taking me to school. I can't get a fix on him. I can't make out any of his moves. He seems to know my mind before I can fashion a reply. He seems to know my every move."

It was my turn to make a wisecrack. "That's because Wilks is a slick Northern cullud boy." He laughed out loud at that remark.

"What I worry about is the fact that he's influencing a lot of the brothers, young brothers, who are hungry to take their place in the sun," Reverend Peck stated. "These brothers feel society is ignoring them, and Wilks gives them that respect and recognition. He's got their number. He knows how bad they want that. He knows what they need."

I pointed out to the reverend that Prophet Wilks didn't preach to the choir; instead, he embraced and welcomed the worst kinds of sinners and heathens. The man promised to save their souls, as well as give them newfound financial opportunities, and divine forgiveness and redemption in these final days of judgment.

He bristled. "I don't like an outsider telling my church what to do. Also, I don't like that Wilks claims his own Word is equal to that of God's. He has no right to do that."

I scratched my head and frowned. "But so far your church has allowed him to get away with that foolishness. I'd be a little wary about a man who says he's God."

He was excited to tell me this. "Now, I know this guy's off his rocker. He tells me he keeps living one life after another. Then he says he's lived many lives. I think it proves he needs to be in somebody's crazy house."

"Could be." I didn't want to follow that line of reasoning.

The reverend went on blasting his foe. "Now, when I think of it, he might be nuts. He said to me after one of the deacon board meetings, 'Are you really waiting for somebody to come down from another planet and save our butts?' I didn't know what to make of that."

"I think Wilks likes to mess with your head," I replied.

His mouth drew taut and hard, evidence of his steely resolve. "Clint, I *will* stop him. When there's a will, there's a way. I trust in the Lord, and He's on my side. He will make a way."

There was one thing I didn't want to bring up, but I had to ask. "Reverend, they say your wife has left you and taken up with Wilks. Is that true? I can't believe it."

He slumped and concentrated on his fumbling hands. "The church has been buzzing with rumors of Geneva and him being together. One of the deacons told the head usher that he saw Wilks and my wife at a roadhouse last week. He says they couldn't keep their hands off each other."

"Do you believe the rumors, Reverend?"

His pitiful stare spoke the bitter truth. "They're true. Geneva always wanted the finer things in life. He can give them to her, but I warned her that those things might come with a high price. She says she doesn't care as long as she gets them. She says she is tired of promises of getting everything in the future. She wants them now."

"I don't think your wife knows who she is dealing with," I said. "Wilks is a tough dog to keep on the porch. He's always catting around. He'll chew your wife up and spit her out."

The reverend kept staring at a tattered globe with parts of the southern hemisphere ripped away. "I know. I know Wilks is no good. She'll get hurt, and I don't know if she can deal with that. She's always been coddled and sheltered from the bad things of life."

He reminded me about the Saturday after Labor Day this year, when Wilks gave an event near Pell City. The gathering was all female: females in SUVs, females in station wagons, females in pickups, even females on tractors. He did his best impression of Dr. Phil among his loyal admirers. Some of the beaus and husbands were outraged. The local newspaper said a group of gals carried Wilks on their shoulders while they chanted his name.

I stood up and went to the window in time to see a white man with a straw hat leading two beautiful stallions down the dirt road. The well-groomed animals were following his lead without any trouble.

"Did you know Wilks sells his sermons on DVDs through the mail?" the reverend asked me.

"No, I didn't. The man's a hustler."

A few minutes later the reverend went out to his car and brought in two large pots, plastic bowls, and three long Italian bread loaves. We placed them on a long table and set chairs around it. He told me to run out to his car and retrieve the shopping bag of cookies, which had been donated by an area bakery, from the backseat. The bakery's owner had said the cookies were two days old, but he thought the kids would like them.

When I returned to the schoolroom, the children had already filed in. I looked at the ragamuffin kids, many of them in shoddy clothes, boys with patches on their knees and girls in faded dresses. Still, they were chasing one another, singing, and holding hands, their faces happy and radiant. It was as if they knew they held the promise of that community's collective future.

I got a good look at their teacher. She didn't look as plain and dowdy as she had at first glance. She was neat, low-key, but very feminine in a Southern kind of way. The reverend noticed me looking at her.

"We want the children to have real, productive lives, not the oppressed ones that the crackers have in store for them," the reverend said.

One little girl in overalls did a headstand while the others watched and clapped. Before long the teacher put a stop to her little exhibition. She also wiped the runny nose of one of the tykes, removing all traces of snot with a tissue. Reverend Peck and I smiled and shook our heads; they were a noisy bunch.

I walked over to the kids and the teacher, who laughed as one little boy with nappy red hair put an arm around her waist while pointing at me with his other hand.

"Who he?" the boy asked the teacher.

Still smiling, the teacher turned to me, her eyes sparkling, and asked who I was.

"This here Reverend Clint," Reverend Peck said, introducing me. "And this here is Miss Addie James, schoolteacher deluxe."

Addie James and I shook hands, because I didn't know what the customary greeting was between a man and a woman below the Mason-Dixon Line. She then prepared the children for lunch, brushing the dirt and grime off their cheeks and hands with soap and water. The older kids helped somewhat, leading the younger ones to the table where lunch was waiting for them. Hot bean soup, bread, a little salad, and cookies for dessert, courtesy of the reverend.

"Little Emory, he's such a sweetie, but his mama doesn't take care of him like she should," the teacher said, pointing to the little redhead running to the lunch table. "She has a lap baby, and that requires all her attention."

As we started to leave, Addie said to me, "Don't be a stranger, suh." That sweet 'Bama lady accent.

The reverend winked when we were out of her sight. I grinned. The last thing I needed was a little romance. That could complicate things. The reverend got into his car, and when I started to cross the road on foot, the driver of the Ford Fairlane gunned his engine and raced toward me, narrowly missing me. I figured that was a warning.

10

A DIXIE RIFT

Sang's Diner, a landmark of fine dining in Carterville, was the meeting place where Reverend Peck had said it was safe to rendezvous. Everything was arranged by the reverend a few days after the visit to the schoolhouse. He confessed he had some pull with the sheriff. The sheriff would be joining us for this latest conference. I was tired of all this cloak-and-dagger mess. To be honest, I was getting tired of all this church intrigue and the backbiting and betrayal by church officials. The only thing holding me to this deal was my friendship with the reverend and the fact that he'd been there for me when I was going through the terrible crisis with Dr. Smart.

I stood under the diner's blinking neon sign, which called to the hungry of this sleepy Alabama town. Once I went through the doors, I noticed the badly printed signs announcing homemade chicken soup, blue-plate specials, fat burgers and thick fries, and mouthwatering slices of apple and peach pie. There were two heavyset black ladies, probably members of the reverend's church, smiling a warm greeting at me.

"Over here, Clint, over here," Reverend Peck shouted, waving at me.

The diner's proprietor, Miss Sang Owens, stopped flipping hamburger meat to come over to see what I wanted, doing a special favor for the reverend and the sheriff. Very stout, she wore her gray-streaked hair in a ponytail and filled out her uniform with a mighty frame.

"Gentlemens, what do you require?" she asked sweetly. The two men, who had arrived early, waited on me before ordering their meal.

"What's good, darling?" Sheriff Frank Means replied, grinning. "This man's from up North, and we got to treat him right. He don't know good food from eatin' up there."

We all laughed. The reverend was uncommonly quiet, almost timid. Miss Sang explained that dinner wouldn't be ready before four in the afternoon, but we could have breakfast or lunch. It was only one thirty. We all settled for her special burgers, which were triple stacked, with an order of fries and a slice of homemade pie. The sheriff ordered a hot slice of peach with a dollop of vanilla ice cream, while the reverend ordered apple with nothing on it. I asked for the same dish the sheriff had ordered, always partial to that sweet taste of peach.

When our burgers were ready, Miss Sang sent one of her waitresses over to our table, a young filly with upturned breasts and a high rear end. She was a real looker, but we ignored her and began to chow down as soon as she set our plates in front of us. I could tell this was serious.

Nobody said a word until we had eaten and drunk a cup and a half of dark coffee. Then introductions were made, and things got down to business.

Sheriff Means, who told me he was in his second term as Carterville's chief law enforcement officer, acknowledged that there was a crisis brewing in his town. He informed me that he had been elected a few years ago to end the brutality of the town's old white sheriff, who had beaten and harassed the Negroes, as they were known then, without any resistance.

"The old cullud folks took the abuse without any fuss," the sheriff said. "When the town elected me, they figured it was a new day. I look at it like this. Live and let live. I'm about compromise. There's still some Klan and militia activity in the area, but I leave them alone and they leave me alone."

"Tell Clint what the trouble is now," the reverend said sternly.

"I'm coming to that, Reverend," the sheriff replied. "See, I know these people 'round here. I grew up with them, know the blacks and the whites. They know my family, and I know theirs. They saw me grow up, knew me when I was a kid, a teenager back in the sixties. At the time, I wanted to join the SCLC under Stokely Carmichael. I went outlaw for a little bit, but the folks reeled me back in. I had to be loyal to my race. Do you remember Stokely?"

I nodded. I recalled that he had coined the term "Black Power" and that he and H. Rap Brown were the militant counterbalance to the more moderate Reverend Martin Luther King and his group of ministers and supporters.

"I think he took an African name and went international," I answered. "Didn't he die over there in Africa some place?"

"That's right," the sheriff said. "That's not me. I'm as country as watermelon."

"Get to it, Sheriff," the reverend said, very impatient.

"Well, the crackers want me to chase Mr. Wilks out of here," Sheriff Means said. "They want him out any way possible. They're getting restless. They want action, and they want it now."

"Why do they want him out?" I asked.

The sheriff, in love with his own voice, didn't want to get to the point. "Reverend Peck, it's a shame what he's doing to your church. Everybody around here knows that ain't right what he's doing. The white folk even know that. They're hoping that situation will come to a head."

"That's not going to happen no time soon," the reverend said, frowning. "He's got the folks fooled."

"What kind of man is Mr. Wilks?" the sheriff questioned. "Is he a sophisticated gal boy, or is he a randy skirt chaser?"

I piped up. "He's a greedy con man, period."

"And a false Messiah. Don't leave that out." The reverend had a score to settle with Mr. Wilks.

"The white planters and the big farms around here are teed off at Mr. Wilks because he's putting ideas into the heads of the black farmers and landowners in this area about how they should make more of a profit from their crops," the sheriff explained. "He's got the independent truckers in on his plan to squeeze more dollars from the market. He's been holding meetings with the young fellas and men and telling them they can make more bucks from their crops to make up for the bad weather, bad crops, and the big money paid out for the new equipment and feed. He's telling them that everything's gone up, so they should get a larger piece of the pie, and the white planters don't like that."

"I think he had political ambitions when he sucked up my church," the reverend said angrily. "Who does he think he is? Dr. King or Reverend Abernathy? That's why he wants my church . . . so he can use it as a political base. Dang! I should have seen it comin'."

"That's not all," the sheriff said, sipping his coffee. "Wilks convinced a group of the more successful black farmers and truckers to join co-ops so they can get a higher return when they sell their goods at market. This makes them more of a profit, so they can fend off any attempts from the white planters to buy up their land when they go broke."

"And that's why they're upset," I volunteered. "That's why the white folks want him out."

"Yessuh, Wilks thinks he's King, Adam Clayton Powell, and Malcolm X all rolled into one!" the reverend exclaimed, his voice getting a little louder, causing patrons to look at our table. "The church has no business being involved in commerce and politics. I've always felt that way."

I disagreed. "I think if Dr. King had followed your opinion, then the civil rights movement would have never existed. Somebody had to take a stand."

"The peckerwoods are riled up," the sheriff continued. "They're mad as a wet hen because Wilks got the farmers and truckers on a work stoppage. He's a very opinionated boy. He's stopped much of the freight traffic in this part of the state. He's blocked food and gas deliveries and halted most of the marketing of the crops in this region."

"Dang, you got to be kiddin'." The reverend was flabbergasted.

"When does he find the time to do his union work?" I laughed.

"I don't know," the sheriff replied.

"Gentlemen, I believe I know," the reverend said eagerly. "When I went to Anniston, he held a service in a field behind the county line that only black boys and men could attend. I looked around, and there were folks as far as the eye could see. Some of the fellas had signs saying in bold print WE AIN'T NO FOOLS ! I wondered what that was about."

"Holy cow!" I was shocked.

The reverend was working up the memory of what he'd seen in Anniston. "Wilks kept shouting at the men, saying, 'Heaven is right here in this world, and so is hell.' I thought that was funny. He kept repeating that line. As he kept saying it, the crowd was going crazy, shouting and hollering."

I shook my head. Wilks was playing with things he should leave alone. It was one thing to want to praise God, but it was another to wish to be God. That was very dangerous, indeed.

"Mr. Wilks has fallen in love with an idea that might lead him into some trouble," I said. "These white folks are not to be underestimated. They'll show him no mercy. He has more guile and backbone than I originally thought."

"Wilks will be dead if he don't stop what he doing," the sheriff suggested. "He's stepping on too many toes. The crackers hate that this Wilks, a Northern nigger, got these cullud co-ops raising crops and selling their goods to the food chains directly. The white planters and big farms hate this, and they hate Wilks."

"And they can make Wilks disappear," the reverend warned.

After this remark, we sipped our coffee and didn't say anything else. Wilks had no idea what forces were moving against him and what extremes they would go to in order to protect their profits. Holy man or no holy man.

11

ABRACADABRA

One night after the meeting with the sheriff, there was a series of fireworks at a healing service a few miles outside of Tuscaloosa, where some of Prophet Wilks's members lived. We drove there to see what the false Messiah was stirring up. He was again dressed in all white, sporting a stylish Italian suit with the customary red rose in the lapel. When we arrived, the band was warming up, going through hints of songs it would play during this evening dedicated to the homeless.

"Welcome, my Beloveds. When are the homeless arriving?" the holy man asked one of his assistants with a team of troubleshooters. "When they get here, put them right out front. I want the audience to see them. Remember, you send them one by one to me, and I'll give them a blessing."

His assistant was lively, eager to do his bidding. "After that, do you want to give them money or food or just shove them out the door?"

Prophet Wilkes's back was turned to a staff member in the wings of the stage, and he was shouting questions at him over his shoulder. At the same time he motioned with his hands, urging his assistant to lower his voice. The rows were filling in, with all kinds of people coming to his event. I guess they were curious about him and his work.

I watched him for a time with Reverend Peck, who stared at him with utter disgust. We then walked farther away from the stage and stationed ourselves in a place where they couldn't see us. This service was being held in a large parking lot. Three police cars were parked nearby, and the officers strolled through the crowd. I didn't know what kind of trouble they were worried about.

The church was full of control freaks, perfectionists whose parents had stressed success at all costs or had withheld their affection in exchange for achievement, sending the message "We love you, but you must do better." Prophet Wilks was one of these folks who needed everything in its place, in a kind of order.

Before long the service got under way. While the band and two choirs performed the classic hymn "The Lord's Prayer," Prophet Wilks was out onstage, trying to stoke the spiritual flame in the souls of those who had gathered. He walked over to the stairs and paused before going on in his praise of the Almighty.

"My Beloveds, every one of us tonight is washed in the blood of Jesus Christ, anointed by the spirit of the living God. Say amen," the holy man said. "It is God's words that flow out of the mouths of the anointed. We are His messenger, and the Lord is saying, 'Send out that message of love and salvation into the land of the sinners.' Say amen."

The crowd shouted a hearty amen. We could see that there was a sizable number of Reverend Peck's congregants there, some of whom he had thought were loyal and faithful to his doctrine.

"God is the same yesterday, today, and forever," the holy man said with a punch in his voice. "I hear chief sinners, some of the people in this area, say somebody should do something about this man. He's trying to mess things up. He's trying to put an end to the natural order of things. But all I want to point out are the things that are wrong and need to be fixed with divine glue. That glue is God's Word. Say amen."

Shouts of amen came back to him. He was pleased, very pleased. While he was speaking, the ushers showed a group of men and women to the front of the audience, where they were seated on special chairs that had been reserved for them. They smiled at him, happy that he had shown some mercy on them.

"They don't want me to tell what is wrong!" he yelled. "They want me to keep quiet, to be meek as a lamb. I say to them, 'You bunch of hypocrites, you bunch of vipers, you bunch of blasphemers, you need to flee the wrath of the Most High, who is coming!' The voices of the anointed will never be stilled. Never!"

The crowd sat there, not knowing how to react. He had never been this intense, this over the top, this manic. They sat there, not clapping, almost holding their breath.

"Say amen. Say amen. Say amen," Prophet Wilks yelled.

The gathering answered him in kind. Now they were with him.

He was still standing at the stairs, not yet having gone down them, but he wanted to make a point about the speedy arrival of Judgment Day and the heavy price about to exacted on the souls of sinners. This was one of the areas in which the holy man was skilled, in issuing warnings.

"My Beloveds, this is the day of the Redeemer," the he said, going back on the stage. "With our words and our souls, we commit to the teachings of Jesus Christ, the song of the living God. He, the crucified one, is coming back again. He is coming back, the King of Glory and judge of all living things. If you knew the day He was coming, would you be ready to meet Him, my Beloveds?"

He strolled across the stage and kneeled down, pointing to the group that had just arrived. "Welcome, my Beloveds. These are those who have slipped through the cracks through no fault of their own. They were hardworking, good-living people who lost their jobs and homes. They need fixing. They need fixing by the Lord. Say amen."

Again, the response was a solid, sincere amen.

"We have a program at our church where we give them a hot shower and clean clothes," the holy man said. "When we first opened our doors, we had a crowd of folks around the parking lot. All for a hot shower, clothes, and a bite to eat. We also give them a place to nap and a haircut, and referrals to employers around there."

The smiles on the homeless people were even broader. They clapped the loudest anytime the holy man paused or took a breath. This was the human side of Wilks, which baffled the reverend. He wanted to paint the man as evil, cruel, and despicable, but there were elements to the holy man's personality that defied a label. That was the unholy contradiction.

He sat down among a row of civic leaders, church officials, and some of the elders of Reverend Peck's congregation. A deacon moved to the microphone, held up his hand, and told the gathering to give freely for the benefit of the homeless. Ladies in all white passed large collection plates along the rows, and once filled with coins and bills, they were handed to others, who took them back stage.

Then Prophet Wilks was back onstage, waving his arms, jumping up and down. "I speak the Holy Word and transform souls. You've seen my work. You know my life. Don't ask questions of the anointed. Don't question if I know God. I speak for God. Say amen, my Beloveds."

"Nobody wants to talk about being hungry and being poor," he continued. "When you bring up those subjects, they turn their heads. But I'm going to get on my holy soapbox and shout to the heavens for those people with means to provide for those who have not eaten and have no money. That's why you're giving from your hearts. That's why you know you're doing God's will."

That same platoon of loyal members of the holy man's army fanned out among the gathering and passed out small red crosses to wear. They were polite but firm about putting a cross in the palm of everyone sitting there.

"This cross is the cure for the wicked world in which we live, suffer, and struggle, my Beloveds," the holy man said, cradling the microphone. "We need the cross more than ever. We need the Lord more than ever. This cross is the symbol of redemption and salvation for the wronged, the poor, and the suffering. Hold on to that blessed cross. Hug the cross. Embrace the blessed cross."

The crowd was getting a little twitchy, as if they were saying, "Enough with the fire-and-brimstone chatter." They wanted the healing to begin. The holy man, sensing they were getting impatient, moved the show into another gear. A chubby woman in pink began singing "Oh Happy Day," and some in the crowd sang along.

"Ah, the world, the flesh, the devil," the holy man murmured.

Reverend Peck nudged me, shaking his head, noting that this show was not as tight as some of those we had seen in Fayette, Cragford, and Fultondale. He was right about the quality of the service. It wasn't as good. I figured the pressure was on Wilks from the big farms, the white planters, and the cops, and he was facing steady resistance from the supporters of Reverend Peck.

"My faith has not been shaken, O evildoers, O blasphemers," the holy man said, giving a thumbs-up salute. "I know the first step to strengthening your faith entails prayers and sacrifice. I know how to pray. O Lord, hear our voices and lead us from sin and despair. We wait on your Word. We need your wisdom and guidance. We seek your truth. But we know that nobody will turn us around. We will not turn our back on you."

With a nod from the organist, the singers started singing the ole-timey hymn "Ain't Gonna Let Nobody Turn Me Around," and the reverend looked at me with a stricken face. He couldn't figure out what the holy man was doing. Was he sending a signal? Was he quietly communicating to the forces who wanted to bring him down? Was he seeking a truce?

"I'm not a perfect man. I'm a redeemed sinner like you, an anointed man of God lifted up by the mercy of the Lord," he almost whispered. "This is from Isaiah, chapter fifty-five, verses six to nine. 'Seek the Lord while He may be found, call ye upon Him while He is near. Let the wicked forsake His way, and the unrighteous man his thoughts, and let him return to the Lord; and to our God, for He will abundantly pardon.' Say amen, my Beloveds."

I turned to the reverend to say that Prophet Wilks wanted to be the Great Houdini, a magician who escaped from coffins underwater and from a straitjacket while dangling over the street from a skyscraper. He knew all the tracks of the mediums, faith healers, psychics, mentalists. The prophet's magic, combined with the Holy Ghost, was just the cure for poor people so desperate for an equal shot at opportunity.

"Yeah, right, Wilks wants to be able to bend spoons like that Jew guy did on *The Johnny Carson Show* years ago," the reverend said. "But the folks with their eyes open will see this nut a mile off. I know guys like this give the big shots at the National Baptist Convention bad ulcers."

Midway through the healing service, after the pleas for the homeless, Prophet Wilks told those who had gathered to stand and take their medicines out and throw them away. He commanded them to toss them into the baskets being passed around by members of the staff.

"Toss off those poisons concocted by the devil," the holy man yelled. "Don't take those poisons into your body. Throw those toxic elixirs away. The Lord will heal you of diabetes, cancer, heart disease, high blood pressure, arthritis, infection, blindness, and nervousness. Just believe in Him. Just believe!"

The staff wheeled a group of handicapped people, war-mangled veterans, and victims of car crashes to the holy zone, where Prophet Wilks laid his hands on their necks and healed them. One man with a walker suddenly hurled it and began a wild dance, which showed he was overcome with the spirit. After the dancing convert, the holy man laid his hands on the eyes of a blind woman who had been guided by a staffer. She threw down her dark glasses and discarded her cane. She crushed the glasses underneath the heel of her shoe.

"Praise the Lord," the holy man said, leaping up. "Praise the Lord. This kind of healing can be yours if you accept the Lord as your personal savior. He loves them that fear Him. He loves them that respect and worship Him. He loves those who keep His commandments. Praise the Lord, my Beloveds."

I grinned. "The guy wants to be big time."

"He's a darn con man," the reverend replied.

After the service ended, we immediately walked to the reverend's car, where we were surrounded by a white planter in overalls and a few field hands. The planter introduced himself to me as Boss Elmer. He was one of the big farmers and had a place outside Aliceville. As he chewed his snuff, his hammy forearm went around the reverend's neck in a yoke move.

"Come closer, nigger. Ain't we treated your people fair?" the white boss growled. "You're letting us down, letting me down. This Wilks boy is raising too much hell."

It was almost pathetic to see the change that came over the reverend. He became very passive, almost Tommish. People looked up to him in this area, but now, when they saw this, his reputation shrank to next to nothing.

"I cannot control him," the reverend whimpered.

"Coon, I don't care if you supposed to be a preacher or what," the boss snarled, then spat juice into the dust. "All these folks like things as it is right now. We don't want no progress. We don't want to make it any easier for outsiders from up North and troublemakers to put fool thoughts in our people's heads. These white folks like it just the way it is now."

For the first time, the reverend glanced at the groups of black people staring at them, wondering what would happen now, so he stiffened his spine. He hated the manner in which the white man spoke to him, like he owned him, like he was his slave.

"I cannot control him," the reverend repeated. "And I don't know if I want to."

"Don't back talk me, nigger!"

The other men drew nearer to the reverend and me. I was wondering if I would be able to get in a few licks before they got me. Needless to say, I was proud of the reverend for standing up to them like he did.

"Maybe somebody on your side should get him in hand," the reverend added. "Maybe he would get the point better if it came from you."

The boss man reminded the reverend that he was his eyes and ears with the niggers. He told him he was one of his best boys, said it just like that.

"Your man Wilks is a threat in these parts," he said. "We can get some fellas to pay him a visit. We don't like him stirring up these young bucks. I know you can control him. I know you can do that, because you hired him."

"I cannot do that," the reverend said firmly.

"What did I say, darkie?" the boss man asked. "I told you to tell this Northern nigger to mind his business and go back where he came from. I'm not going to ask you twice. You get this thing settled in two weeks or else. I'm not playin' with you , Reverend."

The reverend started to talk, to make his plea, but then the boss slapped him hard in the face. A harsh sound that got everybody's attention. Reverend Peck fell down, holding the side of his face, and tried to scramble up. The boss stood over him, stepping on his hand, standing on it brutally.

"Let me help him up," I told the boss and moved around to pick the reverend up. The boss asked me if I wanted to get what the reverend got. I ignored him and hoisted up the reverend and let him put his weight on me as we navigated to the passenger's side of the car.

"He's got two weeks, two weeks," the boss said loudly. "That's all. Then we take over, and you won't like the results."

12

HE ROTE

We split up after that Wilks service. I went back to the motel, since I was completely worn out. With my head throbbing, I plopped down on the bed. It was then that I noticed a note from Reverend Peck on the nightstand, typed and handwritten on the motel's own letterhead. The Cool Sheet Motel. There was a list of questions under a handwritten paragraph, which began, *Notes and questions addressed to the Master of the City of the Dead.*

The reverend had probably been bending his elbow when he wrote this. Drinking. A lot of pastors drank. Or maybe not. It was not great to lose your church, your wife, and your reputation all in one grand sweep.

The first paragraph ended with a quotation. *Life has no meaning. Life's purpose is to suffer for the sins we've committed. All my life I have suffered. Panchi Bor.*

Maybe he had found this quote in a magazine or a book. It was appropriate since he was in emotional pain, suffering on the soul level, the pain keeping him up nights.

Questions to God:

        a.)   *Are you watching us?*
        b.)   *Who are we to you?*

c.)   *Are we an afterthought?*

d.)   *Do you love us?*

e.)   *Do you hate us?*

f.)   *Do we matter to you?*

g.)   *Does it matter how we live?*

h.)   *Do you forgive?*

i.)   *Do you hold a grudge?*

j.)   *Do you hear us?*

k.)   *How do you define* truth?

l.)   *Who created the Holy Ghost?*

m.)   *What do you admire in martyrs?*

n.)   *How do you define a false life?*

o.)   *How do you feel about other Gods?*

p.)   *Do we have the power to heal our-selves?*

q.) *Do you feel sorry for sinners?*

r.) *Do you think we're good enough?*

s.) *What would the elders and the ances-tors do?*

Sitting on the bed cross-legged, I reread the note and wondered what was going through the reverend's mind when he wrote it. One thing was true. The amount of pressure he was under was warping his reason and making him very nervous. When I thought about the predicament confronting the reverend, I realized nothing was cut and dry, nothing was good and evil. Sure, Prophet Wilks was a supreme charlatan and hustler. I'd seen his kind in Harlem when I was a kid.

There was a fly in the ointment. Truthfully, Wilks was not all bad. He was the force behind the organization of independent farmers and truckers in this part of Alabama, ensuring that they would net greater profits from their crops. That was why the big farms and the white planters wanted him gone or dead. The night before, one of the white planters told a radio announcer that none of this mess would be happening if we had the right kind of government.

13
THE OLD GOSPEL

Walking with a bag of groceries bought at the open air market near the motel, I craved a quiet evening alone, without any kind of interruptions or disturbance. Things were heating up between Prophet Wilks and Reverend Peck, along with a mean upcoming showdown was looming between the embattled minister and the council of the elders. Reverend Peck was under a great deal of stress, and nobody had seen him for days. I was frightened for him and his fragile state of mind. Some people could not deal with pressure or crises.

After dropping the bag of groceries off at the room, I walked over to the motel office to see if I had received any messages. There was one, from my loyal cousin from New York. I hadn't received a phone call from the reverend, but I had gotten a surprising call from Miss Addie, the schoolteacher. I guessed her interest in me was genuine.

"Hey, man. What's up?" I said to my cousin over the newly repaired phone in my room. "Anything happen? What's going on with the church mess?"

He swallowed very hard on the other end of the line. "Dr. Smart is dead."

I couldn't believe it. My old foe and mentor had gone to meet his Maker, and I couldn't figure out whether

I was happy or sad. He had made my life hell in that town. In those last days, I had gone to my knees often to deal with his scams and schemes.

"What happened to him?" I asked.

"They say a woman texting in her car hit him during a hard rain," my cousin said matter-of-factly. "Dr. Smart was crossing the street, and he had the right of way. Then the car smashed into him. It dragged him for quite a distance. He was dead before they got him to the hospital."

"I guess there were witnesses," I said, stunned.

"Yeah, but that's not bringing him back. I saw it on the TV, the news report of it, the killing. People told the TV reporter that the woman pulled up to the curb and looked back at the body and drove off."

That scene sounded very sad. "He didn't deserve to go out like that."

"That's not the half of it," my cousin said grimly. "In the end, Dr. Smart lost everything, his money, his church, his wife, his good name. He was clinging to the hope that he would get back on top, that he'd make a comeback."

"I had no idea that he was having such hard times." People would say I should have held a grudge against him, because of all the mess he put me through, but I didn't. In a way, I understood why he had felt so desperate.

"Folks say he deserved it," my cousin said. "He was a crook."

"When is the funeral?" I asked. I was thinking I could fly up to the city and make an appearance.

"They didn't have one," my cousin replied. "He was cremated. They had a little ceremony at a Methodist church on the East Side, and that was it. It was his family who insisted on this."

I couldn't talk about this any longer. "How are you and your family?"

He sighed, his air coming from down deep in his chest. "I'm so deeply in debt, I don't know what to do. My family says everybody's got it hard these days, but I don't care about them. I care about me."

"Did you get laid off from your job?" I asked.

"Yes. That's why I'm going through this rough patch. I was thinking about leaving New York to find work. My brother says I play it safe too much. The worst kind of risk, he says, is no risk at all. And maybe he's right."

I agreed. "Maybe he is right. But what can you do?"

"I'm a jack-of-all-trades." My cousin laughed. "Electrician, carpenter, plumber, baker, painter, anything you need. My brother says that's my problem. I need to specialize. I guess he's right."

"Where do you think you'll move?"

"Out to the Midwest. Ohio, Illinois, some place like that."

He was tiring me out. "Well, good luck. Let me know where you land. I'll be here for some time. I'm trying to help the reverend out. If you can't get me here, then I'm back in New York."

"Sounds good," my cousin replied. "Take care, man."

After I hung up, I looked out the window. The Ford Fairlane was still there. The driver usually camped out through the night, until another car and driver relieved him. I was under surveillance.

I crossed to the bed and sat on it. In no time, I was fast asleep, snoring my head off. I enjoyed about two hours of a good nap before there was a light tapping on my door, then silence, and then a series of loud pounding, followed by shouts. I walked quietly to the door and listened to the voice, but I didn't recognize it. Yet I opened the door.

A woman stepped into the room, her hair greased and pulled back, and stood there. She was dressed very neatly, in colors that didn't shout her name. "I thought he was with you. Have you seen him?"

"And who are you?" I asked her.

She found a chair and sat down. "I'm Reverend Peck's wife, Geneva. I know he's talked about me. He's told me about you. He calls you Clint. Can I call you that?"

"Sure." I sat opposite her, in a chair. I could see she was upset.

Her eyes were swollen and red. "Wilks convinced me to get a restraining order against my husband. Hickory was really mad, because he thinks I left him for Wilks. So the law said for my man to stay away from me. No contact, no verbal abuse, and no harassment."

I didn't understand. The reverend didn't strike me as a violent man. "Did he threaten you? Did he beat you?"

"No. Hickory thinks I'm seeing other people, namely, Wilks," she explained, sporting some nice-size legs in her light blue cotton dress. "I think he's drinking on the sly. The few times I've seen him, he's been chewing on a peppermint, and most folks know that is a sign of a drunk."

I sized Geneva up. Small and pretty. Looked like a chocolate Nia Long, that actress in those comedies. As soon as she got inside the room, she'd kicked off her shoes and wiggled her feet. You could tell she was a country gal.

"I've not seen him in some time," I told her while she pushed up the sleeves of her black sweater. "I'm worried about him. He's not in a good state of mind."

"What's wrong with him?"

I frowned. "He thinks you have something going on with Wilks. Most of the folks around here think that too. Are you messing with him?"

"Look me in the eyes and tell me the truth." She stared at me. "Do you think I'm messing with Prophet Wilks?"

"I don't know. I can't say." Sometimes women could really lie.

"Hickory threw me out because things were going very badly between us," his wife said. "It's partly my fault. When he cut me loose, I dated men from church and in town, but I find myself getting hurt again and again. I'm just a li'l ole country girl who a small-time preacher smiled upon. A gal out here alone is just fresh meat."

I had a feeling that there was more to this story than her version. "Geneva, I bet the reverend is sorry about the way he treated you. He's under a lot of pressure, so much that he's not thinking straight."

She looked down mournfully. "I know he is."

I noticed her bright red fingernails were nibbled to the quick. A bad case of worry and nerves. I asked her if she had ever hurt someone she loved.

She shrugged. "Probably so."

I asked her if the hurt was intentional, thinking how many beaus young girls tossed away when they were at the fickle stage.

"Probably so," she repeated.

"I bet you've seen a change in the reverend over the past few months." I watched her face, and her mouth turned down at the corners.

For a moment, her breath caught. "I remember how Hickory was before all this mess, before he brought Wilks into the fold. Hickory was a loving, caring, honest man. He was a true servant of the Lord. He was always walking, visiting the sick, the poor, and the old folk in town. He was a good man."

"And he's still a good man," I shot back.

She wiggled her bare feet again and grimaced. "Hickory's not a nice man when he drinks. After we broke up, he waited for me to get off work, and when I pulled out of the parking lot, he followed me in his car, driving real crazy and almost running me off the road. He scared the crap out of me."

"Do you know if he had been drinking, Geneva?" I knew how folks could condemn a guy without having evidence.

She pointed at me, scowling. "When Hickory gets his snout full, he can get mean and hard. He bends his elbow, and then he starts to stalk me. Sometimes he makes me very nervous."

I shook my head. "I have never seen anything that tells me that he is a drinker. I have never smelled anything on his breath."

"Hickory kept calling me, calling me, calling me," said the estranged reverend's wife. "He called me over a hundred fifty times one night. This went on for a week. I counted all the calls. I recall he called me over seventy-five times one Friday, when he thought I was with Wilks. He's an intensely jealous man, like I said."

I folded my arms across my chest to ward off fatigue. "Are you sure that he has no cause to be jealous? I can't picture the reverend doing all those things. That's not like him."

"I want to be in love, like all these happy people enjoying themselves," she explained. "Every woman wants that. I have had my heart broken in this marriage. It would be difficult to open up to love again, especially with a man like Wilks. My husband has nothing to worry about on that score."

Geneva looked distant, miles away, through my tired eyes. I was totally whipped from the past few days. "Do you think you can trust again?"

"I don't know." She stared at her bitten fingernails.

At this point in our talk, she told me Wilks's followers were very envious of her during the time they spent together. The prophet kept her close, by his side, permitting her to accompany him to his meetings and healing services. Sometimes she even was allowed to go to his secret shindigs with politicians and other public officials. When they strolled into a room, one could hear a gasp among the gathering, but she added that the rumor that they were intimate was false.

"Do you know what Prophet Wilks would say to me?" Suddenly she pulled back.

"What would he say?" I really didn't want to know. I was beyond emotionally and physically drained. I needed rest in the worst way.

She just kept talking and talking. "Wilks would say, 'Love often feels like a closed fist around your heart.' He'd also go on and on about wanting power. In his soul, he'd say, he knew both good and evil, like any fallen angel."

"The man sounds confused, very confused." My eyes were almost closed. I wanted to go back to sleep.

Again, she wiggled her feet, crossing them and uncrossing them. "Thanks for listening to me rant. I'm in pain, deep emotional pain. Am I overreacting, Clint?"

"No, I don't think so." But I felt if I kept digging up her delicate past, then it would be really embarrassing and humiliating for her.

Wisely, she didn't let me see her cry, but the cracks in her voice were there. "I'm nearly broke. I have zero credit, with little income. I can't rent a car. Hickory had us living way beyond our means. Since I've been out on my own, I've tried to bury the hatchet with him and get past our problems. But he won't let this jealousy thing go."

In my sleep-deprived and unsettled state, I wanted to console her. Part of me wanted to take her in my arms, but I knew she would take it the wrong way. She needed love and security. She needed to feel safe, and I couldn't do that to my friend, the reverend, even if he was out of his mind these days.

The next thing Geneva said confirmed what I was thinking. "Clint, if you weren't his friend, I'd set my eyes on you. You're a very kind man. I know your heart."

Before I could reply, a knock sounded on the door. This was getting to be like Grand Central Station, everybody going and coming, and me getting no sleep. When I opened the door, there was the schoolteacher, all dolled up, dressed in a flowered blouse and pressed red Bermuda shorts. Meanwhile, the schoolteacher quickly excused herself, saying under her breath that she didn't know I was going to have company. When she saw Geneva, she turned tail and got out of there as fast as she could.

14

THE ELDERS SPEAK

That next day, Reverend Peck drove to the motel with one of the elders, who had called a secret meeting of the high council at the home of the influential elder Perkins, a local businessman. I was happy to see him. After we got in the car, the reverend told me about the church issues that would be discussed at the gathering. I then informed him about the chat I'd had with his wife. He was very interested when I told him that she had denied that she had been intimate with Wilks.

The reverend leaned forward and stared in the rear-view mirror at me. "I believe I can talk in front of an elder of the church. But I don't know if she is telling the truth here. After we met with Wilks, she began getting more phone calls, day and night. She'd leave the room to talk on the phone, like she was sneaking around or something."

"Maybe she just wanted her privacy," I suggested as we drove through the countryside.

He grinned. "I know my wife. She was up to something. She'd get on the phone and lower her voice so I couldn't hear, or she'd go to the bathroom and close the door. I know she was going out, cheating. Every other weekend, she'd go out with the girls. I thought about following her. When she got home, she'd be freshly showered or smelling like men's cologne. I don't wear cologne."

"It sounds like you had her dead to rights," the elder said. I didn't know his name. I didn't think it was right that the reverend had started bad-mouthing his wife.

"My wife started smoking and drinking," the reverend added. "Did she tell you that? Folks began noticing her running around town. It didn't look good. Probably that's why I lost so much support from the church."

"I didn't know you were going through all of that with her," the elder said, snorting.

The reverend digested my and the elder's words in silence, but moments later he continued on with his verbal onslaught. "Also, she started wanting sex less than usual. She felt I was boring now. When we did it, she just went through the motions, just lying there. But after she met Wilks, she began doing all kinds of sex tricks, licking this and that, all kinds of odd positions, vulgar and perverted things."

"Yessuh, that's always a sign of somebody steppin' out," agreed the elder.

The reverend reached up and rubbed his ear. "The other thing is she couldn't look me in the eye. My mama used to tell me if a person couldn't look someone in the eye, then she was telling a bald-faced lie. I believe that."

"So do I," the elder said, cosigning to the minister's view.

Instead of throwing the reverend's wife under the bus, as they say, I defended her. "Your wife looked me in the eye, and I believed her. I don't believe she had anything to do with Wilks. I think you're under so much pressure that everything looks shaky to you, including your wife."

"That's good news!" the reverend exclaimed. "I've been at wit's end over this marriage. Maybe we can smooth things over. This is an answer to a prayer."

As we sped past the farms and fields of crops, I also told him about the fast visit from the schoolteacher, and the reverend grinned from ear to ear. I was happy I could amuse him. Both of the men were not surprised that Miss Addie had fled when she saw Reverend Peck's wife sitting there.

"That woman has gone through so much suffering lately," the elder said abruptly. "I don't know whether you know this. Her man was lost with three others in an explosion on an oil platform in the Gulf of Mexico. They say the rescuers found only a hard hat bearing his name. That was about a year and a half ago, and the Coast Guard still lists him as missing."

"That's terrible," I said, shaking my head.

However, the reverend had other things on his mind and abruptly changed the subject of the conversation. He informed us that at the meeting with the elders, he was going to present the worst-case scenario of the false Messiah and his stranglehold on the church.

Finally, we pulled up in front of the home of Elder Perkins. We parked alongside some other cars in a grassy lot across from the well-tended house. We got out, and the reverend led the way. I noticed the same Ford Fairlane parked some distance away from the house. It seemed the opposition knew our every move. There were no secrets.

Elder Perkins welcomed us into his house from the porch and seated us around a long dining table. His wife and her sister served us cold tea and refreshments, then waited for us to get settled down before they left. After a long and strong prayer by Elder Moore, we got right to business.

I was then introduced to the other elders at the meeting: Elder Gilliam, Elder Carson, Elder Heath, and Elder Lewis. Everybody welcomed me into the fold after the reverend presented my spiritual résumé. Not much of a blowhard, Elder Perkins said a few words about the current state of the church and the crisis of leadership that has arisen from Prophet Wilks's new direction and Reverend Peck's old, sturdy worship agenda.

Before we chowed down on a plate of warm butter cookies, Reverend Peck gave a short summary of what was confronting the church under the latest ministry. It was fascinating to watch. He still had the power to persuade the doubtful.

His voice was hoarse with fatigue. "My brothers, you know this passage from First Timothy, the fourth chapter and the first and second verse. 'Now the spirit speaketh expressly, that in the latter times some shall depart from the faith, giving heed to seducing spirits, and doctrines of devils. Speaking lies in hypocrisy, having their consciences scared with a hot iron.'"

"Meaning Prophet Wilks, I take it," remarked Elder Gilliam as he bit into a cookie.

"Yes, that's right," the reverend replied. "Not only is he wrecking the church, but he's also making it difficult to live with these white folk around here. They don't like what he's doing with the black farmers and truckers. It's a situation that can really hurt us and the church."

I looked around the room, which was large and expansive, with a custom-made leather sofa and matching rockers and a huge paneled television on top of a carved oak table. It was a well-balanced space, comfortable and homey, which said the church's elders were doing quite well for themselves financially. There was quality artwork depicting the Lord speaking to the multitudes at the Mount of Olives, the Lord feeding the hungry, the Lord walking on top of the waves, and the Lord nailed to the cross, the nails piercing his tender flesh.

"Brothers, we must not forget that Prophet Wilks delivered us from one of the worst financial crises we've had in the history of our church," reminded Elder Moore, making the silent gesture of counting money. "He reversed our culture of debt and restored us to the black."

Elder Heath then stressed the church's good fortune over any disappointment with the moral shortcomings of the messenger, noting that the man had established a series of debt repayment goals and they had been met.

"Yes, Wilks has erased our debts, but at what cost?" the reverend countered. "True, he's not Jim Bakker or Jimmy Swaggart or Peter Popoff. But I believe he is a false prophet and is preying on suffering people. I believe he's practicing magic and voodoo from some ancient pagan culture. I believe he's a sorcerer, a necromancer."

Elder Moore frowned and held up his hands. "That's going too far. You make him sound like he's the devil's spawn."

"Maybe he is," the reverend said. "I believe he's a seducer of dark demons and occult spirits. He compares himself to the Old Testament prophet Elijah. I believe you'll all agree with me when I say the Bible and the supernatural do not mix."

Just then, the doorbell rang, and the wife of Elder Perkins rushed to answer it. She opened it a crack and then asked in a loud voice if anybody knew a man named George York. The reverend rubbed his hands together with glee and said to send him inside.

A man of medium height and slender build entered the room and greeted everyone. He was wearing a dark suit and carrying three large accordion files. The Perkins woman found a chair for him and placed it at the table, near the reverend.

The reverend shook the visitor's hand vigorously and stood proudly. "Mr. York is an investigator. I believe this man on my right will shed some light on the prophet and the growing scandal that is spreading through our tabernacle. I hired him at my own expense."

Mr. York opened one of the accordion files and spread its contents across the end of the table. "The man you know as Prophet Wilks has many names. He is a felon with a history of criminal enterprises in several states. He is not to be toyed with. Although he preaches a message of hope, opportunity, healing, and wealth, he is a hustler and a con man. They say the prophet keeps a loaded shotgun near his bed."

"Oh, my Lord, what have we brought into our church!" the Perkins woman exclaimed. "I knew he was trouble, just by his face."

"Prophet Wilks has done some time, and we're still gathering all that information from the correctional departments across eight states," Mr. York continued. "If you think he's dangerous, you should be very aware of the group of guys and gals he's got around him. I think he calls them his 'Mega-Beloveds,' and this crew is no joke. You've got among them killers, dopers, gamblers, molesters, and every kind of felon under the sun. They're devoted to him. They have sworn themselves to him by blood and oath. They would die for him."

Elder Lewis and Elder Heath had stunned expressions and covered their mouths. I noticed the reverend watching their astonished expressions closely, as if he had been presented with an award for valor. It was priceless.

Mr. York passed out copies of black-and-white photos of young women to each man. "The man also has a wicked yen for underage girls."

"That's the scariest and creepiest thing I've heard yet," said the sister of Elder Perkins's wife in a shrill voice.

Mr. York read a few lines from his report and turned the page. "The Honorable Wilks has several offices, where teams of very young girls, most of them poor black teens, send out letters offering items of blessing, salvation, such as holy water, while demanding that the needy send a contribution for the Lord to smile on them. Each letter is identical and is mailed to the list repeatedly."

"What do these letters say?" Elder Gilliam asked the private eye. "Do they ask for money? Isn't that illegal?"

Mr. York narrowed his eyes and stared at the church official. "Wilks has an endless supply of prayer cloths, holy oil, and holy water. The factory that supplies these items is a place outside Anniston, a real sweatshop. I bet the church doesn't even know about this place."

"What a racket!" Elder Lewis shrieked.

"What Wilks is doing is deceiving these needy and broken people and giving them false hope," the investigator added. "Wilks tells them they have to wipe the water or oil on their face, chest, or feet, anywhere there is sickness and pain."

Elder Perkins yelled loudly, "It's Satan's handiwork!"

I sighed and rested my head on my arms. "Mr. York is saying the guy is a big crook. He's milking cash from the poor folk and the struggling members of the church's congregation. He tells the faithful that God will bless and help them only if they pay for it. A blessing for some bucks!"

One elder, Elder Carson, took Wilks's side, saying the parishioners had no idea of the difficulty of balancing the demands of the pastoral life with the obligations of the secular world. He also noted that the congregation was trying to figure out Wilks's agenda, because he had taken the church in a new direction.

I couldn't believe him. "That's not an excuse for his actions."

The tide was turning. Another elder, Elder Heath, suggested that Wilks was attempting to address creatively the social problems in this area, such as the plight of the black farmers and their need to be financially independent.

"Yes, Prophet Wilks should be held accountable for his behavior, but we should also weigh the positive side of his plan for the revitalization and renewal of our church," he remarked. "We should go all out to protect him against all enemies. We must support him!"

Elder Carson, a firm ally of the con man, chimed in. "Prophet Wilks did a special favor for our church. There was a great need for black men to join the congregation, and he has brought droves of them back into our fellowship. We talked to him, and he said, 'No problem.' He has got them involved, not only in our church but also in their families."

"He really has been a godsend," Elder Health said, beaming.

The private eye rose from his seat, mustering a smile. "Not so fast, not so fast, gentlemen."

"Yes, Mr. York?" Elder Perkins asked.

The private eye was quick to point out that some of Prophet Wilks's business practices might not be legal and could come under criminal investigation. "Gentlemen, you have a hustler in your midst. He preaches to the poor that wealth is in their house and within reach. He also tells them that all their debts will be cleared up. He's taking advantage of the gullible. I can promise you that law enforcement is looking closely at this fake ministry, especially since he's now on the radio. He wants to go into televangelism on a national level, using the profits gained from your church."

"He's using us, using the church," Reverend Peck shouted. "This fraudulent huckster is ripping us off. We must take back this church."

"Talk about the letters, Mr. York, please." Elder Perkins wanted to give the cause of Mr. Wilks every possible route to justice.

The private eye walked around the table to present a few copies of the letters that were being mailed to people who wrote in to Wilks's offices in Anniston and Decatur with prayer requests. He explained that the prophet asked people to send a contribution for a blessing, then guaranteed the senders a cash sum in no time. The Anniston office had provided a large database in which the addresses were stored. Senders who didn't contribute the cash required were threatened, told that "something bad and tragic" would happen to a family member or loved one.

"That's akin to extortion," Mr. York said as the letters were handed around the table to the members. "This is unlawful."

Elder Heath grimaced and looked at the expressions of the other elders, including that of a smiling reverend. It didn't look good for the Wilks doctrine.

"Brothers, maybe this doesn't look good for Mr. Wilks, but we have to give him credit for the value and quality of his healing services," Elder Heath suggested. "Nobody can doubt the man is a natural healer."

Everyone was quiet for a moment, until Elder Gilliam piped up. "God is not indifferent to the spiritual power of Brother Wilks. God knows that the flesh is imperfect and that sometimes a person needs a miracle to repair or sustain it. God knows that illness and death are a part of the fabric of our lives. Everybody gets sick and eventually dies."

The Wilks supporters were not going to go down without a fight. Elder Heath recalled Prophet Wilks reminding him that healing is God's love as a divine parent of an unruly child.

"Prophet Wilks doesn't claim to be a miracle worker or a guru or the Son of God," Elder Heath said. "The man is a true servant of God. He believes that if God doesn't heal us, it doesn't mean He has turned His back on us, and so the prophet is called in to pinch-hit for Him."

It was a solid one-two punch. Elder Gilliam then listed the maladies that had been cured by Prophet Wilks: cancer, anemia, defective speech, blood poisoning, deafness, multiple sclerosis, female problems, paralysis, blindness, and other defects. The elders on Wilks's side smiled broadly and patted each other on the back.

"So why doesn't Prophet Wilks ever send for the medical records of the people he cures?" the reverend insisted. "Does he do follow-up sessions after the services? How does he know that any of these people are cured? Nobody asks any of those questions."

Mr. York cleared his throat. Then he walked around the table again, passing around copies of documented cases where the healer had failed to provide a remedy for the sick. Some of the elders read the copies intently, while Wilks's supporters laid them down on the table, near their teacups.

"Mr. Wilks put his hands on a woman who was pregnant with her first child," the private eye continued. "The woman had been an alcoholic and was fearful that the baby might be deformed. Although she was healed, she died during childbirth, after excessive bleeding."

"That proves nothing," Elder Heath protested.

"Gentlemen, his faith healing killed a ten-year-old boy with a hole in his heart. The boy had attended one of his healing services right before his death," the private eye added. "Another young woman in her twenties died from an untreated bowel obstruction right after he'd declared her healed during one of his services. I believe the man is a fraud, a fake carnival medicine man."

"God uses him as a tool of His holy power," Elder Gilliam yelled. "Who is this private eye? Why is he saying all these things? I believe he's in league with the devil."

Elder Lewis waved the papers vigorously. "I believe Mr. York has done his homework. I think he has provided all the evidence we need to see that Wilks is leading this church to ruin."

"How do we know that Mr. Wilks is ordained or anointed?" the reverend said loudly, and that set off the men trying to outshout each other. The volume of the ruckus was deafening.

After delivering a sharp slap on the table, Elder Perkins stared at all of them, commanding silence in the room. "Enough, enough, enough. We're not going to settle this issue today. But we have everything out on the table. Thank you for your hard work, Mr. York."

The private eye grinned. "Thanks, gentlemen."

"For a believer, the work of Prophet Wilks is most evil, and to employ God's holy name when perpetrating his wicked deeds is blasphemy," the reverend said, glaring at the man's supporters.

Elder Perkins waved his hands, calling for calm again. "Enough, please. The council will confer in a few days and will come to a judgment shortly. This is a big decision. This determines the future of our church and our community."

The participants sat silently for a time and then filed out to their cars. I accompanied Reverend Peck and the private eye down to where the row of vehicles was parked across the street. The Ford Fairlane was still there. From the front seat a man with a camera was shooting pictures of the members walking off the porch.

"Look, there's Wilks there!" the reverend said, pointing to a tall man in white with dark sunglasses, holding three large black pit bulls on a leash. He was standing near his long black Cadillac, smiling and nodding at the church members as they moved past him.

15

THE GOOD HEART

Things were looking up for Reverend Peck. Word had got out about the secret meeting with the elders, and the congregation was relieved that something was going to be decided about the future of the church, since passions were running high. Meanwhile, Wilks and his crew kept out of sight, that is, until he presided over a funeral of a young farmer who fell into the blades of a harvester. Nobody could see any change in his demeanor or attitude.

"Clint, the white folk want to see me Tuesday afternoon," the reverend said over the phone. "Can you go out there with me? They can be a surly bunch."

I agreed to go. I remembered how they had treated him savagely in that parking lot a few miles outside of Tuscaloosa, and I didn't want a repeat of that.

However, life had another wrinkle for me to confront. I saw her when I was taking out some garbage. She had driven up here in a red Mustang convertible. For some reason, something clicked with her when she appeared on my doorstep the second time. Upon further scrutiny, I realized the schoolteacher's appearance wasn't so plain. Little things about her started catching my eye.

"Hello, Reverend Clint. I must apologize for how I left the other day," she said, smoothing down her blue calico dress. "I shouldn't have gone off like that. Reverend Peck's wife is a friend, so I can't justify my behavior. Forgive me, please."

I was dressed casually in a checkered shirt and blue jeans. "No problem. Were you jealous?"

She clicked her tongue. "No. I can't explain it."

I walked past her and opened the door to my motel room. "Want to come in and sit a spell?"

Her brow furrowed. "I don't know if I should. People will talk. This is a small town, and everybody knows your business."

After a little sweet-talking and cajoling, we entered the small room, which I was starting to think of as my prison cell, and she found a seat. I saw her wiggle her nose, for women have a much keener sense of smell than men.

"Your place smells musty, like you shut the air in too much," Addie said. "The windows are closed. I don't know if the motel guy has somebody to clean up the rooms, but you should do that."

I nodded. "I know. What's the purpose of your visit?"

She was pleased when I opened the door and then crossed the room to get two cool cans of Coke. I handed one can to her, and she smiled.

"Let me put you at ease, Mr. Preacher," she said. "I'm not husband shopping. I did that once, and that was enough, thank you. No, I'm in need of friends who can help me escape."

"Escape what?" I asked her as I passed her a clean glass.

She replied that she would do anything to get out of this dreadful place, Alabama. I could smell her as well: her smooth brown flesh bathed with Camay soap and the scent of a few drops of mail-order perfume sprinkled in strategic areas.

"How could you leave New York City?" she wondered aloud. "I'd give anything to be there, enjoying the shopping, good restaurants, fine movies, good talk. I don't know why you would leave."

I shrugged. That was a question I'd been recently kicking around.

"Lately, I've been just sleeping here," I said wearily, rubbing my eyes. "Reverend Peck has been running me ragged. I've been putting in a lot of overtime, trying to put out fires, going from one crisis to another. And that's okay."

"I don't get you," she said. "You stay down here in this hellhole just to help out a friend. They don't make folks like you no more. Today it's everybody for themselves."

I took a swallow of the Coke. "I try to be always on the side of good."

"Is your family largely in the North?" she asked, letting that subject go.

"Yes, they are, but I don't see them much." I gulped down the soft drink. It was cool and made my throat feel good.

"My parents are dead," she said flatly. "Tell me if I'm out of line. But Reverend Peck told me about the tragedy of your wife and your children. That's very bad business. How are you holding up?"

I gave her my most winning smile. "I get through the days. Most of all, I try not to think about my loss. I have to admit, getting involved with somebody else's problems puts your own in perspective."

She shot me a curious glance. "How?"

"Things are heating up here," I grunted. "I don't want anybody on my side getting caught in the cross fire."

"Do you think you'll ever get married again?" she asked me. "I'm just curious. I know how much that must have hurt you for your wife to do something like that. How could she do that to your kids?"

I didn't flinch. "I don't want to talk about her."

"Do you think you're down here because of her and what she did to your children?" she asked, pressing. Some women wanted to ask questions that went right to the center of your soul so they could see what you were made of.

"I said I don't want to talk about it." I folded my arms.

She blew out a slow breath. "Reverend Clint, do you think you'll ever get married again?"

I grunted and closed my eyes. "I don't know."

"The fact that you're afraid to reveal anything about yourself doesn't mean that I should be like you," Addie remarked. "I'm very forthright. Possibly, I'm overworked. I know I was exhausted when the news arrived about my man being killed in that oil rig fire. You know, I never cried during the whole thing."

I remembered that when the cops showed me into the house after my wife did that terrible thing, I was beyond numb. I was shocked beyond belief. My legs folded up underneath me, and my breath became labored, until it hurt to fill my lungs. But she was right. I couldn't cry the entire time, until I put them in the ground. Then the tears came and came and kept coming.

"Did you hate your man, Addie?" I asked her.

She hunched forward, took a sip of the beverage, then spoke quietly. "Marty—that was his name—got me when I was very young. He had a history of being hard and rowdy. That made me like him more. He was special to me, because we shared a deep sense of being outsiders in this place."

"Did you love him?" I watched her toy with the can.

"No, not really," she replied. "But the loving was good. He had been around. He could be very sweet and tender. But he could be very controlling, rough, and manipulative. It was his way or the highway."

Most Southern women from these parts would have never spoken to me this way. So honest, so bold. I liked talking to Addie, this schoolteacher, because she had an uncommon view of the outside world, rebel thoughts far removed from this rigid, old-fashioned rural culture. It was rare for this community.

"Marty was more trouble than he was worth," she continued. "He was always in control, made me do what he wanted me to do around the house and in bed. He was a professional liar. He lied to me regularly. He told me I was different from other girls. I was so young and so dumb."

I was a big believer in common sense and the practical side of life. That was the case until my wife killed herself and the kids too. I recalled that after my wife did what she did, I couldn't stop washing my hands. I washed them over and over and over. I couldn't get rid of the guilt or the self-hate or the idea that I should have seen it coming.

"I've told you something about me, so it's fair that you should tell me something about you," she said brightly. "Tit for tat. Reverend Peck says you're a very sensitive, compassionate man. Is that true, Mr. Preacher?"

"What do you want to know?" I settled back in the chair.

"About what I just asked." She was persistent.

"All right, I don't think I'll ever get married again," I replied. "I've made a mess of it. Marriage was hard work. Also, to be married to a man of God . . . There is a real downside to keeping the home fires burning. . . . The church and the congregation always come first."

"What were you like before you got the call to become a preacher?" she asked, downing the last drop of the soda water, as they called it around here.

"I did all right with the ladies," I answered. "I always had girlfriends when I was in high school. My parents kept me on a short leash. I treated them with respect. There was never a time when I dated more than one girl at a time. I was a serial dater until I met the woman I married."

We sat for a time in silence. I figured she was thinking about what to ask me next. Suddenly, the guy from the motel office walked up and said the minister who had been with me a few days ago had called but he couldn't get through. I'd left the phone off the hook to get some rest.

"Thanks, buddy," I said, and after he walked away, I called the reverend's number.

"We've got trouble here," the reverend said sadly. "One of my church members just turned himself in for setting fire to the house of an old lady. He was drunk out of his mind. He thought she had planted bad gossip with his wife so she could divorce him. He thought she was lying on him."

I was tired. "What do you want me to do?"

"He's down at the jail, but I'll explain everything down there." He sounded breathless and odd. "Can you get there in a hurry? I'm counting on you."

"Sure, all right." I hung up and turned to Addie. I asked her to give me a lift down to the jail, and she agreed.

Along the way, we discussed all kinds of things: swimming and fishing, local food economies, industrial agriculture, the care of topsoil, the farm work ethic, family farms, growing up outdoors, hiking through the fields, and bicycling down country roads.

"Yes, I suspected you were a country girl, and now I know it," I said and laughed. In that instant, I thought about my routine of playing with the snooze button on the alarm clock, washing up while still half asleep, reading a few passages from the good book, being on my knees in prayer, and eventually having a cup of coffee and breakfast at the diner nearby.

I was jolted from the inner landscape of my head when she swerved to avoid a station wagon full of kids. It seemed her mind was preoccupied as well. She was thinking about this place.

"Farming isn't like it used to be," she was saying, gripping the steering wheel with both hands. "Some of these big farms are growing genetically modified corn and soybeans. I know folks up North like organic, real natural, but I don't know if you can tell what food is what. It's all packaged the same. We down here wonder what this newfangled science is doing to our bodies. Maybe it's breeding cancer and who knows what."

"Maybe consumers will rise up and revolt," I said, thinking about what awaited me at the jail.

"There are good people here in this community," she said. "I remember when if somebody had something bad happen to them, everybody would come together. If there was a storm or a flood, folks would come together and raise a house or a barn without a fuss. They built it out of love and concern."

We pulled into the parking lot near the jail with all the police cars and the vehicles belonging to civilians. I walked ahead of her.

"Reverend Clint, you're a nice fella," she said, catching up to me and touching my cheek.

It was a matter of will. I removed her hand gently, although I secretly wanted her to caress my face. No hanky-panky. We had to be about business, strictly business, because I had the feeling that things were about to explode.

"What's wrong with you?" she asked me.

"This is not the time for this," I replied.

Inside the jail, I went up to the reverend, and he put his arm around my shoulders. The expression on his face was one of alarm.

"As I said, this member of our church set fire to the house of this old woman, Eula Gillespie, who he thought was spreading lies to his wife," the reverend said. "The old woman died of complications from the burns. She was a miserable old lady who had no visitors or no family."

"But what is the emergency?" I asked.

The reverend grabbed me by the arm. "The sheriff and some of Wilks's enemies are trying to lay this crime at the church's doorstep. Jerome Dowers, the guy who set the fire, is one of Wilks's security people. They want to charge him with several counts of murder and arson."

One of the sheriff's deputies came up and showed us into an office, where we watched from behind a one-way glass window as the sheriff asked the man questions about the fire.

"Why did you do it, Jerome?" the sheriff asked.

The black man, whose face was expressionless, glanced at the sheriff and mumbled, "The old lady was a liar."

"That's no reason to burn her alive," the sheriff stated.

"She broke up my family, my marriage," the man said with a sense of great sadness. "She told my wife so many lies. My wife believed her. I prayed for a sign from the Almighty. I talked to Prophet Wilks about my problem."

"And what did Mr. Wilks say?" the sheriff asked, with all the deputies leaning forward.

"The prophet said God's will would be done in these final days," the man said, with his hands clenched tightly. "I knew what I had to do."

The sheriff sat down, facing the man. "Did you take this to mean you should burn her alive? Did you think Mr. Wilks was telling you to do this crime?"

"God told me to do it," the man chanted. "God told me to do it."

"How did you set fire to the old woman?" the sheriff asked.

"We argued, and she said some bad things to me," the man replied. "She cursed me out. I slapped her and doused her with kerosene. She tried to run, but I caught her."

"And then what?"

The man muttered into his tape-wrapped hands. "I lit her up. She was surprised at first. Then she tried to run from the room. The fire just ate her up. She screamed and screamed and pawed at her burning flesh."

"How did you feel when you saw this?"

The man broke down and began to cry. "God told me to do it. God told me to do it. God told me to do it. God made me do it."

Shaking his head, the reverend walked out of the room and into the hallway. He told me the sheriff and his supporters, the planters, were going to use this to get Wilks out of town. The schoolteacher agreed. This poor man would be the instrument for the ouster of Prophet Wilks.

16

SOME DOGS BITE

On the way to the meeting with the planters, the reverend was worried, extremely worried, not only about the fate of Prophet Wilks but also about the fate of his church. The meeting place was at the edge of town, at one of the antebellum mansions straight from the film *Gone with the Wind*, complete with uniformed black men in red jackets and top hats. They parked the car after we got out.

Two strongmen, both with fire in their pink cheeks, escorted us to the great hall, where Boss Chapin, one of the larger plantation farmers in the area, greeted us. He didn't smile or shake our hands, meaning the old order was in full effect. We knew our place. I followed the reverend's lead, because he knew these people and their traditions.

"Ah heah there was a fire set in one of the ole Nigra ladies' homes the other night," Boss Chapin said, looking bigger than the actor Orson Welles at his heaviest. "Did they catch the folks who did it?"

The reverend answered, "Yes, they did."

"An' who was it?" Boss Chapin already knew. He had eyes and ears all over the county seat and beyond. He even had men placed in the sheriff's office, so he knew what was happening before it was known publicly.

The reverend replied, "It was one of our members. It seems there were some problems between him and the lady. I think he's out of his head. I went to the jail, and he didn't make sense."

"One of your own, huh?" The white man grinned. A few of his planter friends wandered back in from outside to take their place behind him. I imagined he was their spokesman.

"It appears that way," the reverend said.

"Is there a direct connection between this man and Mr. Wilks?" one of the other planters asked. "Can the sheriff tie his actions to anything Wilks said or did?"

The reverend looked at him, quite bewildered. "No, I don't think so. The man is crazy, because he thought the woman busted up his home."

Just then, one of the uniformed colored help brought in a tray with glasses of mint julep and proceeded to serve everyone but us. Again, Boss Chapin was sending a signal that we were nothing and would remain nothing in his eyes.

"My beloved mama, bless her sainted soul, often spoke of the Nigras as chillun," the rotund white man pointed out. "She said the Bible mentioned them as the children of Ham, burdened by a divine curse, to be ruled by the white race. Do you agree, Reverend?"

"I didn't know this was going to be a Bible class," the reverend replied, bristling. "What did you call us here for?"

"Don't get uppity, Nigra preacher," Boss Chapin smirked. "As I was saying, the Christian religion is a white man's religion. He loaned it to the Nigras. A good Christian is a white Christian, and anything else is just fake. The darkies don't know how to worship God. Ain't in their blood or in their souls."

The planter was saying the Nigras were brainwashed into looking for their heaven in the sky and in the hereafter, while the white man enjoyed his paradise here on earth. It was so funny. I remembered Malcolm X saying just that in one of his speeches. I didn't know how much some of these whites believed that.

"This Wilks is becoming a real thorn in our side," the white man said. "He's affecting business and profits. I'm tired of these outside agitators and rabble-rousers. Some of these white folk want to do him harm, but we're trying to let him hang himself."

"Darn commies and terrorists," one planter said, staring at me. "Now, who is this boy you have heah? Is this your bodyguard?"

"Yes, introduce us," Boss Chapin said, smiling.

I stood up straight. "I'm a friend. I'm helping the reverend out."

"Where you from, boy?" another white man asked.

I didn't answer, because they knew who I was and where I came from, and they knew why I was in town. I kept silent. The tension rose like a fever but broke when the fat man spoke.

"What you don't understand is that ain't much changed in the Deep South," Boss Chapin said gleefully. "We remember Faubus, George Wallace, and Bull Connor. They had the right idea about you people. We know what they were warning us against. They were warning against these uppity Nigras from the North trying to change our way of life. Nothing has changed the true white person's heart or conscience. They know the darker races are unworthy."

"Look at that mutt Obama," another pal said. "The man from Kenya oughta go back where he came from. This is twenty thirteen. It ain't right being ruled by a man of color. It hurts me to my heart. We can't get a farm bill through Congress. Even the planters would profit by that. Obama should lead the country, rather than hobnobbing with movie stars."

The fat man said that nobody who was white respected him, and nobody felt he was worthy of his high office. He said the white people were tricked into believing he was their last hope, and now they were having voter remorse.

"The white folk down heah had the bright idea of sending the Nigras back to Africa," one planter admitted. "Some of the culluds agreed with us. But we missed our chance to do it early on."

I looked at the reverend, who was frowning at the racist tirade. I didn't like how this talk from these crackers was going. For some reason, I flashed back to my childhood, to the times when I was scared by something and pulled my covers over my head. *Make it go away.*

Boss Chapin pulled out a cigar and lit it. "Preacher, I noticed Wilks has some folk around him, all of them with police records. We've checked with the sheriff. Darn it! I don't like this Wilks man. He's a shade light brown, and he thinks he's the leader. All his men, his trusted men, are darker than him and much dumber."

I could picture slaves huddled against the chill, sad and quiet, in the slush, with shackles around their ankles. Their hands were raw and calloused from swinging the pick or the shovel or from plucking the cotton from the thorny stems. The planters desired those days to come back again.

"I had my spies at one of Wilks's rallies, and he was shouting about how the other side was going to resort to lynching, intimidation, and harassment," the fat man said sourly. "We're the blasted other side. We're not going to take this lying down."

The reverend was getting uncomfortable, very nervy.

"Preacher, you're squirming around like you's a tot." The chief planter laughed. "Do you got to go wee-wee? I can have my man Cephus show you where the outhouse is."

The other planters really got a laugh at that one, some of them almost choking on their tongues.

"Wilks needs his villains, some bad guys," Boss Chapin said, waiting for the laughter to subside. "The clown goes to the press and tells them the Nigra workers and farmers and truckers are being intimidated and harassed, afraid for their lives and jobs, because of pressure and threats from us. That is not the truth."

The reverend rolled his eyes at that remark.

"Listen to me, boy," Boss Chapin snarled. "We don't want no bloodshed. But if we are forced into a corner, we will do just that, and you won't like it."

I felt a big knot coming up in my throat, and I felt like slapping the crap out of him.

He motioned for us to exit the room. "Do you want to go outside, boys?"

We were wondering what was going to happen next. Outside, there was a collection of pickups with confederate flags on their antennas. Boss Chapin wanted us to see all this white power and possible mayhem. It was not lost on the reverend.

While the other planters remained inside the mansion, the fat man walked in front of us, waving to the good old boys. Beyond the yard, he took us to the fields, where the black workers were doing their labor under a bright sun.

"Preacher, you know these boys would love to have a holiday with Mr. Wilks," Boss Chapin said with an angry glare at me. "There are still Klan elements and members of the White Citizens' Council in the area.

They are chomping at the bit. They want to take a swipe at him."

The reverend stood watching the workers and the white overseers, who rode horseback around them and wielded revolvers.

"Can you get Wilks out of town?" the white man asked him.

"I don't know." He was honest.

"Do you want to see him get hurt or killed?"

"No, not really."

Boss Chapin noticed me staring at him really evilly. "I cannot control these boys. They want some Nigra blood. They want his head on a stake. If the sheriff can't twist this fire case into something that gets Wilks to leave, then they'll have to take other measures."

Finally, I spoke up. "Do you think Wilks has a point about how some people treat their workers? Is he lying?"

The white man's irritation flared into anger. "No, Wilks doesn't know what he is talking about. Preacher, you know what these people are like. They have no gumption. They don't want nice things like normal people do. They don't know how to take care of themselves. They don't know how to save money or pay their bills. All their kids know how to do is to tear things up."

"I come from these same people," the reverend said.

The planter took that as an affront. "I treat our workers with kindness and respect. Sure, there are problems, and there have always been. It'll take time for these problems to fix themselves, but not by some commie rabble-rouser coming down from the North."

The reverend was surprised by his softer tone. When he directed us to walk among the workers, I was surprised, but not the reverend. He knew it was a ploy to convince us that we were doing the right thing by serving Wilks up for the slaughter.

He showed us the long building with the tin roof, where there was a double row of cots and lockers. Some of the black workers avoided us as we walked with the boss.

"Sometimes these coons need a boot in the backside because they're so lazy," he said within earshot of them. "They wouldn't do a lick of work if we didn't stay on them."

The reverend waved at a group of workers he knew, and they greeted him. Several foremen were not far away from them.

"The work is hard for three months, but then they have it easy," Boss Chapin said. "All the men want to do is to get drunk and chase after a skirt. All the women want is to take their pleasure and make babies. These Nigras are a lazy, shiftless race. They're like that in the North too."

Neither of us answered him. It was his job to defend the old order of things. *Dixie will never die!* I thought.

Worker after worker looked down at the ground while the planter and the foremen glared at them. I put the question of their treatment to them.

It was always the same answer. "Mister Man treats us nice. We can't complain."

One worker, standing at the toolshed, made a face. He commented on my question when he was sure he couldn't be heard by anyone but me.

"It pains these white folk to have to fool with us," he said, toting a shovel. "We hurt their eyes when we cross their path. Imagine how they feel about President Obama."

The reverend and I walked toward our car as Boss Chapin strolled toward a trio of his foremen. While we got into our ride, two workers leaned into one of the car windows and complained. One man said, "Most folks work so hard, but they don't get paid much. Everything at the store costs so much that our money goes real fast. The white planters keep us dumb—we can't read or figure—so they can steal from us."

The reverend, at the wheel, asked them, "So do you think Mr. Wilks is right?"

"Heck yeah," the man replied firmly. "He's causing them grief. They don't know what to do with him. We support him in what he tryin' to do."

As we drove off, Reverend Peck told me that their way of life had to change, because borrowing money from the planters only kept them trapped. "Whether it's the farmer or the tenant worker, they only know living this way. If they leave here, where would they go?"

Shaking his head, the reverend turned on the radio, and the disc jockey played the James Brown hit "Get on the Good Foot." It was the first time I saw him sway and snap his fingers. I didn't think it was about grooving to the funky soul music. It was just a celebration of getting away from the big house and the white planters.

17

INTERRUPTIONS

Two days later, Addie surprised me with an early morning visit. A pair of bicycles was attached to the hood of her car, and she was dressed comfortably for riding, wearing a yellow Rosa Parks T-shirt, shorts, and tennis shoes. I was not prepared, so we had to stop by a store where I could get something to wear for the trip she proposed to the park in Anniston, where we could ride along the end of the Chief Ladiga Trail.

It was almost an hour-long ride to our destination. We bought sandwiches, fruit, a bag of oatmeal cookies, and a mixed concoction to keep us hydrated. She hated Gatorade and the other sports drinks. Her concoction consisted of water, sugar, lemon, and a pinch of salt.

Addie had family in the area. Her aunt worked for a time at the Anniston Army Depot, and there were kin-folk in Munford, Lincoln, and Weaver. Most of her relatives remembered the fiery times when the Freedom Riders came down on a Greyhound bus in the spring of 1961, trying to integrate white businesses. A mob of angry whites met them at the local bus station, and the tires of the bus were slashed and its windows smashed. When the bus driver realized the whites meant serious business, he raced the bus down the highway, but the mob followed and set the vehicle on fire and attacked its passengers. Many were seriously injured that day.

We unloaded the bikes after parking the car. I loved watching the kids rollerblading, the runners on their serious treks, the ladies walking their dogs, and fellow bikers on their way to the trail.

"Are you surprised, Clint?" Addie asked. "Can I call you Clint?"

"Sure, no problem." I straddled the bike and smiled.

I noticed the schoolteacher had some toned arms and legs, so she must have been taking care of herself in her leisure time. She was watching me navigate the bike, centering myself on the saddle. Her smile was very subtle.

"Comfortable?" she asked me.

"Very," I lied. The last time I rode a bike in Central Park was not a good experience. I was sore and bruised for days.

She was circling me in loops, inspecting my rider form, checking to see if everything was right. I could tell she was deep inside of herself, thinking. "Do you also know why I want to go to New York City? I bet you can't guess."

"No, I can't." I was concerned with the quality of the pedals.

"New York City has a great number of health food shops and stores," she said, grinning. "You won't find anything like that in these parts."

"That makes sense." I started riding away.

There was real confidence in the way she handled her body. "In a way, I don't fit down here, because these folks eat all the wrong things. They eat food that poisons the body. Pork, fat, sugar, salt, all the wrong things."

"Are you a health nut?" She had pulled in front of me, so all I could see was the back of her head and her splendid backside.

"Yeah, I'm a real health nut," she said, slowing her pace to ride beside me. "I try to clean out my system and restore my nutritional balance. I drink fruit and vegetable juices to strengthen my immune system. Maybe you should do that as well."

I laughed. "So you don't like Big Macs or Whoppers?"

"I keep away from fast foods, sugary snacks, and white bread," she said. "I drink a lot of distilled water. Cups and cups of herbal teas. Water is good for you. I can see by your eyes that you don't drink enough water."

I frowned. "I drink when I'm thirsty."

We could hear the sound of the chirping birds about to take flight from the trees into the clear sky. The view from the path was incredible. I was getting to the blissful state where the pedaling and the scenic vista ahead were all I was focusing on.

She broke the trance when she spoke. "I was the tallest girl in my class. I was all legs. That made me totally self-conscious."

"Really?" I tried to pay attention.

"Do you meditate, Clint?"

"No, I don't. Maybe only when I pray."

"That's a good answer. I just thought you looked like a guy who was in tune with your inner self. You're a mystery. I wonder if anybody's ever figured you out."

It was my time to grin. "I don't know."

A sour expression came across her face as she gripped the handlebars tightly. "What about the guy the sheriff is holding down at the jail for burning up the woman? Do you know anything about that?"

"Only what you read about it in the paper."

"This community doesn't want him to get away with murder," Addie said. "He did what he did. I don't know how he can live with himself."

"He's in a special kind of hell already," I replied.

"I hear he's a member of Reverend Peck's church, but I don't ever remember seeing him there," she said. "If he is a good Christian, really believed in the Lord, he'd feel some sense of remorse after what he did. That's horrible. He doused her with gas, I hear, and set her on fire."

"With kerosene," I said, correcting her.

"Still, that's a horrible way to die," she said with a quiver in her voice. "Burning to death is my least favorite way to die. Let me go to sleep in front of a mindless sitcom and gently drift away."

"I guess that's one bad way to go out," I suggested.

"I also heard the man suffers from some mental issues and is easily led," she continued. "They also said he was off his meds when he did this crime. My neighbor said there had always been something a little off about him."

Keeping silent, we sprinted up a hill and down another. I tried to keep up with her. She was in good shape, very good shape. Occasionally, some other cyclists lingered alongside of us, then pulled away, leaving us in their dust.

The schoolteacher was not finished with the subject of the guy who set the fire. "Humans can do some awful things to each other, like this man who torched the woman, or your wife, who sent your little ones to their Maker."

I was wondering whether I should even acknowledge that such a tragic thing had happened to me. She was very curious about my wife's insane actions. One day, I promised myself, I would tell her the entire story so she would not have to probe and pry into that dark tale. It was like picking at a scab.

"You look tired, but you always do," she said matter-of-factly.

With my loyalty to the reverend, I placed myself on call, day and night, to help him out. However, Addie had noticed the dark bags under my eyes, which meant I was skimping on sleep, burning the candle at both ends.

We kept riding along the path, going at a decent pace for a few miles. Every now and then, we'd go into a heart-pounding sprint, and suddenly I'd ease off the pedals. The key to her stamina was her regular late afternoon rides after school, which had built up her endurance and wind.

"Are you stressed about something?" she asked after a while.

"I don't know. These white folks feel this is a turf war. The reverend and the church are stuck right in the middle of it. Someone is going to get hurt. I keep saying that, but I think it's inevitable."

A white guy with a buzz cut whizzed past us with his expensive bike and swank racing gear. I was tempted to race him, but my legs wouldn't have held up.

While the schoolteacher pedaled along the path, she gave me a lightweight lecture on stress. Stressed gals, she noted, tried to get rid of it, tried to get a grip on it, but guys usually ignored it.

"Guys don't know what to do with it," she said, shooting me a look. "They bottle it up, just like you do or like my man did. They can't express their real feelings."

"You paint guys as really bad, like most women do," I said, getting my legs pumping. "As a guy, you do something about some things, but not about other things. Men realize the best thing to do about certain things is to just walk away."

"Sure. That's why men get so many health problems from carrying stress, like insomnia, high blood pressure, anxiety, depression, and ulcers," she said proudly. "Possibly, that's why women live so much longer than men. They exercise, eat right, meditate, and get a good night's sleep. They know how to deal with stress."

I grunted an answer. Some women knew everything.

She was very competitive. I was struggling as we biked along the winding path. My legs and lungs were beginning to burn.

Again, we rode in silence, avoiding some power walkers and some rollerblading traffic. Through the tall old trees, we could see fields of green as far as the eye could see. It was awesome.

"As I told you before, I'm a good listener," she said, a little sheen of sweat appearing on her forehead. "Maybe that's from being a teacher. I pay attention to what men say. A man will never tell a woman what is really true. He will never tell her what he wants her to know. My man was like that. I don't know if you're different."

From what she was saying, I realized this woman didn't trust or need men. But maybe I was wrong.

"Do you think guys understand love?" she asked.

If the schoolteacher ever wanted an occasion to give me a third-degree interrogation, this was ideal. If I let her ramble on and on, she would get me upset. However, being a minister, you got used to people being chatterboxes, just yakking away.

"Love is something you fight for," I said. "Judging from my past, I guess I didn't fight hard enough."

"Why do you think that's the case, Clint?"

"I truly don't know, Addie. I don't know about love. I feel ridiculous even talking about love and desire. After what I've been through, I keep running from one life to another. One day, I'm going to stop and face myself."

"That's pretty profound," she said, compassion showing for the first time in her eyes.

"You asked me about my marriage and the tragedy," I said. "I think I was getting into a rut about the arrangement with us, about the man-and-wife thing, and then this shocking event happens."

"You didn't see it coming?"

"I saw it coming, and I didn't," I answered, chugging along.

"What does that mean, Clint?"

"I knew something was going on with my wife," I said. "There were signs. But I thought she would straighten out and we would make a decent go of it. I tried to look at things from my wife's point of view. I really did. That didn't work."

Narrowing her eyes, she peered at me like she was seeing me for the first time. "But when someone goes around the bend like that, there are more than signs. I don't think you were paying attention to her."

I started pedaling faster and faster. I wanted to burn myself out.

"Maybe I saw everything, and I was just in denial," I replied. "It's tough to admit that you have failed at your marriage. I saw her drifting away from me, and I couldn't do anything. Not one thing. That hurt."

She saw how uncomfortable this talk was making me, so she switched the focus to her emotional woes. "Clint, some women are not ready to love. They're afraid to let their guard down. I was so ready for love. Totally ripe. I wanted to surrender to him. I wanted him to take me."

"What happened, Addie?"

"When you're in love, in real love, it's a great feeling," she said, hunching over the handlebars, matching me in speed. "You feel safe. And it doesn't have to be sexual. He doesn't have to be good in bed. He can be average. But you know he's yours, yours to keep, and that's the reason you love him."

I was slowing down, sweating like heck. "What was your man's name?"

"We'll just call him Spider." She laughed, making up a wicked nickname at her deceased man's expense. "That's a good name for him."

"Actually, I think you still love him."

Her voice was a blend of frustration and caution. "We were overextended, in debt. We were living paycheck to paycheck. We lost our home. I just wanted to get off that cursed merry-go-round."

"What stopped you?"

"I kept thinking he would change," she said angrily. "I was gambling on a dead-end relationship. Things just weren't working out for him. We were about to break up before he took off to go to sea. He had a bad mouth on him, but when he started hitting me, I knew the marriage was over."

I looked up just in time to see three young boys tossing a football between them right in our way, their lithe bodies stretching and bending to avert a collision.

"All breakups hurt," she continued. "You start asking questions of yourself. Why didn't it work? Why wasn't the love strong enough? Why did I choose the wrong man? Why didn't he love me? Do you know what I mean?"

"Oh, yes, I asked those same questions. No answers, though."

She stopped riding and stretched, her long arms going up into the air. "It really soured. He started neglecting me. When he got back to work, all he did was pay the bills. He turned into a drunk. I didn't need that. I want somebody to focus on me. Cuddle me. Pay me some attention."

"I think everybody wants that," I said, stopping.

"Not everybody. Marty used me. He made me feel unwanted. I felt violated and vulnerable. I cried a lot and missed a lot of days from the classroom. Breakups are terrible."

"I know," I answered. "Were you tempted to step out on him?"

She grinned wickedly. "I was tempted seriously twice. One time I came *this* close. I had my panties off, but I thought better of it."

There was a young couple going at it hard and heavy, kissing and petting teenage style in the middle of a gazebo off to our left. We looked at them and shook our heads. So young, so innocent. So full of hormones.

"Did Marty make you suffer?" I asked.

"Sure, he did, and he loved it," she said with malice. "Nobody deserves to suffer. Nobody deserves to be mistreated by anybody. One life is given to you, and you try to fill it with worthwhile people. Some you'll know for the remainder of your days, and others you won't." She paused for a moment, then asked, "Clint, what did you do when your wife acted up?"

I had the map of the Chief Ladiga Trail out and was looking at it absentmindedly. "It starts to hurt too much. You begin to go numb, so you try to fill your day with distractions."

"We're kindred souls, Clint," she sighed, then bent over and kissed my forehead.

I was so sore. I had cramps in every part of my body. She sensed I was all in, totally exhausted. When she said, "Let's start back," I was overjoyed.

Just a few feet from where we had stopped, the mysterious Ford Fairlane was cooling its engine, its two passengers staring in our direction. They had followed us to Anniston. I should have known.

18

NO OTHER HELP I KNOW

Within minutes of our arrival back at the parking lot, the Ford Fairlane pulled up in the space where we were attaching the bicycles to the top of the Mustang. The window on the passenger's side was open. There was Prophet Wilks, dressed in a sweat suit and totally unrecognizable. He was unshaven, was looking haggard, and was smoking a cigarette.

"Come here, Reverend Clint," Wilks called out to me. "It's time that we met. Come on. I won't bite you."

The driver's door opened, and a massive guy, who was bald, got out.

"Help her," ordered Wilks, who then motioned to me. "Come on, Clint. Isn't that what they call you? Please get in."

I got in the car, with its musty smell, after Wilks scooted over. Cautious, I watched his eyes and then shot a glance through the window to see his driver holding one of the bikes down so Addie could screw the lock into place.

"What do you want, Mr. Wilks?" I asked him.

He smiled sinisterly. "Clint, I know everything that happens here, sometimes before it happens. I have eyes everywhere. There are no secrets hidden from me."

"I knew I was being followed," I said.

"I knew we might cross paths sooner or later," he said, grinning.

I watched his driver push the bike into place again and again.

"Maybe I should help," I remarked. "They're having a heck of a time getting that one bike locked down."

He shook his head. "My man's perfectly capable of getting the job done. He was once a professional wrestler."

"Is that so?" I didn't like this guy's cockiness.

He folded his arms like he was bored. "What is Peck trying to do to me? The congregation of the church doesn't want him. They want a change. Why is he stirring up trouble?"

"It was his church," I replied. "He brought you in. He feels betrayed. You did a number on him when he wasn't looking."

"What number?" He acted surprised. Then he stretched out his legs and snarled, "Tough titty!"

The minute his driver finished his task, Wilks waved his hand to make him stop and wait before getting back into the car. I could see the wheels of his mind were turning.

"Are you sure you're doing God's will?" I asked him.

He was silent; then he spoke in a toneless voice. "I know I must be. I know the congregation and the crowds have been receptive to my message. The size of the crowds is getting bigger at our services. That's what Peck and the whites are afraid of."

"Not true." I screwed up my face.

"Don't misunderstand me," he added. "I'm not trying to throw Peck out of the church. I'd be willing to share power with Peck. I just want to have a platform in the community to get myself heard. I want to be someone like you. A seeker. A searcher of the truth."

I didn't think his remark was funny. He was trying to ridicule me. I let him know I was wise to him by giving him an annoying frown.

"Then why are you down here?" Wilks got right down to the heart of the matter.

It was my turn to look at him. He didn't like it.

"All I want is to serve the Lord," I answered. "I want to make the Lord happy and praise His name."

"What is your connection to Peck?"

I looked him right in his eyes. "He's my friend. He needs my help at present. He was there for me when I needed him. How can you be sure about what his congregation wants?"

"Because they told me as much," he replied.

While he was answering questions, I figured I'd pick his brain. "Wilks, do you really believe you are the Messiah, as you're telling folks down here? Do you really think you're God?"

He recoiled . "No, I never said that."

"I think you're misrepresenting yourself," I said. "Do you really believe you can divinely heal?"

"I heal with the power of God," he said weakly.

I shook my head. He was a false prophet, if I'd ever seen one.

"Clint, have you seen the crowds there at my healing services?" he said proudly. "They know I have a direct connection to God. They know He is healing them through me. I heard about your meeting and the man Peck hired to disprove all my miracles. But you see, some of the elders want to believe me. They know the power of the Lord. They know the Lord is a healing God. Don't be afraid for me."

I wasn't so sure of his invincibility. "They might arrest you."

He laughed loudly. "I don't think so."

"Why is that?"

"Because God is watching over me," he said, gloating.

I was angered by his confidence. He didn't know how much trouble he was courting. He could take the entire community down with him.

"Do you want me to die, Clint?" he asked.

"No, I don't."

He snapped at me, his words slapping me in the face. "These white folks want me to die. They want to hurt me, and you want that too. I know Peck wants that."

"Peck wants no such thing," I replied. "He wants you to straighten up. He wants you to give up this farmer business. These crackers will hurt you if you continue to do it."

Again, he laughed. "See, Peck's a Judas. He'll give me the kiss of betrayal. He'll sell me out so he can get back his church. The man's not a fool. He'll let the whites take care of me, and then everything will go back to normal."

I looked at Addie with her tall self, her nice lanky frame, her large brown eyes, and full lips. For a time, I forgot about him, this faker.

"You are the fake," he yelled. "You and Peck are the fakes. You don't do anything for the people. You don't believe in anything."

My silence must have rattled him. He suddenly reversed his rants, his words becoming a psalm of harmony and peace. The man was a nut job.

"Clint, help me find a way out of this without getting myself killed," he said oddly. "Now it's personal. I'm hitting them where they live, in the wallet. I'm getting death threats."

"But you brought this on yourself," I said.

"Not true," he replied, correcting me. "You see how the people live, from hand to mouth. They're beyond poor. They work very hard and get nothing for their labor. That's why I had to step in."

"I can't fault what you say," I said. "I know how poor they are. They live a harsh, miserable life. In that regard, I agree with what you're doing. I don't agree with what you're doing to Peck's church."

"Then save me, save me." It was almost a plea.

I couldn't follow him. He was moodier than my late wife. He could go through several moods and emotions at the drop of a hat.

His eyes were unfocused, going every which way. I could tell he was under a great deal of stress.

"Forgive me," he said, his voice breaking. "I don't know what I'm saying. I'm under a lot of pressure. I guess even Jesus's disciples cracked under pressure, like Peter."

I knew my Bible. I resented the fact that he would compare himself with the apostle Peter, who earned his place beside the Lord.

He looked around the park and suddenly gave the schoolteacher the look of a detective, the probing glance. "Do you love the woman, the schoolteacher?"

"No, I like her." That was none of his business.

"Why not?"

I glanced at her as she stood on the running board of the car, tying the bike down, revealing her backside. "Like I said, I like her. She's not unattractive. She makes me think of my old life, when I was married."

He smiled that sickening smile again. "Nice rear end."

I grunted at his remark. I knew about him being a freak and all.

"You better stay in the good books of the media," I said. "They say you've charmed the press, and you better continue to do that. I know you know how the media works, but they can turn on you in a New York minute."

"I know that." His attitude was smug. You could tell he loved to see his picture in the papers, to see his name in print. He loved being in the public eye.

He told me that his schedule was tight, and soon he would have to go. The staff had penciled him in to appear at one of the local senior centers, where he would bless the old folks and pray with the seriously ill. Just when I thought he was finished running his mouth, he started talking about his flock, the Beloveds, his army of angels, and the Kingdom of the Faithful.

"I want to amass over ten million followers in the South," he boasted. "I want to be one of the leading televangelists, with programs on the TV and radio. Get a good home, a private jet, and an incredible megachurch."

I was disappointed in him. "Ambition and greed will be your downfall. You're not serving the Lord. You're lining your pockets. What are this farming business and the protests doing for you?"

"It keeps me in the newspapers," he said, grinning.

I stared at him in disbelief. "Do you believe in Armageddon, the end of times? Do you believe in the final days?"

"Oh, yes. I kept having this dream where a red angel comes down from heaven, holding a golden key in one hand and an ancient snake in the other," he whispered, popping a stick of gum into his mouth. "The angel unlocks the bottomless pit, and all manner of demons and devils pour out. They plague those on the earth, both the believers and the unbelievers, and the angel sits high above. He waits for the religious dead to come to life. He waits for those who have worshipped the beast and have its mark on their foreheads."

This sounded like the critical verses from Revelations on the Final Judgment. I just listened to him. He was chewing the gum for all it was worth, his jaw really working. The odor of his sweat filled the car, making me pinch my nose. There was something desperate about him. Still, I heard him out. I knew the entire business about that day, when only the day and the hour would be known, not by the angels or the Son of man, but by the Almighty.

"I'm fascinated by the final days, as you can see." He glared at me with crazy eyes. "I love those passages in the Bible. I live for them. This is the only thing that matters to me as a Christian. The only thing."

Suddenly, I heard a loud growl from the backseat. I turned and looked there. The terrifying sound had jarred me back to reality.

"It's Myra," he said soothingly, reaching back a hand to pat the dog. It was a huge black pit bull, showing a savage grin of knifelike amber teeth.

Following this show of animal love, Wilks took my hands, seizing them between his own, as if I was a long-lost friend. He informed me that he had a trio of such canines, but he wanted a commitment from me.

"Can I count on you, Clint?" he asked me.

I didn't answer him. I remained mute.

And so he let go, and I got out of the car. So did the pit bull, Myra, who ran at me with blinding speed, catching my pants in her powerful jaws. The fabric of my pants ripped with a sharp sound.

Wilks laughed like a madman as the driver and Addie looked on with interest. He laughed and laughed while the pit bull pinned my leg against the car.

"She just wants to play," he said, laughing in wheezes down deep in his chest. "She likes you. You must have sweet meat."

Angry, I jerked my leg free. My leg was torn and bleeding. I walked around his car, pulling Addie by the arm. We got into her car, all the while watching Wilks and the driver, who were now doubled over with laughter outside the Ford. It wasn't that funny.

"You know he's crazy," Addie said, scratching her head.

"I know that." I'd resisted the urge to kick his mutt, because who knows what this madman would have done to me.

We looked into each other's eyes, fearful for an instant, but then letting that bad feeling drain out of us as we sat for several seconds in silence. The antique Ford Fairlane started up with two puffs of black smoke, sputtered, and drove off.

19

A SPIRITUAL CONFESSION

A full moon presented itself in the dark sky. I couldn't sleep. I felt the need to pray. So many things went through my mind. There was trouble within my soul. *This is the time to get down on your knees,* I thought, *to kneel before the Lord and pray in earnest.*

In the velvet darkness, there was one beam of light coming through the window from a streetlamp in the parking lot. Its golden ray illuminated a far corner of the room, like a spiritual line reaching from this world to the next. Whenever I questioned God's majestic power, I realized there was something operating in a divine pattern in the universe.

Yes, a prayer was to listen; a prayer was to embrace quiet in the mind. I prayed for peace and serenity in the midst of crisis, obstacles, and challenges. I wanted it to go easily. I wanted everything to stand still and remain as it was.

Sometimes when I prayed, it was as if I was being lifted up out of myself. It was as if I was watching myself from a great height.

One of the things Dr. Smart, a wise man who veered off the path, once told me was, "Every soul is a creation of what God has inspired." His idea was that God would use a soul to work His will and do the deeds of the divine. Only He knew our limits as human beings.

God was never tone-deaf. He often sifted through the frightened prayers of the impatient, the fed up, the manic, the crushed. What kind of Christian would I be if I thought God wouldn't take the time to reply to an earnest prayer! However, I kept God on speed dial. I believed that God was not a busybody, controlling every aspect of life, overseeing everything, but there was an overarching wisdom in our daily affairs.

Prayer was an extraordinary experience. It meant focus, concentration, not imagining events from the past or the future. It meant being really there, in the moment, in the present.

Will you hear me when I pray? All I wanted was God's blessing. I remembered my father, in his work clothes, kneeling near the bed, hands clasped tightly, beer on his breath, asking God to pay the bills. Pops promised he would never, never, never ask for anything else in life.

Somebody said prayer was a man's impulse to open his life at its deepest level. If so, why did prayer work for some people and not for others?

There was a time, a dark, emotional time, when I didn't believe any of my prayers were getting through to God's ear. Nobody's life took a straight line. My life was more zigzagged than the regular guy's. My grief was greater than my faith then. With continuous prayer and the support of our church members, God showed me I couldn't lose my faith in Him, as I believed in the scriptures. He permitted me to find my purpose in life, while I was being redeemed and healed.

Wisely, the Bible said that pain fell equally on the just and the unjust. Everybody in the world suffered. And everybody sought relief from that suffering. In the midst of that suffering, I was filled by a new purpose and saw things that I could not see before. That sense of divine joy and truth filled my spirit and compelled me to go forward. He elevated me with an understanding that raised me above sorrow and grief.

Most people turned to prayer when they were desperate, when they had their back against the wall. My advice was not to pray only when you needed something.

God, will you hear me when I pray? The men and women of faith knew He would listen to their request. Yet some preachers and church members believed prayers were a joke, a mockery between the believer and the divine.

As I sat on the floor, watching the golden ray, I recalled a spirited talk I'd had at a bus station with a nun who supervised a hospice for terminally ill cancer patients. It was providence. Her banter had put me at ease. While she'd talked about the need for grace, she'd told me about her wish to end all pain and suffering through prayer and service. I'd agreed with her, saying that we sometimes lost track of the joys of life because of the abundance of suffering.

"Will you join me in prayer, brother in Christ?" she'd asked, kneeling right beside a bench in the bus station. I followed suit and became her partner in prayer.

The nun held my big hand in hers and recited the Hail Mary prayer, her gentle, almost girlish voice echoing through the room. "Hail Mary, full of grace. The Lord is with thee. Blessed art thou amongst women, and blessed is the fruit of thy womb, Jesus. Holy Mary, Mother of God, pray for us sinners, now and at the hour of our death. Amen."

People crowded around us, several of them joining in our prayer to the Almighty. The nun, in full regalia, smiled warmly at me as I recited the Lord's Prayer. In no time, there were about thirty people either watching or kneeling, until an officer walked up and told us to break it up. The nun smiled again, hugged me tightly, and went on her way.

"God bless you and keep you, my brother," she'd said before disappearing into the crowd of people hurrying to the buses. I never forgot that day.

O Holy Redeemer, I needed to know you, know who you are, what is required of me. I believed He would show himself to me. God guided us; we were His chosen instruments.

Whether I was reciting the Lord's Prayer or the Twenty-Third Psalm, I used prayer as a gesture of profound thanksgiving. I used it as a means to ask questions and express doubts.

Shutting my eyes tight, I asked Him, *Is the voice Wilks hears inside his soul yours? Is it your voice?*

It was probably not of the Almighty, but his own demented voice. Wilks probably had a warped revelation that he would change his holy service and life. That was the mystery of God. Everybody wanted direct communication with the Lord. Maybe it was like the temptation of the Lord in the hot desert by Satan, who made Him promises he couldn't keep. Or maybe it was like the burning bush appearing to Moses, a divine telegram.

I thought of Ephesians 6:12. "For we wrestle not against flesh and blood, but against principalities, against powers, against the rulers of the darkness of this world, against spiritual wickedness in high places."

I knew all about the satanic principles. I knew to look back and see the signs of the words and deeds of this fake prophet. The devil did exist, and he was real. I recalled the devil and his clever salesmanship with Adam in the Garden of Eden. I saw his increasing power everywhere in the countryside, even behind the pulpit, even in the sacred confines of the church.

Three nights ago, the reverend had burst into my room at the motel. I'd been having a slight pity party, looking at the black-and-white photos in my wallet, the ones of my crazed but beautiful wife, Terry, and the kids. He'd walked in here, shouting about Wilks and the devil and his minions. He'd yelled about one of the elders being grumpy and asking him to leave his church, saying it was private property.

"Clint, you don't have a clue," the reverend had said.

"Don't you believe God is a loving, just God?" I asked him. "Do you believe that? I feel God's presence in the good *and* the bad. That's why Wilks confuses me so."

With a smile as cold as Alaska, the reverend looked older, somehow seeming frail and nervous. He said that at one of the meetings with the elders, he'd told them that he would take matter into his own hands.

"What does that mean, Reverend?" I wanted to give him a piece of my mind, but he was off balanced. I wondered if he was having some sort of breakdown or something.

He stood by the door, like he was a crook on the run. "I'm not going to let Wilks take everything away from me. I'm just not. My life has been very hard, and all the piety and sincerity have been kicked out of me. I'm not going back to what I once was."

I was silent.

"Did you know you've got one of the Wilks guys hanging around here?" He was fidgety.

"Yeah, I know. I saw him through the window."

"Why don't you call the cops?" he asked me.

"He's harmless," I replied. "He's not harming anybody."

He said he was going to have it out with Wilks in a meeting with the elders and the entire congregation. The church had to decide who it wanted to lead them. Peck or Wilks.

"It's about time," I answered. I wanted to go home.

"I've been thinking about the fact that the devil is among us," the reverend said quietly. "Wilks has been corrupted. He has been won over and has gone over to the side of Satan. Lucifer is whispering to him constantly about how he wants to run things."

I was confused. "Are you saying Wilks is a fallen angel?"

The white planters saw Wilks as a huge, beastly ogre with sharp horns, foul breath, a pitchfork, and a spiked tail. In their opinion, he'd been sent from up North to stir up the colored help. Peck thought of Wilks like that too.

I recalled Wilks saying in the parking lot that day I hopped in his Ford, "I simply do what God tells me to do."

"You're walking up the wrong road," I'd assured him.

Wilks had laughed. "Maybe they should cut that part of my brain out. I want everything corrected, where nobody gets the short end of the stick. Is that wrong?"

As the picture of Wilks dissolved in my mind, the reverend was peeking through a crack in the door. "All I say to Wilks is, 'The Lord rebukes thee.'"

With the church turning on him and time running out with the planters, the reverend found himself between a rock and a hard place. Still, I prayed for Wilks, that he would be redeemed and spared. *Fat chance of that.*

When all of my memories were cleared from my mind, I turned to the serenity of prayer. I recited the Lord's Prayer very slowly and deliberately, making each word count, ignoring my sore knees. *Praise the Lord. Amen.*

20

AMONG THE THORNS

It was billed as one of the community's biggest events, next to the well-attended regional fair, the standing-room-only area football bowl game, and the arrival of the popular fall carnival. Church members passed out flyers and nailed up posters proclaiming the second leg of Prophet Wilks's "Common Sense" tour in Wilson, Alabama. The reverend called me and asked me to go with him to the service. He wanted to collect more evidence for the showdown at the meeting with the congregation and the elders, to be held in a few days.

"I'm trying to put a good face on this whole thing," the reverend said during our call. "Wilks is right when he says the church is forcing me out. All the church mothers are laughing at my expense. They're laughing at me about losing my church, losing my wife, and losing my standing in the community."

"Don't do anything foolish," I said. "Right will win out. You can't do anything about the past. It's futile to regret anything."

I listened to the reverend rant and rave, but Wilks knew the measure of the man. When we were in the Ford, he had talked about Reverend Peck's love of bean pies, pigs' feet and yellow rice, a plate of spicy deviled eggs. He'd done his homework. He knew about his fondness for his old blue Oldsmobile, his romantic insecurity about his wife, and his fear of the white planters.

"Wilks will get himself killed if he takes on these peckerwoods," the reverend remarked. "He needs to call in the NAACP or the National Urban League. That's what they do. He's got all these young bucks up in the woods planning and plotting against the white folks. He cannot win. The white folks think he's a commie or a terrorist."

"Is that what the planters are telling the press?" I asked.

"Yes. You can't mix God with politics," he replied. "The last person who did that was Reverend Martin Luther King, and you see what it got him. Wilks's got a target on his back."

I brought up how Wilks's dog, Myra the pit bull, had attacked me in the park. Wilks had seemed to enjoy the animal's assault on me, laughing and almost cheering her on.

"He's got three of them, three black pit bulls," the reverend said. "I was in town, and one of them tried to bite me. I kicked it hard in the side. One of Wilks's men pulled a gun on me, but the fool got the dog on a leash."

"I was not so lucky," I replied. "I had to go to the doctor to get a shot. You never know what the dog might have. Rabies or anything."

The reverend went back to his favorite topic, the Gospel and the subversive work of Prophet Wilks. He compared Wilks's work again to a virus that has run its course in the bloodstream of the demoralized church, corrupting it but not defeating its holy tradition.

"It's like the passing of a bad fever," the reverend suggested. "Truthfully, God will destroy the wicked. Wilks told me he is God's bonus to me. The Almighty sent him to get my life straightened out, to restore his faith, to strengthen my call. How do you like that?"

"He's nuts," I said.

"I don't trust the man's psychological development," the reverend added. "I don't know if he knows the difference between good and bad."

"I think he knows the difference," I said.

"Listen to this, Clint," the reverend said. "Wilks told me he is a legit leader. He asked me how I could account for his success if he had not accepted Jesus as Lord and Savior in his life. I wanted to tell him that the devil is always working his plan. He added that he'd accomplished goals that you, a true man of God, have not been able to reach."

"Let's go to this service in Wilson, Reverend," I replied. "I want to see him in action."

Half an hour later the reverend's car pulled up to my motel. I trotted out to take my place in the backseat. One of the reverend's supporters, a man I had never seen before, occupied the front seat. We covered the distance from the motel to Wilson in about forty minutes and then tried to find a space in the crowded parking lot.

Following a fruitless search up and down the lot, we parked on a side street near the building, which had been a movie house for the colored back in Jim Crow times. Our mystery passenger told us he remembered his parents going to see picture shows there a long time ago.

Once inside, we sat together on the second floor. We had good seats, unlike some of the others, who had to peek around poles and columns to see the stage. The crowd was bigger than when we last saw him.

There was an enormous portrait of Wilks, with his jaw jutting up like that of a Caesar, behind the raised podium. The choir, which was split up on two sides of the stage, was dressed in all white. Music came from a tape of old gospel hymns going back to the churches of old. The same organist came out and took his place in front of the instrument, and a guitarist joined him, while two staff members did the final checks on the microphone.

Slowly, the organist stood and waved his hand, and the choir sang one of the old-time hymns, "Take My Hand, Precious Lord." A group of dark-suited faithful walked to seats lined up behind the podium, while the uniformed ushers kept others moving in an orderly manner to chairs below.

The volume of the hymn decreased as Prophet Wilks stepped onto the stage and clapped in time with the music. Some acknowledged his arrival with shouts and cheers. He put up his hand in an almost regal fashion to let them know they existed.

"I say to you, praise the Lord," the holy man said.

"Praise the Lord. Praise the Lord." The shouts came from the front rows in the hall. Every seat was filled, with standing room only again. Some of the faithful had slept for hours near the hall, waiting to hear the prophet speak. There was an overflow crowd outside the hall, satisfied to listen to the words of the prophet on loudspeakers. It was an orderly, polite gathering.

"America is a Christian nation," the holy man said. "America has no boss, no king, but Jesus."

"Amen to that!"

"I want to acknowledge that this program is being broadcast on fifteen radio stations and by satellite feed to over thirty countries," the holy man added. "Praise the Lord. Can you say that, my Beloveds?"

"Praise the Lord!"

Prophet Wilks, dressed in his customary white, was a bit more energetic than the last time. "As Christians, we must stand for something. If we don't stand for something, we will fall for anything."

"Amen!"

The organist provided a little light riff while the holy man continued to talk about his beliefs. "As Christians, we believe faith is very important in our lives today."

"Amen!" somebody shouted after the others had quieted.

"As Christians, we believe we have a personal responsibility to share our beliefs about the Creator with nonbelievers," he said firmly. "We believe Satan exists. We believe evil exists."

"Praise the Lord!"

"As Christians, we believe eternal salvation is possible only through God's grace," he declared. "We believe Jesus Christ lived and died for our sins. We believe God is the Creator of all things. Is there anything wrong with that so far, my Beloveds?"

A very thin, wig-wearing woman jumped up and yelled, "Teach the Holy Word, Prophet Wilks!"

The holy man walked to the organist and looked at him. "As Christians, we believe God will come back and judge all of us, believers and unbelievers. Right, my Beloveds?"

"Hallelujah!"

"I watch the TV, and they say this is the message of the Christian Right," the holy man noted. "They say this is the message of the Christian Coalition and the Moral Majority. They say this is the message of Pat Robertson, Jerry Falwell, and James Dobson. No, this is wrong. This is the message of the Holy Bible. This is the message of the Holy Word."

"Hallelujah!"

Now his voice was filled with power and spirit. "Dearly Beloveds, I have worn the crown of thorns, I have been beaten and spat upon, I have been kicked and slapped, and I have been talked about and slighted.

But I'm a true Christian. I am a true warrior of God. I refuse to run like a scalded dog. No, no, no, I will stand fast and raise my head. I will serve Him that sent me. Let's say amen."

"Praise the Lord!"

Several people yelled amen.

"What is the penalty for sin and becoming a follower of Satan?" he asked the audience. "What will happen to sinners? No, don't answer that, my Beloveds. Let me give you some inside information."

"Teach us, Prophet!"

With a slick finger wave, Prophet Wilks signaled the organist, and the hall filled with an eerie, dark sound. "Oh, my Beloveds, Satan is making a comeback. Satan, the father of lies, is licking his chops and sizing up new targets. He's changing his game plan and revising his goals. He's using Plan B, and it's working."

"Hallelujah!"

"In this world, he will tempt you and lead you into sin and evil," the holy man whispered. "But he will not prevent you from being redeemed or saved. Ignore him. Don't get into an argument with him, for he is the great deceiver."

"Teach us, Prophet!"

He wiped his face with a handkerchief and tossed it into the audience. There was a fight for it before two security men broke it up. His hands went up when the applause and the roaring were at their highest pitch, and then he made a flapping motion, as if he were an angel high above the earth. After this, he stood still, straight as a single blade of grass.

One of his staff members walked up to him with a golden cross the size of a magazine and gave it to the holy man. He nodded majestically.

With a move worthy of a dancer, Prophet Wilks held the cross above his head and shouted, "The Lord paid for our sins with his divine blood. The Lord paid for our sins to redeem us. He did this for us, and now He wants an accounting. Matthew, chapter twelve, verse thirty-six, says every idle word and deed would be accounted for on Judgment Day. He says we will be judged by everything we say and do on the Last Day. Can someone say, 'Praise the Lord,' my Beloveds?"

"Praise the Lord!" someone in the gathering yelled.

"O my Beloveds, we can be certain there is a Judgment Day and everybody on earth will be there. Amen!"

"Amen!" The roar of the crowd almost shattered the roof.

"How will Judgment Day be, my Beloveds?" he asked in a still voice into the mic. "St. John says it all. He gives us a vivid description of the Last Day in the last book of the Holy Book. He says it all there in the book of Revelations. Everything."

"Teach us, Prophet!"

He was clutching the cross just so the amber lights fell upon it, creating a spooky shimmering effect. It was like the cross was acting as a conduit, a lightning rod, for the electricity or the heavenly power to surge through the holy man. This eerie effect wasn't lost on those in the crowd, who recognized that this man had been sent by the Almighty to appear in such a way.

"John says, 'And I saw a great white throne and Him that sat upon it from whose face the heaven and the earth fled away, and there was found no place for them. And I saw the dead, small and great, stand before God and the books were opened, and another book was opened, which is the Book of Life, and the dead were judged out of these things which were written in the books, according to their works. And the sea gave up the dead which were in it and death and hell delivered up the dead which were in them and they were judged every man according to their works."

The holy man strutted across the stage, holding the cross in front of him, making high steps. A warrior of God. The cross still glowed.

"The Bible says, according to their works, according to their works," he said, his voice thick as honey. "Not everybody will enter the Kingdom of Heaven. What excuses will you give for your sins? What will you say to repent on that final day?"

He hopped up and down and launched into a spin, whirling around and around like a child's toy.

"O my Beloveds, do you know the signs, big and small, that tell us He is coming?" the holy man asked them. "Do you know them? It's important that you know them."

"Praise the Lord!"

The holy man stood with the cross in one hand and the mic in the other. "Knowledge will disappear, and ignorance will rise. Adultery and fornication will be common sports of the wicked and idle. They will be performed in the open, in public, where everybody can see. The young will be full of rage and vulgar. Don't you see that now? In the papers?"

"Amen!"

"I'm not finished," he told them. "Men and women will turn against each other. Gains will be shared only by the rich, with no benefit to the poor. Wealth will increase greatly, but the rich will not be satisfied. Sudden death will be widespread. The young will not respect their elders or authorities. Family will not matter. The leaders in power will be the worst of us and will trample the rights of all."

"Amen!"

Somebody yelled that this could be seen in Washington and in the Congress. Some laughed.

"Evil will seem to triumph," he cooed to his flock. "Men will begin to look like women, and women will begin to look like men. Plagues and depravity will rule. The Antichrist will reign. There will be great and big disturbances on the earth—earthquakes, floods, drought, heat waves, killer winds, deadly snows, and fire belching from the land. These are the signs of the Last Days."

"Amen!"

"Every religion teaches us about the day of reckoning, or Judgment Day," the holy man noted. "What can we do to be saved? How can we avoid, as Matthew says, being separated by the Holy Shepherd and being on His left, as goats? We want to be sheep on His right hand. Don't we? Don't we, my Beloveds?"

"Praise the Lord!"

"We don't want the Lord to say, 'Depart from me, ye cursed, into the everlasting fire prepared for the devils and his angels,'" he said. "We don't want to be sent into eternal punishment. We want to be with Him, to be counted among the righteous comfortable with eternal life."

"Amen!"

"The Lord promises that the universe will be renewed with a new heaven and a new earth. This is what He promises. This is the world to come. Don't you want to be saved, my Beloveds?"

Again, the holy man waved the cross, the light catching it perfectly, above his head. The cross symbolized the resurrection of the Son of God from the grave. When he hoisted the cross, there was a great murmuring among the audience. He was a God-sent man.

"Be in the world, but not a part of it," he said tenderly. "The world is Satan's playground. His world consists of pleasure, sin, immoral practices, vice, and indecent behavior. You don't want none of these in your life."

"Praise the Lord."

He leaned over at the end of the stage. "Make your life right with God. Resist sin and temptation. Line the devil in your sights and say, 'The Lord rebukes thee.' The devil can be beaten. He can be beaten with a good verse from the scripture and a pure heart. Did you know that?"

"Amen!"

Suddenly, a deacon cried out and did the holy dance, and an usher tried to fan him, but he kept pushing her away.

"Practice kindness. Practice tolerance, and don't say unkind things about your neighbor. Toss any hate, jealousy, or envy from your heart. Never lie. I mean, never lie. That's when the devil knows you're a true friend."

"Praise Him!"

He held the cross as if it were a baby. "Join together. Be a force for good. Don't trust your emotions. They are fickle and short-lived, like quicksilver. Don't be overconfident. Don't be vain. Don't be proud. Vanity will make you fail. Don't talk down to your brothers and sisters. Never."

"Amen!" Some short bursts of clapping broke out.

"And, my Beloveds, fill up on the things of God," the holy man added. "Embrace holiness and salvation. Steer clear of all things evil and wicked. Prepare for Judgment Day! Judgment Day is at hand! It is coming soon, very soon."

One of the staff members ran up to him and mopped his sweating brow. He was tired and was trembling and still rambling. A member of the choir jumped up and down, pranced around, and banged a tambourine. The place was in a state of bedlam.

The holy man gave the cross to an usher and raised his hand. "Let us raise our voices in thanksgiving to the Lord. Move away from the evil of this world. There is a battle going on. Like I said before, it's a war between good and evil. God will be victorious in this world."

His legs almost folded up. He held the mic tightly as he walked back and forth across the stage, an usher trying to keep up. It was almost as if he was in a trance, in a mental fog.

"My Beloveds, are you saved?" The holy man staggered across the stage, toward the exit. "Can you be saved? What will you do to be saved?" The last words echoed throughout the hall, like feedback from a sound system, and the crowd went wild. The show was over.

21

FORWARD OR BACKWARD

On Friday of that next week, Addie asked me to talk to her class about Harlem, the hip black neighborhood in New York City that was the home to so many writers, painters, and musicians from the last century. She especially wanted me to lecture them on the Harlem Renaissance, Marcus Garvey, Duke Ellington, the Apollo Theater, Malcolm X, and Reverend Adam Clayton Powell. I agreed to do it in order to witness their young faces light up when they learned of the wonders of the big city in the North.

"I hope I can do them justice," I said over the phone. "I've never taught little kids. I've always respected you folks who can harness their boundless energy."

She laughed. "It's a special skill. Teaching is a talent."

I arranged to be driven out to the school. During the ride to the small, battered schoolhouse out in the sticks, I looked out the window and thought about how these people survived despite living in houses with little heat, having no medical care, often not having enough to eat, and putting hand-me-down clothing on their kids. The parents of these poor kids made just enough money to survive, not to thrive. Some of the workers slept on the floors of those lucky enough to have a shack large enough to accommodate more than one family.

Upon arriving at the school, I paid the driver, a man who ran a car service that went through the poor black sections of the region, a necessity given that the white cabs steered clear of the rougher, tougher places where the darker people lived. Addie walked down the steps, greeted me like a visiting celebrity, and ushered me into the main classroom.

The classroom had not changed. The familiar portraits of the Kennedy brothers, Reverend Martin Luther King, President Obama, and the civil rights icon Rosa Parks still hung on the far wall.

Eager young black children, ranging in age from eight to twelve, sat behind the desks, waiting for my performance, waiting to hear about the big city. The schoolteacher had primed them to listen to me, a keen observer of life in New York City, and Harlem in particular.

"We welcome Reverend Clint Winwood, a resident of New York City," Addie said, introducing me to the children. "He's going to talk to us about Harlem, the so-called Black Mecca of America. Its rich history as a cultural and political place is something we should know."

One of the students clapped at that point, and the others followed suit. The schoolteacher waved her hand to silence them.

Finally, she said, "Let's make him feel at home." Addie wanted to call the shots.

Then the kids applauded as if they were welcoming a circus act, like a tightrope walker or a trainer with big cats or some fool letting a guy throw knives at him. I loved it. I loved their energetic joy, which reminded me of my own slain children.

Addie pointed to a map of New York City on the front wall, then circled the neighborhood of Harlem, at the northern tip of the island of Manhattan. She was smiling at me as I opened up my prepared notes on Harlem, the black capital of America. The students looked at me like I was bringing them the sacred Holy Word from the Mount of Olives. I loved it.

"Harlem is an incredible place in these United States," I said softly. "Black people came there at the start of the last century, as a part of the Great Migration, seeking a better life. They were trying to escape the hard Jim Crow laws here in the South."

Addie rolled up the New York map, then stood in front of the blackboard and wrote the words *Jim Crow.*

"Who knows what these words mean?" she asked the students. "Show our visitor that we use our heads for more than a hat rack."

A few hands went up. She chose the little boy who was waving the most vigorously and shouting that he knew the answer. Some of the others chuckled at him.

"Jim Crow was a group of laws that kept Negroes from being equal," the little boy said. "The white peoples wanted to keep us in slavery. Pa tole me that."

Addie was very proud. "And that was segregation. Remember when I explained that word for you children? What is it again?"

"Seg-reg-shun?" a small girl with pigtails asked her.

The same little boy who had answered the first question wanted to reply, but the schoolteacher selected someone else.

"We'll try to let other students answer," she said to them.

"That's when the law tries to keep people apart, you know, like the white apart from the colored," another girl, with acne, said firmly. "They make them eat apart, sleep apart, pray apart, and even ride the bus apart."

I walked to the blackboard and scribbled the word *Harlem*. "During the 1920s to 1930s, Harlem saw a lot of writers and artists celebrate our culture, traditions, and history. It was like James Brown singing, 'Say it loud, I'm black and I'm proud.' Everybody was proud to be black then. This was called the Harlem Renaissance."

"I told you about that last semester, right?" Addie asked.

They nodded and agreed with her, but their eyes were on me.

I continued my lesson. "Some of the names you should know are Langston Hughes, Claude McKay, Zora Neale Hurston, Countee Cullen, Rudolph Fisher, Jean Toomer, Nella Larsen, and James Weldon Johnson. Their creations are still important to us today."

"Remember I read Langston Hughes's poem 'The Negro Speaks of Rivers' last week?" the teacher said. "What did you think of the poem?"

The children roared their approval. I could tell they liked it.

"Also, we sang a song written by James Weldon Johnson at the start of Black History Month. What was that song?" she asked them.

A bucktoothed lad bounced up from his seat and lisped, "Ah know. Ah know. . . . 'Lift Every Voice and Sing.' I like the words to it."

"Harlem went through tough times when the country was hit with the Great Depression," I went on, erasing the words *Jim Crow* from the board. "The Depression was when the stock market and banks crashed and there was no money. There were no jobs. Everyone was desperate."

The boy who was the prized student piped up. "I bet the folks down here didn't suffer that bad. We could eat off the land."

I corrected him. "But if nobody had any money to buy the crops, everybody suffered, even the farmers. There was no cash around at all."

"Where did you live in Harlem?" another child asked.

"I lived off West One Hundred Sixteenth Street and Lenox Avenue when I was young like you," I replied. "Harlem was a different place back then. It was a close community with pride in itself. Most men worked as waiters, porters, bellhops, redcaps, elevator boys, mechanics, and clerks."

"What is a bellhop?" a girl quizzed me.

"It's a guy who carries luggage at a hotel, sees after the needs of the guests, and makes everybody comfortable," I answered.

The class was getting restless. One little girl, well dressed for this area, put her hand up and asked what was there to see in Harlem for people who were visiting there.

"There is the big Hotel Theresa, where Malcolm X stayed, and even the Cuban president Fidel Castro had a room at the place," I said. "Langston Hughes's house is still there, and there's an area called Strivers' Row, the Apollo Theater, the Schomburg Center for Research in Black Culture, and various stores and shops along West One Hundred Twenty-Fifth Street. A number of museums are in the neighborhood, such as the Studio Museum in Harlem, the Museum of the City of New York, and El Museo del Barrio. There is a lot to see and experience."

"What people did you look up to when you was a kid?" a boy asked me, and all the children's eyes turned to me again.

I thought it over. "I admired the labor leader A. Philip Randolph and Reverend Adam Clayton Powell, who was a Harlem congressman for many years. Later,

I adored Reverend Martin Luther King and was very hurt when he was shot."

The class assured me that the lesson on Reverend King was one that they had absorbed. Two boys recounted the bloody march between Selma and Montgomery, fire hoses and police dogs tearing the tender flesh of the black protestors. I smiled at their knowledge.

Addie sensed that the class wanted to take a break, especially the younger children, so she asked if they wanted to celebrate the birthday of one of the little boys, Gilbert, and they shouted that they were ready. Gilbert was the scrawny boy with the buckteeth. Addie brought out a large chocolate cake and a tub of vanilla ice cream. She told me that she had stayed up all night making the ice cream with a hand-cranked machine and rock salt.

The class sang "Happy Birthday" to Gilbert, who was beaming with delight. His voice tinny, he joined in with the revelers. The boys bounced a few balloons around in the air, while the girls watched and giggled. Several of them began to chase each other, like all young kids did, playing tag, until a knock sounded on the door.

A teenage white kid, dressed in a blue uniform, stood at the entrance to the classroom. His hair was blond and shaggy, and it hung over his ears. He appeared startled when he saw me, a big black guy, walking behind the schoolteacher. Addie led the teenager back into the hallway, and I followed.

"This is a wire from the school board in the county seat," he said in almost a whisper. "They said that I should make sure you got it. It was important for me to put it in your hands."

"Do you have to wait for a reply?" Addie asked him, tearing open the envelope. He said no and trotted away to his car.

She was very quiet, absorbing the words on the page. A slight tremble went through her body. Her eyes leaked onto her smooth brown cheeks.

"The idiots on the county school board want to close three of the rural elementary schools, including mine, to meet a budget shortfall," she gasped. "That's crazy. They could find the money if they wanted to support the schools. They didn't have any public hearings on this matter."

"What can you do?" I asked. "What can anybody do?"

"Listen to this." She read from the letter. "This action of closing the schools has been a very difficult decision for us all. It isn't anything we take lightly. Many of our neighbors' children attend one of these schools."

"Is that true?" I wondered aloud.

"No, it's not. The three schools on the chopping block are far from the towns and very rural. They are in poor black communities. This is the work of the planters who are trying to pressure the black farmers and truckers to back off from their demands."

I wanted to say words of comfort and support to her, but I didn't want it to be taken the wrong way. She covered her face. I could tell she was very raw emotionally.

"I asked the school board if they could seek a funding increase so we could sustain the schools," she added, tears now streaming down her face. "They said they could not, because the whites in the adjoining communities could not bear any more taxes. I argued that we needed school supplies, including textbooks and writing instruments, but they made more cuts, including eliminating five full-time teaching positions, and gave no pay raises. We've not received a pay raise since I've been here, and that's been for six years."

"What can you do now?" I repeated.

"Nobody cares. Nobody cares if you're poor," she lamented. "Nobody cares. If you're poor, you're nothing. You don't count."

We stepped back into the classroom and silently watched the kids play and chase one another. One or two of the children looked at Addie's face, but they didn't ask what was wrong. I imagined they had seen her cry before, many times.

22

THE HARD SELL

The Prophet Lamar Wilks was big news in these parts. On the next day of my Harlem class lecture, he was interviewed by a local TV station on his work with the black farmers. I found his face splashed on the newspaper below the fold. I read the article with great interest.

The Atlanta Free Press – *Fall Sunday Supplement*
By Victor Biller

Fate has not dealt Lamar Wilks a winning hand in a long time. He is in the fight of his life with two mighty opponents: one the formidable pastor of the influential church he's taken over and the other a group of no-nonsense white planters seeking to run roughshod over local black farmers and truckers in a power grab.

Still, Wilks greets the day as if he has nothing to worry about. He's staying in the large house of one of the local matrons, the widow of a liberal white congressman who served only one term. When the Atlanta Free Press *team arrives, the thirty-nine-year-old, freewheeling minister is sitting in a red satin bathrobe, his bare feet in furry house shoes, sipping cool mint tea. Even before the interview takes place, he waxes eloquently about gun control, Iran, the trendy Kardashian women, health care, the Syrian madman, out-of-control meteors, dementia, and the quirky San Francisco 49ers football team.*

After an all-night rally against the region's greedy big farms and the good-ole-boy trucking monopoly in an adjoining county, attended by over fifteen thousand angry people, he relaxes by slumping back on the sofa, two chilled slices of cucumber on his aching red eyes. A young woman, all dressed in white, removes the soothing vegetables and puts the cup of tea again in his hand.

Wilks knows he is the voice of reason in a community that has been ruled by prejudice, ego, and the hoarding of political and financial power. "This poverty is real, but many in this place would rather ignore how much pain and suffering the poor are enduring," he says. "The Buddhists believe life is actually an illusion, but I know this is real, much too real."

When asked about the lack of stress on healing and salvation, he refuses to get cagey. "I've seen so many people suffer and die in this kind of life. It's a hopeless, punishing existence. There is no difference between this and living in a poor slum in the inner city. I know the Christian doctrine preaches about a generous spirit, but many churches are concerned only with themselves, concerned only with their financial well-being. The church must step up whenever it sees suffering and lack."

But that doesn't mean Prophet Lamar Wilks is so forthcoming when he speaks about his upbringing or his past. When interviewing the controversial minister, one will constantly be frustrated by the confusing stream of consciousness spewed by the man when he discusses the years gone by. He reveals that his par-

ents lived for the sake of their family and their children, but he refuses to disclose his birthplace or the number of siblings he has.

"My mother was the matriarch, always in control," Wilks says, watching his trio of pit bulls stroll through the house. "I recall her chasing my father out of the apartment with a mop. Did you know my mother once entertained troops in Vietnam with Bob Hope and Juliet Prowse?"

Questioned about her name as a performer, he reluctantly admits that her stage tag was Doris Carroll. The pastor confesses that it was his secret desire to join the foreign service or be a big-time broker with a lavish room at the Plaza or the Waldorf. Or a man of impeccable reputation giving the prime-time sermon at the Cathedral of Saint John the Divine, where one of his idols, James Baldwin, was eulogized.

"I've got a progressive agenda," he says, taking another swallow. "I'm not breaking away from the conservative values and traditions of the church, only expanding them. I'm a nonconformist, but I want to serve God and humanity. I'm called to serve."

Another pretty girl with bangs and long legs, in white, brings him a piece of a cherry blintz on a saucer and a bottle of chilled ginger ale. One of the bodyguards, in one of his trademark white suits, stretches out on a lounge chair and winks at him. He nods approvingly.

"I wanted to go to Spelman or Howard, but my father thought that was a waste," he confesses between bites. "I was all over the place. I didn't know what I wanted to do. I tried to join the army, but they rejected me because of a detached retina after a high school boxing match."

Purring from the taste of the treat, he admits to a huge sweet tooth, a weakness for Tootsie Rolls, Almond Joys, Baby Ruths, Milky Ways, Snickers, Sugar Babies, and Raisinets. There are three Black Cow suckers on the table before him. He gobbles the blintz down while saying the community is about to become a circus. He doesn't explain that.

Wilks suddenly perks up when speaking about the prevalence of poverty in this rural community. "Certain moments have defined my life. Once, when I was hungry and without shelter, I was given a tattered suit from Goodwill by a thrift shop owner. It was very cold. A bitter cold winter in New York City. I found a crumpled ten-dollar bill in one of the coat's pockets. I lived off of that for days. I was overwhelmed with God's presence at that moment. I had asked for His mercy, and He had provided. Nobody who has not done without can know what it's like. It's hell to be poor."

"Why the push for the homeless and the poor in this area?"

He takes a sip of the tea before answering the question and explains he had a sore throat until Tuesday. A bug, no doubt. "A black person down here is more than three times more likely to be poor than a white person," he replies. "It doesn't matter if the black person works hard and puts aside something for a rainy day. He cannot get ahead."

He stares at the pretty young girl with the bangs as she bends down to go under the coffee table to retrieve a shoe. "Most of these people here are poor. The planters use the poor blacks against the poor whites and vice versa. I called them on it, and they don't like it. God didn't intend for any of His children to suffer through this life, no matter what color they are."

Asked whether the planters were trying to reach an agreement in good faith, to iron out the differences in sales and distribution, the controversial minister rolls his eyes and lowers his voice.

"Believe me, I wanted to think there is a sense of friendship and fellowship between our two sides," *he says.* "I hoped this community, black and white, rich and poor, would come together as a family of the faithful. An agreement, a settlement on these issues, would be in the best interests of everybody. However, there's so much that still divides us."

Something happens to the sound equipment. Wilks rises to his full height and stretches with a loud yawn. There is no doubt that this situation is wearing down his resolve and patience. A staffer makes the adjustment on the machine, and the interview continues.

He carries his cup to the kitchen and asks one of his assistants to pour him the remaining portion of tea. Walking briskly, he returns and sits down to face the reporter.

"I want to end poverty, suffering, and loneliness in exchange for freedom, justice, and peace," *the minister begins after clearing his throat.* "The Lord doesn't like lack. He wants us to walk in step with His plan for us. As you travel through life's journey, you understand failure is often not a defeat or a setback, but a road to a greater triumph."

Wilks grunts loudly when the reporter says he is trying to begin a movement similar to that of Dr. Martin Luther King and the civil rights campaign in the South. The reporter congratulates him for being an inquisitive man, larger than life, with a kind of spiritual hunger that knows no boundaries.

"Some say you've gone rogue, that you're trying to do everything yourself," *the reporter adds.* "Some say *you're presenting yourself as the Savior, with your theatrical road shows and dramatic healing sessions. They also say you're putting yourself and your members at odds with the church establishment. And that establishment might not support you when the going gets tough."*

Wilks frowns and grins. "Are you calling me a quack, sir?"

With a smirk, the reporter reminds the minister of the string of black churches that were burned in the mid-1990s, noting that the establishment might not want a similar retaliation for Wilks's political activity of this sort.

There is no life behind Wilks's soulful, distant eyes as he launches into a defense of his ministry. "I've always acknowledged my weakness, my sins, my unworthiness. But the Lord forgives."

Nothing is said in response, so the minister continues his rant. "We elders and leaders in the service of the Lord must tell the youth the painful and troubled pasts of our lives. It has not always been easy. I've never tried to present myself as more than I am. I'm a sinner saved by grace. That is all."

Prying into the opening that Wilks gives him, the reporter asks the minister about his so-called sketchy past, those things the media and the religious community know but are reluctant to discuss.

"First, let me tell you that I've got a terrible memory," Wilks jokes. "Most of the people in my inner circle know that. I think most people in the service of the Lord do. I'm sorry about my amnesia concerning certain things from my past."

"So there are things you don't want your congregation to learn?" the reporter asks firmly, with a bite. "There was a car crash where some people were killed. Do you remember that?"

The minister leans forward, forms his hands into a steeple, and focuses on the journalist. "I won't talk about this again. There was talk that I was behind the wheel when a car containing several of my relatives collided with a van on the Pennsylvania Turnpike several years ago. They say I was drunk. But the fact is, I wasn't driving, nor was I drunk. I was in the passenger's seat when the van swerved into the southbound lanes on the highway and slammed into the driver's side of the car. My aunt was pronounced dead at the scene, and two of my cousins died later at a nearby hospital. I remember the driver of the van got out, staggered around, with blood streaming down his face, and looked into the car. I think he was in shock. Then he went back and stood against the smashed van. The cops say accidents are common on that turnpike. Later, I was cleared of all wrongdoing."

The reporter wants to press Wilks on the facts. "That's not how I heard the story told. That's not on the official record. That's your account of what happened."

"That's all I'm going to say on that matter." *Wilks is resolute.*

"Aren't you afraid that you've bitten off more than you can chew, Reverend Wilks?" *the reporter asks him point-blank.* "This is the South. Things can get out of hand very quickly. Aren't you afraid for your life?"

The minister sips from his cup and makes a serious face. "To be afraid is a very human thing. I used to be afraid of change, of time, of being alone, of defeat, of failure, of the unexpected, of dying. But no more. I've died already, and the Lord brought me back to life."

"What does that mean, Reverend Wilks?"

Wilks adjusts himself in the seat and crosses his legs. "My grandfather, who was a fan of FDR and the

New Deal, always quoted Eleanor Roosevelt's words on fear and change. He'd say, 'You must do the right thing that you cannot do.'"

"What are you saying, Reverend Wilks?" the reporter asks. "Don't you know your actions can have frightening implications in this area?"

The minister's attitude is defiant and bold. "I'm not afraid for myself. All I want is for the local black farmers and the poor workers to decide and speak for themselves. I don't want them pressured. Sure, I'm afraid of what might happen if things go the way they have in the past. It'll not be good for anybody. That's why when you say 'frightening implications,' I know what you mean. Somebody will get hurt or killed."

"Again, I ask you if you're afraid for your life?"

Wilks stands up and starts shaking hands with the publication's staff and the reporter. "I expect nothing. I demand nothing. I'm grateful because I've been given the miracle of life. I pay attention to those blessings that have always been there. I pay attention to those that sometimes go unnoticed and unappreciated."

"Reverend Wilks, you did not answer my question," the reporter insists.

"Nancy, show these people out," the minister says as he escorts the reporter to the door. "Just remember, truth doesn't make things easy. It makes them possible."

23

HOLY DISOBEDIENCE

Something was always happening. No sooner had I read the interview with Wilks in the Atlanta publication than a hard knock sounded on the door. I was in my pajamas, still half asleep, and cranky. The voice of Reverend Peck boomed from the other side of the door, alarmed and frantic, saying the sheriff had one of the young girls in custody and the naive girl was spilling the works.

"Who knows what they will do to get the lowdown on Wilks?" Reverend Peck said as he walked into the room. "The planters feel their backs are against the wall, and they're desperate. They're throwing money at the sheriff so he can make something stick."

I stretched my arms above my head and yawned. "So what do you want me to do? If the law has the girl, then what can be done? Maybe we can get a lawyer to get her out, but that's it."

He sat on the sofa and crossed his legs. "We need to go down there and see what's what. This girl is one of my church members, and I cannot fail her. Her family is counting on me."

I poured myself a cup of coffee. "You cannot go down to the police station every time a church member is brought in. The planters know what they're doing. They're wearing you down. Once you go down in nervous exhaustion, that'll leave Wilks exposed. They're slick. They know what they're doing."

He shook his head and coughed. I could see he was running himself to a frazzle. Running and chasing schemes and plots. While Wilks seemed not to worry about anything, the old minister was trying to keep his church together and protect his members.

"Want a cup of coffee?" I asked, standing near the pot.

"Yeah, all right." Reverend Peck asked me if he could bring Addie along, because she might be of some help with the girl. I agreed.

"Did you read the Wilks interview in the Atlanta paper?" I asked him.

He said no but added that Wilks was going to get himself killed, along with a bunch of his gang. The publicity he was trying to wrap around himself would be futile in preventing what was his fate. Angry and desperate, the planters were plotting something special for him.

I was tired of talking about white folks. "Is there any word on your wife?" I asked him, watching him frown.

"Ex-wife." He said it like it was so.

"You haven't divorced her, have you?"

He folded his muscular arms and made a serious expression. "You know I haven't. I just feel like she is lost to me. She belongs to someone else. Not me."

"Why do you say that?" I asked him.

"She lied to you. She is back with him. She moved back into Wilks's house shortly after she came by your place. She lied to you, my friend. I hope she rots in hell. I hope he rots in hell too."

I took my pants that were folded over a chair and tucked them under an arm, then ducked into the bathroom. I could hear him through the door of the bathroom. He was still raging out there, cursing her out, cursing him out. I could feel the manic energy coming from him.

"You need to get yourself together, or you won't be able to help anybody," I said, my voice sounding hollow through the crack in the door. "When is the last time you got a good night's sleep? You seem like you're about to crack. The planters are counting on that."

He slumped on the sofa and put his head down. "I know. I know. I'm a wreck, but then, you told me that the last time we talked. I'll rest after all this mess is over."

I removed my pajama top, filled the sink with water, and splashed some of it on my face. He was still ranting out there. I had stubble, so I shaved with one of those plastic razors. There was a loud knock on the door. He was impatient, urging me to hurry up and dress. The girl's life might be in danger. At least that was how he put it.

It was maybe three minutes before we were in his car, listening to the news about the gun nuts threatening the president, an earthquake hitting Japan, the U.S. food supply being endangered by a drought, an Air France jet sliding off the runway, and a drone taking out a terrorist in Pakistan. The silence was killing me. The minister had his moods, up and down, dark and light, calm and frantic.

The minister totally forgot to pick Addie up. He was in his own head, in his own world. He believed he was under siege, in a war of good and evil, and he couldn't fail the girl. He had to protect her.

We pulled into the parking lot, between two police cars, Reverend Peck immediately noticing one of the big Cadillacs owned by a planter. Something was up. He turned to me with an alarmed expression and said the presence of the planter scared him, especially since the girl was in the custody of the sheriff. Anything could happen.

He marched into the station, past two cops, and demanded to see the girl, remarking loudly that she was a loyal member of his church. When the woman behind the desk didn't move quickly enough for him, he started walking toward the back of the building, where the prisoners were kept.

"Wait here until I call you," the reverend ordered.

One of the deputies held up a hand, blocking his way. "You can't go back there. Sheriff's conducting business. And he has company."

Reverend Peck cocked his head and growled, "Does this business have to do with the girl? Don't mess with me. This is illegal. You have no warrant. You have no right to bring her in."

"We can do anything we want, Reverend Coon," the lawman said.

"You know this ain't right," the minister snapped.

Suddenly, the sheriff appeared, elbowed his way between the men, grinning like a vacuum cleaner salesman, trying to make peace. "No, no, no, that ain't the way to talk to a man of the cloth. If Reverend Peck wants to see one of his members, then he should see her. We're here to oblige. We want to make everything go smoothly."

I was standing there, dumbfounded. This was what I hated about the South, thinking that this kind of stuff could still go on, and nobody could do anything about it.

I guessed my face wore the annoyance that I felt inside, because the sheriff waved me on as well. He led us down a long hallway, decorated with medals and awards, to a room separated from another room by a window. The girl, seated at the table in the other room, couldn't see us. I found a seat next to the reverend and stared at the girl. Her kinky hair was all over her head, her eye was bruised, and her full lips were busted. My eyes went to her feet, which were bare and ashy.

The sheriff went in the room, joined there by a uniformed cop and a plainclothes policeman. The lighting was pretty bad, but everything was visible. An older woman, dressed in clothes geared more toward a summer picnic, took notes on a legal pad. They faced the girl, who still sat at the table, a look of raw terror in her bloodshot eyes.

"Martha, the church of the prophet is more of a cult than a church, ain't that right?" the plainclothes gentleman asked. "Ain't the man a false prophet?"

The girl didn't appear to be clearheaded. She was probably foggy because they hadn't let her sleep. "Naw, suh, I don't know about that."

"They say the prophet is out of his head, slightly psychotic and paranoid," the deputy said, looking at the woman taking notes. "Did you see any of that, missy?" The girl widened her eyes. "What's *psychotic?* Did I say it right?"

"Plumb crazy," the sheriff shouted. "A nut job."

"Naw, suh, I don't know about that." Her voice was real small.

"Darn it, gal. What do you know?" the uniformed cop yelled, and the girl flinched. "We can't be wasting time with you."

The sheriff walked around so the girl could see him dead on, see the grim expression on his lined face. "We made a deal here. You know what we want. You know more than you're saying."

"Yeah, talk," the deputy yelled at her full force.

The girl stared at her crooked toes and spoke quietly. "Nancy an' me know we is fall from grace. The prophet say all the nonbelievers need to go through the change to see God. We know not to question him. Some of the man assistants been botherin' us, so we tell him, and he say they won't be botherin' us no more. We believe him. We believe everything the prophet say."

"Why do you feel that way, girl?" the sheriff asked.

"Mr. Wilks ain't Jesus Christ, the Redeemer. He can't walk on water."

The girl beamed. "The prophet cannot sin. God knows his soul, and he's one of the anointed. The prophet always say so."

"Do you know how we found you, girl?" the deputy quizzed her.

"From the papers," the girl replied quickly. "But I told the papers I don't hate the prophet. I'm not happy at all about all of this. He has done a lot of good for a lot of folks who really needed it. I don't think the prophet is an evil man, but maybe some of the fellas around him are doing Satan's work. Maybe the locals are doing something wrong by lumpin' him with them."

The sheriff threw up his hands, ignored her, and turned his attention to the men. "This girl's been brainwashed. Just like the other ones. What do you call Mr. Wilks? You got to hear this, boys."

A wide smile split the girl's bruised face. "Sometimes we call him Daddy. He likes that. That makes him happy."

"And what does he call his flock?" the sheriff asked.

"We are his Beloveds," came the sweet, innocent reply.

This entire chat was getting to the deputy, who wanted some action, wanted something to pin on the false prophet. He was pounding his ham-like fist into the outstretched palm of his other hand, like he wanted to beat it out of the girl. He hated nigger stupidity.

"Were you considered a team player?" he asked.

"Team? What team?" The girl acted dumb, but she wanted to drag everything out. She was praying for the cavalry to arrive.

"Did the men with Mr. Wilks take your cherry?" the uniformed policeman demanded. "Did they rape you?"

"Naw, suh. Naw, suh." The girl was stubborn on that point.

"Now, word reached us that you was with some young girls from the congregation who act in what they called a manner of prideful behavior, and they told you all to take off your clothes in front of the members," the sheriff said. "Do you recall that?"

"Naw, suh, it wasn't lak that."

The sheriff was fed up. "Then how was it?"

"Were you tortured or the like?" the deputy asked, pressing.

"Naw, suh. Naw, suh. The men did the punishment to the men, and the women to the women," the girl explained. "If we did wrong, the church say we need to be punished. The prophet's assistants kept tabs on the members who was grumbling or complaining about the way the church was going."

"We had some girls who say several of Mr. Wilks's men had sexual affairs with them," the sheriff insisted. "We have evidence of those abuses. The girls say they would beat their families if they exposed them. They was afraid the men would take it out on their kinfolk. Did you hear of that?"

The girl kept staring at her feet. "I heard it, but it doesn't make it true."

"We heard about sexual relations, all kinds of weird mess," the deputy insisted. "You never heard about that, girl?"

The girl stared at the cool glass of water that the sheriff drank, and slowly slipped into a trance. "The men loaded us into buses and took us to meetings where the prophet's assistants talked nonstop about duty, loyalty, and service. At some meetings, there was only a few of the young girls there. None of the older or senior members was allowed. I think everybody knew what was happening, but they turned a blind eye to it. The assistants gave us something to drink in little plastic cups. It always made my head throb and made me wobbly."

"Now, this is what we want," the sheriff said excitedly.

I turned to the minister and saw that he knew this was a setup to get Wilks up on a felony charge or to drive him out of town. The planters had it all rigged.

"We girls didn't want to be belittled in front of the others, so we did what we was told," the girl said quietly. "We thought we was being tested. We was scared. Some of the girls told me some of the older boys got on top of them and wiggled while the assistants watched."

"Where was you during all of this?" the deputy asked.

"I was scared, like I said. When I first refused to do what they wanted, they made me scrub the floors, clean the toilets, or take out the trash. If I gave them lip, they made me stand in the corner with no clothes on. They broke me down. I didn't want the girls to hate me. None of the girls wanted to be hated or shunned."

I couldn't figure out whether the girl was telling the truth or not. Reverend Peck knew she was not. He knew this girl and her family and their background as poor sharecroppers.

The girl wanted only to be pleasing in their sight, to make them like her. "We girls know how to make mens happy, or at least some of us did. The older girls loved to be touched, looked at, or, as the prophet called it, 'adored.' Some of the girls saw it as a chance to have raw sex, and they didn't care if the mens looked upon them like tramps. It didn't matter that some girls was not yet mature womens."

The deputy's eyes glowed, and he rubbed his hands together. "How old would you say the youngest girl was?"

"I don't know about that," the girl replied. "All we girls wanted to feel special and loved. Don't most young girls want to feel like that?"

The sheriff ignored her remark. "Go on, girl."

"The mens offered us girls drink, rum and Coke, in those little plastic cups," the girl continued. "We drank it all up, wanting to please them. I was special. The prophet say so. The mens talk soft to me, real gentle. Call me sweet honey baby. The boys around here is brutes. They don't know how to treat a girl. They all want one thing, just like Mama say."

"Go on, girl," the sheriff said eagerly.

"Some of the old ones, who had lived a bit, had no lead in their pencils, so they just had to watch the fun. They got a good eyeful. All them pretty young girls with nothing on. Wiggling and prancin' about. One of the mens' head was near my privates. I told him no, and one of the assistants say she being saved special. He left me alone. It didn't take much to turn them on."

The girl kept an eye on the water. The deputy left the room, winked at us, and returned with a pitcher of cool water. She watched him as he poured a cup for the uniformed cop.

"Can't they see she's got a powerful thirst?" Reverend Peck said angrily. "This is torture. They don't do this even with the terrorists."

"No, they do worse," I said, groaning.

"There was some huggin' an' kissin'. Some older girls touched the mens in certain areas where they knew they would get heated up. We girls had no say in any of this. So much of it was just huffin' an' puffin' an' nothin' goin' in. That was all right with me, because I wanted to save myself for my honeymoon bed."

"Was there drugs?" the sheriff asked her. "Did you see any drugs?"

"Any meth?" the deputy demanded. "You do know meth when you see it?"

"No, I didn't see anything like that," the girl replied.

"And where was Mr. Wilks during all this time?" the sheriff asked. "Was he telling everybody what to do?"

The girl shook her head. "No, I didn't put up no fuss. I did what I was told. The prophet was always watching me, looking really hard. Some girls was doing hanky-panky, but a lot of us was not. The prophet didn't pressure us."

She added that one time was really special. It was when the prophet said some sweet things to her, really beautiful things, kissed her gently on her forehead, and stepped away to let the others take her to the bus. Her face was glowing when she recalled the moment.

"And what happened when you talked to the papers?" the deputy asked. "How did they treat you then?"

The girl covered her face, sobbing. "The girls and womens humiliated me during services and meetings," she said between tears. "They say I acted selfish, allowing the enemies of the church to reign victorious. They sat away from me. Nobody spoke to me. They acted like I was invisible."

"And where was Mr. Wilks then?" the deputy wise-cracked. "Why didn't he come to your aid? You fell out of favor, didn't you?"

"Naw, suh," she replied.

The sheriff leaned over the table and snarled, "Why didn't you leave the accursed place? You know the church was not doing God's will. You knew that, right?"

The girl's eyes were redder, and her tears flowed. She wiped them with a tissue the deputy handed her. "Suh, I thought about leaving, but where would I go? Where would I be safe?"

"It sounds like Mr. Wilks was your pimp and he was running a cathouse. Did you see money exchanged?"

"Naw, suh. Naw, suh." She was firm with her answer.

Behind the wall of glass, Reverend Peck shook his head in disbelief, wondering why Wilks would surround himself with a bunch of idiots and jailbirds. He also recalled that the man had a big ego.

"Why would these fools choose these young heifers, who are young enough to be their own daughters?" I said aloud. "They're asking for trouble."

The minister laughed. "A fruit is better when it's ripe, not green."

In the room, the sheriff and his men stood, staring at the frightened girl, confident that they had cracked the felony case of Mr. Wilks. The head lawman took a step forward, held up two sheets of paper, saying they were from the prophet himself. He told the girl that Mr. Wilks knew that she was being held in police custody and that other young girls had been placed in safe houses around the area, pending an investigation by law enforcement agencies.

"To those who are trying to destroy what the Lord has divined, I say no earthly influence will take down the mission of salvation and redemption," the sheriff read from one of the papers. "I'm leery about the ones who have been singled out by the authorities. You who have been chosen by the Maker to serve Him and now side with Mammon, you have my pity and concern. I know you girls are innocents, so young and so pure. Oh, my Beloveds, by going to the other side, you're making a really stupid decision. There is more to this than you know. The stakes of this moral and spiritual battle are high. There are all kinds of evil among these people of wealth and authority. Turn away from them. Give them no assistance. Give them silence. Don't help them!"

Trembling, the girl avoided all eye contact, her gaze darting all about the room. She touched her temple, as if in pain. "Do you have any aspirins?"

Meanwhile, Reverend Peck kept telling me it was a setup, but he knew he couldn't put pressure on these people to stop the nonsense. He said over and over that the law and the planters were going down a horrible road, where everything could blow up and nobody would profit. The girls, he acknowledged, were working with the law, being willing dupes, and the planters continued to plot to get rid of the prophet.

I turned my attention back to the girl on the other side of the glass. She was mumbling something. She was crying, barely able to contain herself.

"I was never pressured to do anything I didn't want to do," the girl muttered. "I believed in the prophet. He said we were a disappointment, and he was right. Some members say they saw tears in his eyes after he was brought before the church. He never allowed nobody to do anything violent or rough with us girls."

The deputy pointed at the girl and shouted at her. "Bull crap! We don't want Wilks here! We want him to leave and go back to a place where his kind belongs. We don't want any more of his rallies or the protests. We want him gone, gone, gone!"

Just then Addie entered the hall, her voice loud and defiant, and she then walked into the room with two reporters and a photographer. She asked the sheriff if she could get a little time with the girl. She called her by name, Martha. I sat there as she told the lawmen that she had taught both Martha and her younger sister.

"I can't allow you to do that," the sheriff protested.

Addie, looking good in her gold business suit, wasn't having any of it and glared at the girl. "Martha is a liar. A good liar. I know you, girl, and your sister. She's a liar too. The truth ain't in you! You'd do anything for a profit. You've got all these folks fooled, but not me."

The girl wiped away her tears and stood. "These peoples know I'm telling the truth. All I'm doin' is tellin' the truth."

"Sheriff, you can't accept as fact everything coming out of the silly mouth of an impressible young girl," Addie said, addressing the head lawman. "Lives and reputations are at stake here. This girl just wants to get some attention. You should get her to take a polygraph and see if she's telling the truth."

The girl pouted. "I know I'm tellin' the truth."

Remembering that the girl was an unruly troublemaker, Addie tried to rush her and shake her. It had nothing to do with Wilks. She couldn't let this girl get away with her accusations.

"Martha, why are you saying these things?" Addie protested. "Do you know you're playing into their hands? They have one goal, and that is to destroy Wilks and his church. They want to stop his work with the black farmers. How much did they pay you? What did they promise you and the girls?"

The girl, rattled by Addie's direct talk, stepped back. When she did that, the sheriff and the deputy made sure to keep the schoolteacher from the girl. Meanwhile, the uniformed cop intervened and grabbed Addie by the arm.

"We're going to ask you to leave, all of you," the sheriff said, ushering Addie, Reverend Peck, and me out of the rooms and then through the station. "This is not helping matters at all. Leave us to get to the bottom of this. Believe me, justice will be served. Believe that!"

24
CERTAINTY

After we were thrown out of the police station, we gathered in the parking lot to talk about the brewing Wilks crisis, feeling the eyes of the authorities on us. The sheriff was staring at us through the window and motioning wildly. Addie noticed the cloudless sky, looked up with a smile, and said we shouldn't talk here anymore. She was pumped up from the quick excitement of her verbal battle with the white men.

"Look at those white folk staring at us like we got tails," Addie remarked, holding out a hand to me. "Can I take Clint with me, Reverend Peck ? I want to talk with him. It's a serious matter."

"I see you have your cousin's car again." The reverend glanced around her car, an ancient light blue Chevy Impala. "Does that car still run? You had trouble with it the last time."

I looked at the jalopy, old and a little rusty. We laughed at Addie's vintage ride, joking in a good-natured way to let off the emotional steam from the grilling we had just witnessed.

"I've got to visit some couples who are having a bit of trouble," Reverend Peck said as he got into his car. "Call me, Clint, after you finish your business. I want to get your advice."

I nodded, waved farewell to him, and got into Addie's car. She watched the reverend drive off, noticed the shadows in the windows of the police station, and shrugged. I hadn't noticed the straw hat in her hands, a cute little number. Finally, she pulled out of the parking lot and drove north.

"Reverend, I can tell when you're thinking of your dead wife," she said, almost blurting it out. "Your eyes get distant and cold. Almost blank."

"I wasn't thinking of her then," I said. "I was thinking of how they're badgering that girl in there. She doesn't know anything."

Ignoring my remark about the girl, she made a turn at the row of stores near the center of town. "I don't want to talk about her. I want to talk about you. When are you going to rejoin the human race?"

I clenched my jaw, getting pissed. Reverend Peck often asked me if I was making progress getting over the tragedy, if I prayed for a holy resolution and a spiritual healing. "Time," he would say, "heals all wounds." Where had I heard that before? There was nothing new in anything anybody said about my grief and healing concerning the tragedy. Nothing new.

I remembered the answer I gave him on one occasion. "I don't need to suffer after something like this." At least that was what I believed. I told him this was not me. I wanted to go on without all that grief.

Addie waited for the light to flash green. "Clint, I can be a very jealous person. Do you have many ladies in the big city?"

I was getting a little nervous. "No. I find dating can be a chore."

"Why is that?"

"Women want to ask too many questions. They want to pry into your life, and sometimes you don't want to be so revealing. As I told another woman not that long ago, women like to rip off scabs, see what is underneath, and get into your emotional pain. Men mostly want to keep that part of them as private as possible."

Addie tugged at her ear. "She must have really hurt you deeply."

A car turned in front of her from the middle lane, getting close and just making it onto a side street. The idiot almost took her bumper off. Still, that got her attention for once and removed the focus from me.

She looked at me sideways. "Do you like women? You're not gay or something? Sometimes after a mess like what happened to you, a man starts to pitch for the other team."

I grinned. "No. I like women, but I can't be bothered with a female who tries to take over my life. That has been tried. It didn't work."

For some reason, I was thinking of a childhood treat, a big pitcher of red Kool-Aid, with a tall glass full of cracked ice. Her words shattered my vision of juvenile bliss.

"This is a very difficult period in my life," she said, cutting the steering wheel real hard. Minimal power steering. "I've got a fella who calls me now and then. He works as a lineman for Alabama Power. Dangerous work. He treats me all right, but I want more."

"More what?" I asked her.

"More excitement, more fun, more frolicking."

I laughed. "*Frolicking?* What does that mean?"

"Adventure, big adventure. Crazy adventure."

"So maybe this guy might be the ticket for you to have those adventures, those big adventures," I said, watching the buildings go past. "Are you serious about him? Is he the one?"

She made an odd sound low in her throat. "Mr. Lineman has a lot of girls, many of them. He treats all of them nice. I backed away from him because I don't want to get in a line to get his attention. Like I said, every now and then he calls me and asks me if I'm seeing anybody steady. He doesn't want me to get serious about him, but he doesn't want me to go on with my life."

"What about your old man, who was killed in the oil rig fire?" I asked her, noting the bewilderment on her face.

"Oh, him. He didn't want me to take birth control," she said, her dark eyes narrowing. "No pills, no IUD or jelly, no foam. He really wanted me to get pregnant, but I didn't want to do it. Maybe God didn't want him to be a father, so He killed him."

"Oh, man, why did you marry him?"

Her lip curled in malice. "Because I loved him at the time."

Heaving out a sigh, I returned to looking out the window. This was why I didn't like to talk. It stirred up so many skeletons.

After a pause, she asked me if I liked children. "Do you like kids after what happened to you?"

"I guess if I loved the woman and got married again, I'd think about it," I suggested. "Children are a serious matter. You have to be ready to do the parental role and do it right."

Swallowing, she became pensive. "My folks were together for almost forty-five years. They were very happy. My own marriage went through a lot of ups and downs, because everything came to a head. It just stopped. . . . The love did. I need to change my life. I need to learn how to raise hell. That's why I think New York City would be the best place for me."

"New York is very tricky," I remarked. "It's not for everybody."

"I could get used to it . . ." she replied, her voice trailing off.

"What kind of man was your late husband ?"

Addie said nothing at first; then she let loose, describing her oil rigger in detail. She needed to talk about Marty, so I let her. Often, she repeated the same things about him, going on like a Chatty Cathy doll, as if she was obsessed with the man. "In so many ways, I married a man like my father, just like him. My ex loved to be in control. He was very bossy. He always wanted to be the life of the party. He called the shots, and you had to go along with him, period."

"Did you ever think you'd marry a man like your father?"

"Clint, no way. I was just hoping to find a man who would treat me nice, like a lady. Now, you are totally opposite. You're not like my papa. You don't talk much. You got to pry things out of you."

"You're right. That's not me," I said quietly.

She chuckled. "In these parts, having a love affair is a matter of making do. No poor black girl has any illusions of making a decent marriage last in these bad conditions. Life here is very hard. And people start to indulge in their worst selves, lying, cheating, stealing, coveting, and even killing. Everybody just wants to survive. That whole business of survival takes a big toll on anything positive and permanent."

"I see what you mean," I replied.

"Are you the kind of man who runs away at the first sign of closeness and intimacy?" she asked, listening to the motor start to cough. "There's plenty of them around here. If you tell them you're getting sweet on them, they hightail it out of there so fast that your head will spin."

I felt uncomfortable. I didn't know where this was going.

"I'm not a quitter," I answered firmly. "I've never been."

The schoolteacher knew how to throw a verbal curveball. "Clint, when did you have sex with your first real woman?"

I frowned. "I don't think that's nobody's business, not even yours."

"Do you think Reverend Peck is an Uncle Tom?" she suddenly asked.

That was a strange and frightening insight, one that I'd considered more than a few times when I saw his behavior around white people. He was too passive, too compromising.

"Do you think he is?" she asked, pressing.

"Honestly, I don't know. I told him the other day that he places too much value in the kindness and compassion of these white people he is dealing with," I answered. "He thinks these white men are more Christian than they are. They're not thinking about making the lives of these poor folks better. He cannot see that."

"That's why some folks think he's an Uncle Tom."

The old Chevy sputtered twice and died on the side of the road. I was really worried, because I didn't know a darn thing about cars. Brakes, transmission, spark plugs, generator, battery, motor oil. I knew nothing.

We both got out. I lifted the hood, and the motor belched clouds of hot steam. With a keen expression, I looked at the insides of the car as if I were an expert mechanic. She smiled, knowing I was pretending to be a grease monkey, as the people up North call them.

Three cars whizzed past, never slowing their pace. A pickup truck, with a rebel flag attached, honked at us, and a little white girl gave us the finger.

We sat on the overheated car and watched the parade of automobiles rush along the road. It wasn't as hot as it had been earlier in the week.

"I guess many black people down here think the North is the promised land," I said, turning to her. "As a Northerner, I can be honest. When you're down here, you think every door of opportunity will be open to you when you go up there. The North is not easy. The white people have a different set of rules to keep you off balance. They have different ways to keep you in your place."

She grimaced, surveying the rural Alabama landscape. "It can't be like it is here. The devil has us by the throat."

The sun was getting high up in the sky. I thought about my bigger concern of solving the dilemma in Reverend Peck's battle with Wilks and the church leadership. Now I couldn't act on any impure feelings, such as pursuing an intimate relationship with the schoolteacher. Sex and lust could control people. In most men, physical desires could run amok, and I didn't want to do anything to tip the balance in our friendship. Still, I wondered how many men could be loved by a woman over time.

For Addie, I was an escape, a dream she had made up, a vision of freedom and opportunity. Sometimes I felt her stare at me like I was her savior. I didn't want to assume that role.

If I had my way, I'd get out of here as quickly as possible. Flee as far away as I could. The situation with Wilks and Reverend Peck was absolutely hopeless. I had a bad feeling that nobody had a future in this thing.

After the brief parade of vehicles, Addie called the tow-truck man over in the county seat, telling the driver the location and the problem with the car. Silently, we stood by the car, watching for the truck and getting hungrier by the minute.

"Do you know how to bake a sweet potato pie?" I asked her as she fanned her face with the hat.

"I'm an okay cook," she replied. "But I don't do pies."

I shrugged, a pity. I wanted a slice of pie with a dollop of vanilla ice cream on top. She saw the pie lust in my eyes.

The tow truck pulled up in a swirl of white dust. Its driver hopped out, wiped his brow, and walked over to the car. He looked under the hood and pronounced it dead. Motor had overheated. Battery was lifeless. The car went up on the hook and was cranked to its height behind the truck.

We all got in the truck, the slim driver all smiles, and the cab was quiet until he broke the silence with a compliment about what a perfect couple we made. He was all gushy about love in its purest form, how it was very rare, and how he had loved his waitress wife, yet she had left him to go to California with a shoe salesman.

I was afraid to live; I was afraid to love. With all the time that had passed, it was crazy that the pain of the tragedy had penetrated the bottom of my heart and nothing seemed to get it out. Even Dr. Smart had said I was young, so I had the right to be happy. *Don't relive the past.*

"How long have you been together?" asked the driver, starting the truck. "I love to see young people so comfortable with each other."

"You noticed that too?" she said, winking at him.

This was forbidden territory. I didn't know how incompatible we could be. I knew she was a teacher devoted to her children, but I knew nothing of her as a woman or a lover. In these parts, the rumors already linked us together as lovers, as potential marriage material.

"What does your man do?" the driver asked her. He could see I was not the talkative type. I wasn't a person who did small talk.

"He's a reverend," she said proudly. "And a good one too."

The driver glanced at me, sizing me up and wondering how I deserved such a wonderful woman.

"Why don't I drop you off at your place?" he asked. She gave him her address. I looked at her in surprise. In all this time, I'd never been to her house.

When the truck stopped in front of her house, there was the familiar Ford Fairlane sitting across the street, with two men in it. I got out and helped her down. She told the driver she'd give him a call tomorrow. He handed me a sweat-stained card with his name, the logo of his towing company, and the phone number.

"Thanks a lot, my friend," I said, smiling.

The driver nodded. "You're a lucky man. You've got a lovely lady there. I'll have something certain for you tomorrow. Call about noon."

I waved to him and started down the walkway. Addie noticed the car with the men, whispered something, and defiantly stood on her porch.

It was odd standing this close to this woman. I hadn't said anything when she talked about our imaginary relationship in the truck, but I wondered what that was all about. Something had clicked in her mind. I think that was the moment she decided to stake a claim.

"Those guys in the car . . . from the park," she said.

"Yes, I know. It's the same ones."

Following our adventures, I had to give her the benefit of the doubt. I had to give myself permission to fall in love again. Still, I didn't want to be a sinner leading a double life. *Willpower.*

"When are you going home?" she asked.

"Back to New York? I don't know." I could imagine Addie in New York City, bewitched by its pace and variety. If I had her there, I'd fix her dinner, take walks in Central Park, see the sights, go to plays and the movies, and do the whole business of romance.

"Do you miss it, Clint?"

"Yes, I do. I've reached my limit of living someone else's life. I want my own life back. It's nearing time for me to leave."

We stared at each other, our eyes locked, both of us wanting to touch. Her lips seemed swollen and appealing. She searched my face and eyes with her stare, actively and passionately. She was aroused. I felt it too. I fought down a fleeting image of Terry nude, with her arms outstretched, in our marriage bed.

Men could be so dumb. And not very attentive. It was the first time I noticed her brown hair was pulled and braided. I touched her gently on the arms, and she shivered, almost wantonly. For the first time, I felt she was falling in love with me.

"Clint, I want to leave with you," she said, grinning. Her eyes were glistening with tender tears.

It wasn't that Addie owned the first mortgage on my heart in terms of love. But I had been celibate since my wife killed herself. I wanted to hold her tight and kiss, but I didn't want to make a move too soon.

Boldly, Addie placed her hand under my chin and kissed me softly in the doorway. In the afternoon sun, she put her arm around my neck and placed her satiny mouth against mine again and again and again. The men in the car had seen enough. The Ford Fairlane drove off, sounding a single honk of the horn.

25

CHANGE AND OTHER CREDITS

We soon ended up back at my motel because Addie was very aware of her snooping neighbors. We called the front desk, got the number to a rib joint down the street, Sweeney's, known for its juicy barbecue, cole slaw, and collard greens. Addie ordered four bottles of beer as well. When the delivery boy brought the food, we overtipped him and his smile lit up the doorway. As he was leaving, Addie saw that the Ford Fairlane was parked in the lot, hidden between two vans.

"I hope they let us eat in peace," she said, laughing, unwrapping the wax paper around the still steaming ribs. "I wonder if they follow Reverend Peck this closely. If they do, he probably wants to shoot somebody."

I was still chuckling at some of the jokes she had told us in the tow truck. She liked them down and dirty. I didn't mind it. The driver had got a kick out of such a pretty woman telling such filthy jokes.

"Tell me about yourself, Addie," I said, twisting the top off of a beer bottle. "Tell me something I would have never guessed."

"All right. I feel you're my protector, healer, keeper." She grinned. "I'm really glad that I met you. I see what kind of person you are. You've made some real friends here in this town. Folks know what you're made of, and they like that."

I took a swig. "I thought you were going to talk about you."

"What do you want to know?" she asked. "I'll tell you this. I'm not going to tell you everything about my life, especially not the most interesting parts. Maybe I'll tell you those tidbits when I get to know you better."

Things revealed themselves to you during this life. I had learned desire was not necessarily bad or wicked. But lust could be dark and even perverted. Lust meant the easy fulfillment of urges and drives. Lust was a nephew of sin and temptation.

"Clint, what do you do for sex?" she asked, tearing into a saucy rib. "You're mostly alone. I never see you with any women ."

I pitched a forkful of greens into my mouth and nodded for her to let me finish chewing. "I haven't had the time for any leisure."

"You're boring," she said in a hushed voice.

Making a face, I shrugged and lifted the bottle. "Marriage is great when you first get into it. It's red hot. You can't get enough of each other. But after kids and the passage of time, it gets cold and you get into a rut. When I was married to Terry, I knew I wasn't perfect, but I didn't cheat on her. I didn't cheat on her, even though she would come into our bedroom with some man's fluids dripping down her thighs."

She shoveled more slaw into her mouth. "Did you want to cheat?"

"Oh, yeah. I prayed often to remove that lust from myself."

"Did you want something different?" she asked me.

"Often, but I knew that would go against my vows," I said.

"Now, while your wife was doin' her thing, how was she treating you?" She sprinkled a packet of black pepper on her greens. "I wish I had some hot sauce. That would really go good with these greens."

I put the bones back into the container and wiped the sauce off my hands. "Terry used to love to tease me. She wiggled her butt around the apartment like she was a stripper trying to entice a customer. I hated that. I wanted to pry her legs apart so I could make love to her, but I knew better than that."

"That must have been torture," she said.

I said, "There is a point when love is over, and we reached that point of no return. Our love was finished."

"I told you I don't know whether I could marry again, and that's the reason," she said. "Too many things can go wrong. Some of these country preachers act like a woman cannot get by unless she is married, tied up to some man. If there is any value in marriage, that is not it. It's supposed to be about two adults who are untied and venturing out into the adventure of the real world."

"Nicely put," I said, smiling.

She watched me drink from the bottle. "Reverend, I'm a funny kind of woman. I don't put much stock in either love or sex. I don't give them much importance, but I'm not saying I am not feminine and don't love the idea of love."

"I can see that," I said.

Her stare was on my lips, which I thought were my least appealing feature. She seemed to be memorizing their shape or color. It was spooky.

"With these fellas, I don't want to be anybody's mother," she continued. "I want everybody to do his and her share. There are a lot of no-count men in the Deep South. Also, I will mess around with a fella only if I want to. Most guys get on my nerves."

"Do I get on your nerves?" I asked playfully.

"Not yet." She looked out the window onto the parking lot to see if the Ford Fairlane was still there. She had done this before. She had been constantly on the watch for the car after our encounter in the park.

"Most women want security and predictability," I noted. "Women want to feel safe and comfortable."

"Not all women."

She drank from her beer bottle and let the quiet enter the room while she peered outside at two white men unloading something from a truck.

"Do you think you're bitter about men?" I asked her.

"No," she replied.

Again, her attention turned to the men, who were putting something into large bags. She got up and stood by the window.

"Have you ever hit a woman?" she asked.

"No," I said firmly.

"You ever hit your wife?" she asked, going down that same road. "Heck, she gave you every right to do it. I know sometimes you felt like punching her out."

"But I didn't," I said.

She didn't leave the window. "You ever made love with a white woman?"

"That's none of your business," I answered.

Finally, she walked back to her chair and resumed drinking.

"I bet you could hit a woman if she pushed you enough," she said confidently. "You seem like that type. Talking just as politely and then just go snap and hit a woman."

I shook my head. No way. There was no way I could do something to any lady that could be called immoral or degrading. The schoolteacher walked around the table and over to the couch, carrying the trash she'd accumulated from the meal. I took the trash from her, walked it to the wastebasket. My eyes followed her as she walked to the window.She looked back at me over her shoulder. It was a lovely picture.

"I guess I can say if it weren't for my wife, I would have had the perfect marriage," I joked. "Some of my fellow clergy said I was too good-hearted and gentle with her. I answered them by saying I loved her too much. Too darn much."

She really got comfortable. "Clint, do you think I'm asking too much of these guys around here? I know this area, and the type of man I want just does not exist here. You know what I mean?"

"I guess," I said, thinking about the Wilks predicament.

"I'll tell you what they lack," she went on. "They lack self-control, so therefore they lack good character. If a man gives in to every urge or lust, he possesses not only a bad character but also bad judgment."

Most people suffer from some bad choice or make a wrong move in their life, I thought as she rambled on about horrible decisions that you had to pay for later on in life. I remembered what one of the nuns at Bishop Coolie's funeral had said about the majority of human beings. They had a basic nature that was moral, and they were inclined to do what was right.

"I think that's the problem with Reverend Wilks," she observed. "He makes decisions based on impulses and wishes that can benefit him in the short run, but that trip him up in the long term. I think you see my point."

Addie was always the teacher. "Yes, I do see what you're getting at," I answered. "But I think there's more than that. Wilks wants it both ways. He wants to get the attention and the notoriety, but he wants it from a community that is very conservative and traditional.

One that doesn't like change. That doesn't like progress."

She sat the beer bottle on the table near the couch. "If the sheriff gets one of the girls to say what they want them to say, the community will turn against Wilks like that. These folks don't like moral failings from outsiders or strangers, especially from a man of God. They'll forgive a man from here, but different rules apply to outsiders."

"Then Wilks is in trouble," I said. "Wilks is not flexible."

Change. "Change," Dr. Smart used to say, "is something millions of people struggle to do and most fail at." Although most people thought they were hardwired to do something different, it was the old habits and routines that tripped them up. As he would say, "There is stuff we can change about ourselves and stuff we cannot." He'd add, "Focus on the stuff you can do something about."

"Clint, that's what I like about you," she said.

"What is that?"

"You sit there and listen," she replied. "All women want is somebody who will listen to them, especially men. I guess you do that a lot when your church members come to you with their problems."

"Sometimes." I looked at her closely to see if she was joking or being serious. Sometimes it was hard to tell.

"Reverend Peck doesn't understand Wilks cannot change," she remarked. "He's not changeable. He's not flexible. That's why he's doomed. They'll find him dead under some strange circumstances."

"Circumstances, eh?" I kept thinking about she had been watching in the parking lot. The men were out there and were watching our every move.

I thought she was a little tipsy from the beer. She was talking too much, and some of it didn't make sense.

"Remember the other day you asked what my biggest fear was?" she said, holding a half-empty bottle aloft. "It's childbirth. I'm deathly afraid of getting pregnant and giving birth. Every woman I've talked to about it says how painful it is. I don't know if I could stand that."

I grinned. "Coward."

"But the women say they forget all about the pain the next time they get pregnant," she said and laughed. "Isn't that funny? I teach kids, yet I'm afraid to have one?"

"Not so funny." These were the kinds of secrets you would never tell anyone unless you were drunk or high.

"What's your biggest fear?" she asked. This was the second time she'd asked me. She had asked me the other day.

"I don't know." I repeated the answer from the other day, taking a seat on the couch.

Suddenly, she was on the couch with me, taking deep breaths, placing a slow, wet kiss on my cheek. Her mouth went to my throat, her tongue tracing a moist trail along my stubbly skin. I allowed myself to go with her advances. She could feel my hands on her body and was trying to remain calm and cheerful despite the beer in her. I thought briefly about disrobing her, seeing her naked for the first time, but I ruled that out. Still, the suit she wore would not be that hard to remove. As I said the sentence, "I will hurt you," she wiped away a few tears from the loneliness she had been enduring with the series of frog princes in her life.

We didn't tear off our clothes, but instead enjoyed the intimacy and passion that came so easily without stripping ourselves bare. I finally realized the divine connection between affection, caring, attention, and appreciation of the other's nature. What these things meant. What these things meant to sustain the life of a soul.

"I will hurt you, Addie," I repeated.

I finally understood what the Maker was saying to me in that moment: if you want joy, give joy in return.

With her head tossed back in the glow of passion, she straddled me, clutching my neck with both of her lovely arms, rocking and wiggling her bottom while thrusting and blending in a way I'd not done since I lay with my late wife, Terry. It filled me with the most marvelous heat.

"Is this all right?" she asked me breathlessly.

"Yes, y-yes, y-yes," I stuttered.

She stroked my face, saying all these guys were color struck and dated only light-skinned gals. Banana yella. Lemon pallor. Her skin was the color of cocoa, solid chocolate brown.

"You like me, Clint?" she asked, pouting. Sometimes she had a face like a naughty angel's.

When the door buzzer sounded, I got up and tripped over a pile of magazines and newspapers on the way. I stumbled as I went to answer it, but just as I reached the door, the first bullets whistled past me after shattering a window. Addie stiffened and then slid to the floor behind the couch. I crawled along the wall. She was scared out of her wits, so I motioned to her to stay down.

One of the lamp shades had a bullet hole in it, as did the wall above the bed. Four shots. We got still, remaining close to the floor. We heard footsteps go away from the door, down to the parking lot, and then came the slamming of car doors. There were two gunmen, not one.

I stood up, went to her, and hugged her. I could feel her trembling along her spine; I felt every tremor of terror.

After the car started, another gunshot sounded, the bullet of a much larger caliber. Glass broke, and a huge hole appeared in the wall near the bathroom. I reached for the phone to notify the sheriff. He probably knew about the shooting already and had the description of the gunmen and the getaway car. He knew everything that happened in his town.

26

HALLELUJAH REALNESS

The sheriff and his crew were going through the motions, dusting for prints, measuring the distance from the yard, collecting spent shells, and so on. We both knew it was all for show. Addie was still at the motel when Reverend Peck arrived, nervous and frantic, and eager to show he was cooperating with the law.

"Reverend, this thing is going from bad to worse," I said, gritting my teeth. "These crackers tried to take our lives. This is more than I bargained for."

Annoyed, the reverend gave me the evil eye. "You've got to be kiddin' me. You're not going to bail out on me now. The church needs you. I need you. You told me you're not a quitter."

I listened to him politely as the lawmen dug into the wall to get the shell casings, aware that we should not be talking this way around them. But I was angry, mad at the attempt to snuff out the lives of people who were not directly involved in the tug-of-war between Peck and Wilks. Or the ruckus with the planters, for that matter.

"Where's Addie?" the reverend asked.

"She's in the office, trying to collect herself," I replied. "She's still rather shaken. Getting shot at is not her idea of a pleasant evening."

"I know. It means these good ole boys meant business."

I walked the reverend out to the lot and gave him a piece of my mind. "I could give a darn about them and these farmers. I could give a darn about the pissing match between you and Wilks. People could get hurt, and neither one of you cares."

"I care," he said, with a catch in his voice. "I asked you once before. Can I count on you?"

"Count on me? What do you mean?"

"I want you to be there when everything goes down," the reverend said. "It'll get serious. These white folks are desperate. When I call on you, I want to know you'll not fail me."

My mouth turned down in disappointment. "And Wilks? What about him? Are you going to throw him to the wolves?"

What the reverend said was something he had said before. It was as though the replay was completely rehearsed and on a tape loop.

His eyes became hard and fierce. "Wilks lost his faith a long time ago and can't accept certain things about the nature of God's work. If he were a true man of God, he would be much more uncompromising about evil. He wouldn't play games with the devil."

I wasn't buying any of it. "Aren't you playing them as well?"

"No, I'm not." He was firm on this point.

"Some of the folks here think you're Tomming for them," I said, voicing what was not to be said. "They think you sold your soul to the planters. They think the planters pull the strings on you."

He gripped my arm and hissed a slow no. "Sure, they want to finish him off. They want an end to this farming mess. It's not my fault. The church and the community have turned on him. They know him for the fake that he is. And then there is this jailbait business. . . ."

I waved my hand and put my finger to my lips. "I saw some of their dirty work when they tried to get these young girls to lie about him. He's a man in love with himself, in love with his own voice. He's bogus, but I know he's not a molester. He's a lot of things, but I believe him when he says he did nothing wrong with those girls. I saw one of them take the third degree from the sheriff and his boys. It was not a pretty sight."

"What do you want to do?" he asked. "Remember I was there, Clint. I saw how they handled that situation and it was heavy handed, to say the least."

"I'm thinking about leaving," I said. "This is getting a little crazy. Everybody around you and him is in a lot of danger. They're making stuff up. They're shooting into the places where we live. I don't need any other invite to hit the road."

His smile was oddly cold. "Do me a favor. Stay a little longer."

"Like how many days?" I asked.

"Until Monday. Everything should work itself out by then."

I frowned. "Let me think on it."

Then the reverend launched into his holy tirade. "Satan is cunning. There is a false apostle among us, and we're in the grip of evil. The devil and his minions know they're in for a good fight. It's a fight between good and evil. You know that."

This was a lot of hogwash. "Nobody respects a fool. You shouldn't let these folks run over you. The church and the community see what you do. There are no secrets in this town."

Smarting from my last comment, he started reciting a favorite verse, Jeremiah 23:16. "Thus saith the Lord of Hosts: 'Hearken not unto the words of the prophets that prophesy to you: they make you vain; they speak a vision of their own heart, not from the mouth of the Lord.'"

"Are you still referring to Wilks?" I asked.

"Heck, yeah. He's going to get us killed," he said.

"Reverend, when did you see him last?"

"He was in town, plain as day, walking those three vicious pit bulls on Main Street," he said. "He was smiling as he led those growling and snarling dogs on a leash. Folks were jumping out of his way. You could tell he was loving the attention."

I laughed at the idea of him wearing his white suit with the rose, walking downtown in plain view of those white folks. He was poking his thumb in the eyes of the rich white bosses. He was something else.

"Wilks had a rally scheduled for the black farmers in an orchard outside of Dixon, but he changed it to the armory outside of town," the reverend said. "The planters have hired gangs of vigilantes to bust up his meetings. Wilks knows this."

I was very curious. "When is this meeting supposed to happen?"

"Tonight. But I caution you against going there."

"Why?" I asked him.

We walked to his car as we talked about the meeting. "Just don't go. Anything can happen. These white folk are riled up, and nothing good can happen when their backs are against the wall."

"Does Wilks know about this?" I was wondering which side he was on. The reverend knew something that he wasn't telling me. He didn't answer the question.

After Reverend Peck drove off, I found Addie sitting in the front office, still shaken. I told her what the reverend had said. She was firm about going to the rally, saying she would make some calls.

"Are the police finished with your room?" she asked.

"Almost." I told her I'd tell her when they left. I knew she had some clothes there. The sheriff had already questioned her.

The rally was scheduled to take place at the Old Townsend Avenue Armory outside of Dixon. It didn't go off as planned, for Wilks was late arriving there. His assistants had hired a security team to man the rally, and they stopped and frisked those who attended the event. Another squad of armed men lined the aisles, and the ushers showed people to their seats. The tension was high within the walls of the armory.

I admired Reverend Wilks's smarts. I saw why he had chosen this building. With its heavily fortified brick structure, it would be able to withstand any kind of high-powered blast. Nobody in their right mind would make a play for him in this three-story armory, which just happened to be listed on the National Register of Historic Places. The grand hall, where the rally was held, had a raised stage, with seating for about six thousand, and balconies for the dignitaries and public officials. A group of union leaders sat in the good seats, where they could make their approval known.

When Addie and I arrived, we were patted down, with our arms held high. Nobody recognized me, which was a good thing. As we were being seated, the 1936 film *Song of Freedom* was just concluding on the large screen at the front of the hall, the black freedom fighter Paul Robeson singing in his deep baritone voice in the final scene, in which his character, Zinga, a black dockworker in England who had sung himself to international fame, came home to his African people to improve their lives with his knowledge of the outside world. The gathering, both black and white, clapped at the positive message of the film.

The large screen was hoisted into the rafters, and there was a burst of activity behind the curtains. Everybody noticed the massive posters of farmers, black and white, and poor folks all shaking hands in a show of cooperation and solidarity. There was also a big poster of a small, grinning black child in raggedy clothes holding a bowl of fresh, succulent fruit out to a consumer.

A well-dressed white trade union representative brought out a black farmer, who talked about how the planters had conspired with the bank to take his land, which had been in his family since the Civil War. Now he and his family were working for others, doing seasonal work and making just enough to survive.

"That ain't right, nah, suh," the farmer said. "Somebody got to do something. We got to make them do right by us. We got to stand tall."

After the farmer shuffled off the stage, the thin widow of another farmer took the microphone and told them her tale of woe. "My man, Jerome Huff, lost our land to the bank too, but the planters allowed him to farm it, but they took most of the money," she said, sobbing. "That's all we knowed. Plowing, planting, growing the crop up, and harvesting. When the farming was done, Jerome took to doing odd jobs, doing the blacktop on the highways and cutting timber in the bottom land. They say a big tree fell on my man, and we carried him home and he died."

A gasp went through the audience. She listened to the people whisper among themselves before she continued her story.

"I remarried to a good man, another farmer, but the same story is repeating itself all over again," she said.

"We're about to lose our land, our home, our future. He's out of town now, trying to get a fair price on our crops. I appreciate what Prophet Wilks is doing. Nobody else was doing anything about this. Support him. Get behind him. That's all I have to say."

The clapping gave her a weak smile, and one of the ushers showed her off the stage. The booming sound of a tape of the old hymn "Take My Hand, Precious Lord" filled the armory, and everyone knew what that meant.

Suddenly, the lighting turned amber onstage. A spokesman for the Association of Southern Black Farmers walked to the mic, waved his hands to quiet the uproar. He cleared his throat, swallowed hard, and began his introduction of Prophet Wilks, who was the main attraction of the rally.

"Brothers and sisters, it's a great honor for me to be able to present to you a man who is not only a profound messenger of God, but also an ardent activist for the civil liberties and equal rights for all. I give you at this time . . . the prophet Reverend Lamar Wilks. Let's give him a hearty welcome."

The crowd rose to their feet and applauded Wilks, who strode regally across the stage in his trademark white suit with the red rose. He nodded to acknowledge their greeting. He stopped to take it all into his soul. When the applause didn't end, he stepped to the side of the podium and gestured for the gathering to sit down.

"My Beloveds, I'm so happy to be here," Wilks said, adjusting the mic. "I want to save souls. I want to lift the poor. As I stand here tonight, I remember my visit to some of the most impoverished areas in this region, moving among these farmers, the descendants of slaves now struggling to survive. It was my traveling throughout this area that made me think things out.

When I went there, I saw the planters get alarmed and wonder why that colored man was here. You know, hate gets in the way of any progress."

Someone yelled, "You got that right."

He took his time and pointed to where many of the farmers were seated. "You are my flock. You are my people. I say this. We must have economic freedom as well as spiritual freedom."

Shouts reached the ceiling and rocked the armory.

"If anything is clear in this struggle, this country and this community must respect your labor. Farming must be listed among the priorities of this society. If you do not farm, we do not eat. Your labor of planting and harvesting serves humanity. Black farmers and truckers are at the end of the food chain, insulted and humiliated, and this must be stopped. I want everybody to have enough to eat, to have a roof over their heads, to provide a good future for their children. God hates the misery of the wretched and the poor."

A group of the farmers and truckers and their families jumped up and down, waving their fists in the air. Their yells soared above them. Even the trade unionists, including some guys from the AFL-CIO and the Teamsters, rose in tribute to his words.

Wilks gave a deep chuckle. "Yes, sir, we used to kneel when they passed. We used to still our tongues when they spoke. We used to lower our gaze when they looked our way. No more. We are men and women, all grown up, and we deserve respect. We deserve to be heard."

"Speak the truth, Reverend," one man screamed.

"Wait, wait. We've got poor white folk doing as badly as our black folk," the holy man said, grabbing the mic tightly. "We must have our economic rights, our economic freedom, better housing, higher wages, higher profits from our crops, and better health care. The planters pit us against each other. Things have got to change!"

Wilks strutted across the stage, going back to his healing meetings one last time, but he caught himself before he got totally back into his showman mode.

"You are here tonight to say no to the planters who say if the poor folks truly followed the Bible, then there would be no problem," Wilks said and smirked. "The planters say everybody should know their place. We say now is the time. I've watched you fight for equal rights, and I've witnessed your campaign to sit at the table among the planters. I come to you, the farmers and the field workers and the truckers, for you are my strength. I came south to fulfill my holy mission, my duty to the Savior."

"Be our voice, Prophet Wilks!"

"Tell the truth about the rich bosses!"

Defiant, Wilks said he had tried to bring all the parties together in a compromise that was positive and meaningful. Then he launched into a tirade about the rich planters and their love of money and comfort.

"What does the Bible say about the rich?" he asked the gathering. "The good book says, 'It is easier for a camel to go through the eye of a needle, than for a rich man to enter into the Kingdom of God.'"

"Teach, Prophet Wilks! Teach!"

He bent over the stage and shouted at the adoring crowd. "Why can't we have hope, happiness, and human dignity? God wants us to have all these things. In the scriptures, He says that the lack of those things is a sin. Remember this. Reverend Martin Luther King said, 'All labor has worth.'"

A worker from the union tapped his finger on his watch from offstage, signaling to Wilks to cut his presentation short. Wilks looked at him and frowned. He looked like he was having so much fun.

"The struggle never stops," the holy man said quietly. "Stick together. Unite. Live in a way that does honor to our children, our families, and our community. We have tremendous challenges and obstacles ahead. Never lose hope. Never lose your will to fight. I close by saying, power to the people. Power to God!"

Crossing himself and then giving a fisted salute, Wilks returned the mic to the stand, bowed, and walked off to the cheers of a standing ovation. We shook our heads. This had to be frightening to the planters. Now something would happen.

27

THE LEPER

It was two days later. I remembered it well. Addie and I were talking on the phone, and told me about her recipe for chili, one of my favorite dishes, and described how much hot sauce she used to spark up the flavor. Terry, my late wife, was an expert at making chili. I missed that about her, among other things. Then I told Addie what Reverend Peck had hinted about in our early morning phone conversation: that Wilks had imported two lawyers, with their staff of enforcers, to quiet all the talk.

"Reverend Peck said he talked to Wilks last night, and Wilks said these guys knew how to deal with rats," I said. "Wilks said they cost an arm and a leg, about four hundred fifty dollars an hour, but they were worth it."

Addie was concerned. "I hope they don't do anything to the girls. They're just doing what they're told. The sheriff is putting pressure on them. They're just stupid country gals."

I couldn't help but think about the poor girl who got grilled by the sheriff and his boys. She had seemed so pitiful and helpless.

"I know that," I said. "Things are percolating. They're going to blow pretty soon, especially after that rally. Wilks didn't do himself any good with the planters and other white folk around here."

Addie asked me to be quiet for a minute, then told me she'd call me right back. I asked her what it was, what was so important, but she hung up on me.

I went to the tiny fridge and got a glass of cold milk. Somewhat alarmed, I sat on the couch, looking out at the empty parking lot and the traffic going past on the nearby highway. Something didn't feel right. My hair was straight up on my neck, and it felt downright spooky.

Then the phone rang. I was so glad that the front office had got the phone repaired in my room.

Addie was out of breath, almost sounding in a panic. "Wilks has been shot. He got shot in downtown Dixon. It's in the paper and everything."

"Shot!" My hand trembled on the phone.

"Downtown . . . shot and really hurt bad," she muttered.

I stood up against the wall, with my legs feeling like jelly. "Addie, let me call you back. I want to go over to the office and get a paper. This is shocking. It's unbelievable."

Addie sounded resigned. "I knew it. I knew it. It was only a matter of time. You can't stir up these white folk and think you can get away with it."

"Addie, I'm going," I said, pulling on my jacket. There was a little chill in the air. "Call you back."

"Promise?" Her voice was small, like that of a little girl with a lollipop.

I hung up without replying to her question and darted to the office. Winded, I got the paper from the guy, who took my money, but not before making a smart remark about the wisdom of putting your hand in a wasps' nest and not expecting to get stung. I ignored him.

Back in my room, I sat down and read the whole grisly story about a hatted woman walking up to Reverend Lamar Wilks on a crowded downtown street in Dixon and shooting him once in the back of the head shortly after seven in the evening. The downtown shooting had scattered people along clogged Pome-granate Avenue, near the row of shops, stores, and the movie theater.

I read where one witness saw the whole thing, how the woman walked up behind the controversial minis-ter and shot him at close range. The woman watched him fall to the pavement, stepped over her victim, and got into a sedan driven by a white man. Other wit-nesses said the car turned around and headed back the way it had come.

The rest of the article concerned Wilks and the church, his healing meetings, his work with the home-less and the poor, and his talks with the planters on behalf of the black farmers and truckers. The reporter didn't really go into detail about the tense labor situa-tion, but he stressed the lurid revelations of the young girls who came forward about possible illicit sexual relationships with Wilks.

My eyebrows lifted when I read one line in the body of the article, which suggested that one of the girls' mothers might have taken matters into her own hands, rather than wait for the sluggish legal system.

Trembling, I folded up the newspaper and placed it on the table. As I drank the milk I'd poured, I saw the old Ford Fairlane pull up outside. It drove right up to my door, and Reverend Peck got out. Life was full of surprises. I didn't know what to make of this.

The minister pushed his way past me and into my motel room. He was worked up, his mouth going a mile a minute. "I guess you heard. Wilks has been shot. I told him not to do that darn rally, but he wanted to do it. I told him. I told him, but he didn't listen."

"Is he dead?" I asked him.

"Heck if I know," the minister answered.

"What do you mean?" I quizzed. "Didn't you go to the hospital when you found out that he had been shot? That was the least you could have done."

The minister scratched his head and wore a curious look. "I didn't find out until about midnight. They took him away to a hospital over in the next town. I think the planters had something to do with it."

"Do you know who shot him?"

"Witnesses say a black woman shot him in broad daylight, and she got away in a car driven by a white man. That's all I know. The sheriff hasn't been helpful. He won't tell me anything."

I was getting angry. "The sheriff has to tell you *something*. Wilks is your friend. You hired him at your church. I don't get that."

Reverend Peck looked down at the floor and said in a quiet voice, "I warned him. I told him these white men were not fooling around. You don't fool around with their bread and butter. He acted like he was made of iron. He acted like he didn't care."

"I know Wilks cared," I replied. "He was scared."

"A couple of Wilks's men drove me out here to tell you," the minister said, knowing that some things were better said in person. "I'm going back to the sheriff to see what he knows. If I don't get any satisfaction, I'm going to the planters. I know they know something. I think they're behind all of this."

"Be careful," I said. "I wouldn't trust these crackers."

The minister reached into his shirt pocket for a clean tissue. "Wipe your lip. You've got a milk mustache. Are you going to be here? Tell you what. Stay by the phone. I might need your help later. It's not over by a long shot. Somebody knows something that they're not telling me. I'll get to the bottom of this, Clint."

"I'll be here," I said, walking him to the door. The minister was out on his feet, beyond tired. He wobbled out to the car, and off they went. The first thing I did was to call Addie and fill her in on the news.

28

STRANGE AS IT SEEMS

The mystery of the Wilks shooting rocked me. I got the afternoon newspaper, and went back to the motel, where I devoured every word of the Wilks tragedy.

The Carterville Chronicle
Lamar S. Wilks, Forty-Six, Minister, Activist, Dies
By Todd Garrison

Lamar Wilks, the controversial minister and activist, was shot yesterday on a busy downtown street in Dixon and died last night at a local hospital. He was forty-six.

Reverend Wilks, who arrived in Carterville only two years ago, was in Dixon on labor business, acting as a negotiator between planters and black farmers, when he was gunned down, the local police said. An autopsy is planned.

Despite his popular healing meetings and community rallies, Reverend Wilks captured regional attention when he took up the cause of the local homeless, the poor, and the disenfranchised. Blending the common touch of Reverend King, the blistering rhetoric of Malcolm X, and the organizational skills of Saul Alinsky, he attacked the issues of economic power, educational and health reform, poor housing, and social inequality. Scores of black farmers rallied to Reverend Wilks when he spoke out in a campaign to lift the lot of poor workers toiling independently or for the benefit of the largest farm corporations.

Little is known about his background and his life before his stay in this sleepy town in Alabama. Local police say an investigation of the shooting continues. No suspects have been apprehended. A memorial service is planned at the local armory, and an overflow crowd is anticipated.

29

CHANGE IN THE WEATHER

At the service, behind the curtain offstage, Reverend Peck held his cell phone to his ear, grunted a few times, and then put it into his suit pocket. I played his sidekick and watched the chaos. One of the pastors from one of the neighboring counties was onstage and was going on and on about the slain minister's desire to house the homeless and heal the sick. Other reverends, church officials, union representatives, and local politicians were huddled in groups, and one after another, they peeked out at the standing room audience.

"Reverend Wilks, who was sometimes called the prophet, lived to see this area reach its potential," the visiting pastor said. "I met him several times during his healing sessions. He was always very intense and serious about bringing salvation to all of God's children."

An usher whispered that the crowd was wrapped all around the armory, with some of the overflow standing in nearby parking lots, where they could hear the service over loudspeakers.

Finally, the visiting pastor finished, folding up his notes, and turned to walk off the stage. Above, there was a close-up black-and-white portrait of Reverend Wilks cradling a frail, aging woman. I thought he would have loved this sentimental touch. Four choirs from the biggest churches in the area swayed and rocked on raised platforms, singing the sorrowful hymn "Mary, Don't You Weep."

"Prophet Wilks called us his Beloveds because he cared for us so, so much," a younger church member said, reading from cards. "He was always there for us. He comforted us. He loved us. And we came to love him."

Some of those in the audience waved their arms, testifying that she was speaking the truth. Bracketed by countless banks of flowers, the large gold coffin sat there below the stage, closed and regal. A few organizers predicted the service would go on for four hours, given that everybody wanted to speak, including the governor, a state senator, a talk show host, two union officials, and a gospel singer, who said she knew Reverend Wilks from the old days in New York City.

Another older farmer, who had formerly been a sharecropper, wobbled up to the stage. He was dressed in work clothes and looked like he wanted to spit out snuff somewhere. "All of dese folk heah . . . all dese folk heah," the farmer said, shielding his eyes from the bright lights, for the service was being filmed by public television. "You knowed what I lak about Pastor Wilks? He knew there was somethin' about makin' a crop with your hands, gettin' callouses, bendin' over in de fields till it feel lak it wont to break. See, he often say there something 'bout tilling the earth that equal to sewin' somebody up lak a doctor. All work have dignity. He knowed that. Ain't nothin' to be 'shamed of ef you do a good job. That's mah piece. Rest in peace, Reverend."

The gathering gave him a standing ovation. Even those onstage were touched by the farmer's simple wisdom and compassion. The farmer nodded slightly, then walked off the stage.

A tall, dark woman in casual clothes went to the microphone. She smiled and started talking. "Prophet Wilks recruited me in Atlanta, at a National Urban League conference. He gave a workshop about the power of organizing and voting. He talked about the blood and sacrifice of our forefathers in the South, talked about having pride in who we are, talked about knowing the issues and taking action. I was impressed by him, especially as he was a minister. I avoided church like the plague, but I was surprised by him and how he thought. He said we are an incredible people when we concentrate on something. If we were united, there was nothing we couldn't do. He said we were unstoppable, adding that we must demand accountability, not just from the whites but also from our own people. I think Prophet Wilks was a great man, a very great man."

The choir sang one of his favorite songs, "How I Got Over," as one of the ushers helped the woman from the stage, sobbing. I was surprised at how deeply Wilks had touched these people's lives. They saw him as one of them. They saw him as a guiding light in this dark, dismal place.

I talked to Reverend Peck while the politicians and union people praised the myth of the man. One man, from the trucker's union, talked about his moral strength, courage, and compassion for the poor. He recalled how Wilks had arranged for food to be trucked in for a group of senior centers when the companies stopped delivering for nonpayment. The seniors welcomed the reverend like he was the Messiah.

Finally, Reverend Peck took the microphone, and everybody wondered what he was going to say, because the whole area knew what the battle for leadership had cost both men. They had been close friends, but the struggle for control of the church had left them at each other's throats. Many of them thought Reverend Peck had sold Wilks out to the evil whims of the white planters. Even Addie had said as much to me the other day.

A smattering of applause greeted him as he delivered the longest speech of the service up to that point, apparently without notes. I realized the reverend had been preparing for this day for a long time, and now it had come.

"We're gathered here today to say farewell to a proud and mighty soldier of God," he said, starting slowly. "Pastor Lamar Wilks was a strong warrior of our people and a capable ambassador in the service of our Lord. The manner in which he passed from this mortal coil troubles me and causes me the deepest grief. He refused to let others set the limits of his involvement in the struggle for equal rights for all of God's children. He was fearless and aggressive, sometimes to a fault."

"Amen. That he was, brother," someone said.

"Pastor Wilks served the voiceless and the powerless," he went on. "He was willing to make his voice heard, even though he knew it could cost him his life. He made up his mind that he would no longer bow down and be a slave to any man, to any boss. He refused to back down, even though he knew how much was at stake."

Some of the old church members yelled, "Amen," and shouted that he should teach even if he had to tell the bitter truth. I was absolutely stunned at how he praised his foe, lifting him up to the heavens before the man's admirers and supporters.

Wiping his face, Reverend Peck gripped the mic while he spoke glowingly about his opponent. Every now and then, I could swear he would look at me to see what my reaction was.

"The day before he was killed, he talked about amassing our support behind those who truly believed in the Christian way, truly believed in the humanity of all people, rather than those who were trying to buy our votes and our influence," the reverend noted. "He said we were facing serious obstacles that would threaten our community. Every offer, he said, must be weighed seriously and carefully. We could not settle for leftovers."

The audience went into riot mode, clapping like crazy. I saw what he was doing. He wanted to regain his church by auditioning as the heir apparent to the man he had hired. He wanted them to see why they had selected him as their leader so many years ago. It was working.

"Wilks was somebody who spoke our language," the reverend said, really pouring it on. "He understood us and our needs. He knew we didn't have to wait for others to come to our aid. As a soldier of God, he realized we possessed the power to heal ourselves. I was so proud of him, so very proud of him."

A shout went up. "We knew you were, brother."

Oh, Lord, I never knew how much Reverend Peck hated the man until now. With his kind words of tribute, he was carving Wilks up right before our eyes. Many in the crowd understood what he was doing and that this was his last revenge.

Reverend Peck reared back on his heels and let out a cry that went through the souls of most folks assembled there. He looked dead at me and laid out the most poisonous barbs, the one he had reserved to hurl at the corpse in the pine box beneath the stage.

"What you folks don't know is that Pastor Wilks couldn't live a lie," he said, bristling. "He had courage and couldn't lie. He didn't love himself that much. In-

stead, he cared about you people, the poor, the homeless, the voiceless. His enemies know he could have
taken the easy way out, but he didn't. He knew that lies
would hurt the community more than the truth ever
could. He settled for the truth, and that is what killed
him. I truly believe that."

The church was silent. The audience was trying to
catch up with his thoughts. They were confused, but
the words sounded good.

"It says in the scriptures that we are our brother's
keeper," he added with a growl. "Wilks knew that too.
He could have felt like a lot of us do. I got mine, so let
them get theirs. He came down here from the North,
from his cushy life there, and reached back and tried
to help someone else. You can say a lot of things about
Pastor Wilks, but you can't say he didn't care. He made
a difference in the life of this community, and that is
what killed him."

"Tell the truth, brother!" many of the members
yelled in unison.

"Amen, Preacher!"

"God created us all," the reverend said calmly. "God
created us equal. Pastor Wilks understood that. Some
folk in this community did not and refuse to do so
now."

"Don't stop now, Preacher!"

"Teach, brother! Teach!"

"In this community, which is slow to change, Pastor
Wilks was a bold and courageous fighter for the rights
of all," he said. "He suffered and sacrificed and was
loyal to the cause. He lies here today, martyred and
murdered and mourned by all who love this country
and the Lord. Farewell, Pastor Wilks. The fight will go
on. The fight must go on. We know the Lord will say,
'Now you will rest, you good and faithful servant, and
now you will be with me in paradise!"

The crowd hollered and gave a sanctified scream, which let the reverend know that he had been taken back into the fold and that he had done justice to the popular holy man and his life of glory. I couldn't take it. I hated hypocrisy. I knew the reverend meant none of the things he had said, and it was all meant to make him look good in Wilks's reflected glory.

Turning his head, Reverend Peck saw me leave the backstage area. He made a little motion for me to stay, but I left, anyway. The whole thing stank. I wanted no part of it. As I was leaving, the choir was performing another hymn in preparation for the next speaker.

30

NO HARD FEELINGS

Outside in the parking lot, I paced back and forth, trying to collect my thoughts. I couldn't go back in there. It was a sham. The man was a pariah when he was alive, and now they were throwing roses and lies around like he was Adam Clayton Powell, the clever dandy who represented Harlem in Congress. Shortly thereafter, Reverend Peck walked out, accompanied by the sheriff, who waved me over to his patrol car.

"Gentlemen, I'd like to drive you over to the station," the sheriff said, grinning with nicotine-stained teeth. "I think you'll be interested in what I have there."

Surprised, I looked at Reverend Peck, who shrugged. I hoped this was not a trap. What did the planters and the law have in store for us?

We got in the patrol car. The sheriff was yakking up a storm, but we were quiet. We were racking our brains, sorting through the tricks and ruses he could concoct. The reverend kept glancing at the blacks milling around the cars in the parking lot, attempting to sneak a peek at the action inside the patrol car. They were very suspicious. Many of them who had been inside the church took the low road in their mind, thinking the law had taken us into custody and was driving us to jail.

Although the drive from the church to the police station was a short fifteen minutes, everything seemed to be in slow motion. I had a chance to really ponder my trip to the South, what kind of man the reverend was, the great battle for the leadership of the church, and the predicament of Wilks. Was this trip worth it? What did I learn about the reverend and the community?

We parked near the building. The sheriff led the way, whistling the raucous lyrics of a Willie Nelson song. We followed, cautious and very nervous about what this moment would bring. A group of deputies stood around the reception area, turning to watch us, but it was all right because the Negroes were walking with the boss.

"This way, boys," the sheriff said, striding like a drum major.

We stopped before a large window reinforced with heavy mesh, and beyond it, there was the reverend's wife, dressed in man's clothes, with her hair slicked back, seated at a table. She looked like she was disturbed.

I kept forgetting his wife's name. She looked much different from when I first saw her. Intense, petite, not much taller than five feet, she seemed much smaller than I recalled her being the last time we met.

"Why is she in there?" the reverend protested. "What has she done?"

"Let her tell you what she's done, Reverend," the sheriff said, turning the knob. "Do you want him to go in? You might want some privacy."

"He's my friend," the reverend said. "I want him in there."

Once in the room, I kept out of the way, and the sheriff and his boys stayed away from the action. The reverend pulled up a chair and faced his wife with a dark, questioning stare.

"Honey, why are you in here?" he asked her.

Her eyes glazed over. "Hickory, Wilks lied to me. I thought he was the greatest thing. He made me all kinds of promises that he had no intentions of keeping."

The reverend repeated his question, glaring. "Why are you in here?"

Then his wife shut her eyes and rolled her head back. "Lamar flat out lied to me. He told me he needed me, he loved me. Once he did what he wanted to do with me, he went on to another woman and dropped me like a hot potato. I kept calling him at the place where he was staying, but no answer. I called him over and over and over. He never returned any of my calls."

"What does this have to do with Wilks?" the reverend asked.

"I had no pride," she said, tears coming to her eyes. "I heard the rumors. When Wilks finally called me, he lied again and said that the girls who said he was with them were lying. But that wasn't all. I could see Lamar was cracking under the pressure and they were going to convince him to leave. And I didn't want him to go. I knew I had to do something."

"But what does this have to do with Wilks?" the reverend asked again, pressing.

His wife sat up and folded her arms across her chest. "I wasn't going to let him leave me in this hellhole," she explained. "Not with you, not in this sorry town. I'd had enough of all this mess. He promised me he would never leave me, and he gave me his word. That means something to me." After a dramatic pause, she turned to me and asked, "Clint, would it mean something to you?"

I nodded yes.

"Lamar fooled me again," she snarled. "I saw his men carry a bunch of suitcases out of the house. I knew he was moving out. He was leaving, and he was not going to take me."

Without missing a beat, the sheriff chimed in, in the middle of her confession. "Heck, the planters only wanted to scare the nigger, but your wife decided to settle the score. She chose to shoot the darkie in the head and end it all."

Our mouths dropped open in shock. The reverend's wife had shot Wilks! She had shot Wilks! The deputies saw our surprise and laughed at our collective astonishment. It was unbelievable. We both just knew the planters had killed Wilks, but never in our wildest dreams did we think it was all because of a lover's spat. The reverend's wife!

Sensing he had the upper hand, the sheriff had a manila folder under his arms with Wilks's name on it, containing everything he'd done in town and in the area since his arrival. The lawman said he had one on me too. Every move I had made, every place I'd gone, every conversation I'd had.

"Reverend Peck, your wife had been seeing Wilks since last spring," the sheriff said. "They met regularly. She was with him for about seven months. They met in small motels, roadhouses, and out-of-the-way hotels. I had them followed for their own good."

"For their own good?" I asked. I was curious.

"The planters wanted to do something bad to Wilks," the lawman said. "I protected your wife from all that. I told them that killing her would only backfire."

"Lamar said he loved me," his wife said absently.

"Did you know your wife was going to a head doctor in Anniston?" the sheriff asked the reverend, staring at him. "She's been going to him for five months. I don't think she took her meds."

The reverend sagged. "I didn't know that."

His wife asked for a cigarette. "Remember you asked me when I started smoking? Lamar got me started. I did anything he asked. I loved him."

That got the reverend's attention. "You *loved* him?"

Her eyes sparked for a second. "Yes, I loved him. I knew Lamar was a con man and could talk himself out of anything. He was a silver-tongued devil. But I didn't want him to sweet-talk me."

The sheriff put the folder on the table and stared at the reverend's bewitched wife. "But you shot him. You shot Wilks. What's the matter? He deserved it. He was a loudmouth and deserved what he got."

She glanced at the reverend's expression of defeat. "When I shot him, it made so much noise. *Bang!* Everybody ran off in different directions. Lamar just fell forward, a bright red puddle under his head. As I turned around, people started running toward us from the driveways and behind cars. But when I waved the gun at them, this made them back off."

Smiling like a friend, the sheriff placed his big hand on the reverend's shoulder, assuring him that everything would work out all right. However, the reverend had to hear him out.

"Wilks is not dead," the sheriff whispered. "He's awake and alert. They operated on him for four hours. It was a close call."

The reverend's wife had confessed, so the lawman was in control of the situation. He would ignore her words. She didn't matter. He had bigger fish to fry.

The reverend's wife was dumbfounded. "He's not dead?"

"No. They have him over at one of the local hospitals outside of Anniston," the lawman said to the reverend's wife. "We have a favor to ask of you. Think this over carefully before you choose."

"What is it?" Reverend Peck asked. "What difference would it make?"

I didn't like the sheriff and his evil schemes. I knew where this was going. Even before the plan was discussed, I realized this was something the planters had thought up, and the sheriff was the man to put it into action. The planters knew the reverend was trapped by his ego and his crazy love for his wife. I knew the reverend would agree to anything to save his wife. The man was thinking hard, weighing the odds, even before the sheriff opened his mouth.

"Reverend, you asked what difference my plan would make," the sheriff said, patting the reverend on the shoulder. "You ask what has changed. Wilks had a death wish. We got rid of a pain in the butt, and you get back your church."

I shouted that I didn't like this. The whole community was in an uproar. Some of the church members had vowed revenge, threatening the lives of anybody involved in Wilks's death. Innocent white folk could die. A race war could start.

"Don't do this, Reverend Peck," I said strongly.

The sheriff rolled his blue eyes upward and growled, "Boy, you need some perspective. You need to get with the program. The reverend has no choice in the matter, and if you choose to open your mouth, you can end up like Wilks."

"Do you set my wife free?" Reverend Peck asked quietly.

"Yes."

"Will she be charged with shooting Wilks?"

"No, not if you do what we say."

I walked around to face the reverend. "How could you do this? I respected you. If you do this, I'll have to wash my hands of you."

The sheriff laughed. "Gentlemen, get him a wash-cloth." And his boys got a chuckle from his remark.

Explaining his plan, he told the reverend that the shooting of Wilks was a "gray area" where the community was concerned. It was the opinion of the planters and the moneymen that there was no harm in the crime. He'd talked to them last night, when he learned of the attempted murder. They said, "No harm, no foul." They considered this a win-win situation for them and the community at large. They felt they could get a settlement between all parties involved without him being in the way.

"Do not do this," I pleaded with the reverend. "These white folk will have something over your head forever if you do this. If you step out of line, they'll just let the truth of the shooting out and you're finished. Think about that."

"I love my wife," he said, looking at me. "I love my church, and I love the Lord. I'll do anything to save them."

His wife, tearful, slid her hand beneath his hand, but he withdrew it. She was looking at him with tender, soft puppy-dog eyes. That expression wouldn't have worked on me, but it was another matter with him.

The sheriff winked at his men and smiled at the reverend's wife. "Reverend, you're doing the right thing. I would say do what's agreeable for you, but we have an emergency here. We have a crisis. All we want is for you to get the loudmouth out of town. We have a plan, I think, a very intelligent plan. The planters have donated a van to transport Wilks from the hospital to this small airport outside Birmingham. All you have to do is to see that Wilks gets on that plane and away from here. Everything has been fixed for you. Then you come back, and we'll see that you get treated right."

I had trouble taking my eyes off the reverend and the sheriff. They were scum. I couldn't believe the reverend was going to go for this scheme. His wife wasn't worth it. He had lost his church. He should have to earn it back.

"Wilks is alive," his wife said, very puzzled. "How could he be? I shot him in the head."

"Point-blank," a deputy said, smirking. "You're a good shot."

I could barely control my anger. "Peck, you're the fake, not Wilks. At least he believed in what he did. You know better. You're letting them make a fool out of you."

"I have no choice," the reverend said.

"And he loves me," his wife said, smiling like a tot.

The sheriff asked his men to throw me out, not wanting me to further influence the reverend, because I might persuade him to go public with the shooting and his wife's part in it.

"I knew you loved me, darling," his wife said, all passive and easygoing. She was no fool. She knew she was getting the best end of the deal. It was not every day that you could shoot a man and get off scot-free.

After the reverend had a talk with his wife, he stood along the wall, pulled from his wallet a snapshot of his better half in a hip-hugging swimsuit, and ripped it up. Still, love made men foolish.

While the deputies pushed me out of the room, I made one last plea to the reverend, who kept shaking his head no, no, no. I felt very defeated. I had been a fool too, for coming down here. *Verily, verily. Why doesn't God stop him? Why doesn't the Lord make him chose the right way?* I thought. So many people could get hurt by this vile situation.

I asked one of the deputies if I could use his phone to make a call. I needed to call Addie. I couldn't keep my mouth shut. Now, this was very odd. But I thought of the last moments before the bullet struck Wilks's head and what he must have been thinking.

31

NAPPING IN THE DEVIL'S BED

Over the next four days, Reverend Peck worked on me, promising me the moon, lying to me, and every plea fell on deaf ears. I had lost all respect for him. I didn't understand why he would do something like this to his church, the community, and to his good name. All for a woman who didn't care about him, who had openly spoken about her love for another man, and had made a fool of him in public. How did you reverse words and deeds, put everything back like it was?

"I know you don't think much of me after what I've done," the reverend said during a private meeting at his church. "But think of Wilks. If you leave him here, he'll die. He doesn't deserve that, no matter what he has done."

I thought long and hard. "I'm finished here."

"That's it?"

I couldn't make things right. "I need to go home."

"Hear me out, please." The reverend was not that shrewd. He tried to hit the soft spots in my heart. "The white folk are giving us a chance to fix everything. It's not a perfect solution, but it will do just the same. You could take Wilks home to his people. They're giving you free passage home. That's money that doesn't have to come out of your pocket. Think about it."

I couldn't wrap my head around it. "Where will he go?"

"I think he has people there in the city," the reverend replied. "The sheriff has been in touch with a cousin, who is a lawyer or something. Said he would take care of him."

"Whose idea was this originally?"

The reverend cleared his throat. "Boss Chapin. Remember him? He's so glad to get rid of him. He didn't want to kill him, but this is the best way for everybody. Wilks vanishes, and that's that."

"I don't like it," I said with a bite in my voice.

"Come on over to the hospital and you'll see things more clearly," the reverend said. "They'll explain stuff over there. You'll see what you're up against. All I ask is that you think it over."

Against Addie's wishes, I went to the hospital, which was not far from the county seat. The reverend was pleased. We drove there with the sheriff. A sprawling, two-story brick building, the hospital owed its funds to the generosity of the planters and their moneymen. I'd always hated the antiseptic smell of hospitals. They reminded me of the bad days, when I spent a lot of time in one with my family.

Dr. Noel Kazam, the man responsible for the care of Wilks, met us at the door, dressed in his white outfit. He shook the sheriff's hand vigorously but didn't shake mine. He talked to the lawman, stationing himself between both of us.

"Your boy is lucky to be alive," the doctor began. "The fact remains that only five percent of people who sustain a gunshot wound to the head survive. He's very lucky."

As he talked, we walked through the sterile corridors, past the other doctors, the nurses, and the attendants. Sick patients lay on gurneys along the hallway. At one point a nurse interrupted him, demanding his signature on something, and then she left.

"It's a penetrating head injury, and most kids do better than grown-ups," the doctor said, looking at the chart. "We had him in a medically induced coma after we admitted him so we could work on him. He's probably lucky, because the location of the wound saved his life."

The reverend turned to me and said that God had saved his life.

I wanted to hear the doctor's story on Wilks, not anything from this man. How did he live when the woman shot him point-blank? Was it a miracle?

"Anybody can die when shot in the head," the doctor added. "But usually people who are shot in the back of the head do better than those who sustain a massive wound from side to side. Let me explain it. A bullet traveling from back to front takes out some tissue from the brain's two hemispheres, but sometimes it can leave essential functions intact."

"Is he paralyzed?" the sheriff asked him.

"We don't know that yet," the doctor replied. "We don't know whether he'll have sufficient muscle control. We do know memory and speech are controlled by different areas of the brain, and we're still trying to determine what areas were destroyed."

"Is he conscious?" I asked.

The doctor fell silent, then continued. "He is now, but he goes in and out. We're pleased that he can move his limbs on his right side and can respond to voices. I think we're so fortunate that the brain stem was salvaged, so that the basic functions of breathing and heartbeat weren't affected by the gunshot wound."

The sheriff chuckled. "So maybe it wasn't a good shot, after all."

We all thought that was a vulgar thing to say. The doctor frowned, because although the patient was a black man, all human life should be respected.

"All I'm saying is that if he had been shot multiple times, he would have been beyond saving," the lawman explained.

The doctor ignored him and continued. "After he was resuscitated, evaluated, and stabilized, the doctors did a very good job before he was taken to surgery. Part of his brain was swelling, so we put a drain into his head to extract the excess fluid. I think he's doing well, considering all that he has been through."

"Can we see him?" the reverend asked.

The doctor opened the door to a room and allowed us to enter. Inside was a man with bandages around his head, hooked up to a heart monitor. There was an oxygen attachment under his nose. His eyes were closed. A slight tremor went through his right leg, causing it to twitch involuntarily.

A nurse tucked the covers over his lower extremities. "That's only natural. It's a good sign. He'll recover."

"She's right when she says he will get better," the doctor noted. "But we don't know how much function he will get back."

"That's a shame," the sheriff said harshly.

"Also, he will be blind," the doctor said.

Suddenly stricken with sadness, Reverend Peck bowed his head. He'd talked with Wilks about a truce, but the man had said it was out of the question. I knew that. Maybe the sheriff was correct when he said that Wilks had a death wish.

We followed the doctor out of the room. I recalled Wilks telling me something once, quoting the orga-

nizer Cesar Chavez: "Our lives are all that really belong
to us, so it is how we use our lives that determines what
kind of men we are." Also, I thought about how the
sheriff and his boys had treated the reverend after the
shooting. He *was* their Big Tom nigger. He was their
Judas nigger, a spy among his own people. Addie was
so right about him.

While the sheriff talked with the doctor, I huddled
with the reverend, still focusing on the man in there
fighting for his life. I couldn't stand hearing the reverend explain why he had to go along with the scheme of
the planters.

"Am I wrong?" he asked me.

I didn't respond at first. Finally breaking my silence,
I said, "Reverend, you need to watch your step."

"Clint, you'll never understand why I did this," he
replied. "I love my church. I love my wife. I had to do
it for my good name. I didn't want my community to
heap shame on me or her."

I groaned. I'd heard this all before. He had said this
before at the police station, lying to protect his church
and wife. What he didn't know was that someone, one
of the heavy thinkers in the church, had contacted the
NAACP and the National Urban League. There was
an FBI investigation under way as well. He would get
caught; I was sure of that.

"I hope you can keep your mouth shut," the reverend
said.

I didn't say anything. All I cared about was Wilks,
the fallen leader, his mourning church, and the outraged community. He had wanted to stir things up.
He had wanted to organize and build an answer to the
bad politics and the poverty, like in the old days of the
movement.

"Can you keep a secret?" he asked.

"I don't know." I recognized disappointment and defeat when I saw it. The reverend had given up on living the good Christian life.

The reverend touched me on my arm, reciting a verse from the good book, Jeremiah 14:14. "Then the Lord said unto me, The prophets' prophesy lies in my name. I sent them not, neither have I commanded them, neither spake unto them; they prophesy unto you a false vision and divination, and a thing of naught, and the deceit of their own heart."

I started to walk away. "You need to stop that. You hide behind the scriptures. How can you explain your foolishness to your church? How can you explain this to the community?"

"Again, am I wrong?" he said, raising his voice.

"Heck yeah, and you know it." I stared at him.

"Just because it's not the whole truth," he explained.

"Huh?"

"You'll do the right thing, Clint," the reverend said. "You always do. If not because we're friends and on the same side, you'll do it for the sake of Wilks. I know he deserves better than this."

"That's crazy," I answered. "Don't bank on that."

"Another thing is that no all-white, all-male jury would convict my wife for shooting a troublemaking loudmouth," the reverend suggested. "This is a man, a snake in the grass, who had deceived her. Nobody in this community would fault my wife."

"I see that," I said, watching the white men conferring.

Eventually, the sheriff shook hands with the doctor and patted him on the back, then walked over to us. He had a wide smile on his red cracker face, like he had hit the lottery.

"We can take him out of here the day after tomorrow," the lawman said. "They want to make sure he is stable enough to travel. We'll have him packed up before you get here. The hospital will assign two guys to ensure the journey to the airport is without a hassle. Everything will be all right. Reverend, you'll be ready to do your part. I want you to go along to make sure the trip goes smoothly, and you'll report back to us."

"Yes, I will do just that," the reverend said.

"And your wife will be out before you get back," the lawman added. "I know you'll like that. Does that suit you?"

"Good, good." The reverend beamed.

"Now, are you going to do your part, my friend?" the sheriff asked, pointing to me. "The plan doesn't work unless you do your part. You have a responsibility to your pal here. And to Wilks, the gentleman in that hospital bed there. I'll not try to convince you. I'll let Wilks do that."

I glared at him and the reverend. I kept my mouth closed.

The sheriff said he'd drive us back to the reverend's car, and then he waved to the nurses, blew a couple of kisses to the pretty ones. I got in the patrol car and scooted next to the door. So many things were going through my mind. I wanted to make my decision without the reverend's input. There would be a couple sleepless nights before the last chapter would be written on my Southern spiritual adventure.

32
THE WRAP-UP

It rained steadily for days after the confrontation at the hospital. I was surprised the reverend left me alone, exerting no pressure, seeking no debate. If there was anything I knew, I was certain I wanted to get out of this accursed place. As a friend, I felt I had done more than I could really do to bail the reverend out of the mess at the church. Addie was lobbying me to let her come with her to New York City. She wanted the move badly. The school gig was ending, and the children would be split up into several regional schools. Her work was done.

After I got down on my knees to pray, I sat on the bed and read the Bible. Sometimes it could provide a sense of peace in a time of chaos. My eyes fell upon the following verse, 1 John 3:18. "Let us not love in word, neither in tongue; but in deed and in truth."

I remembered Wilks in that hospital bed, drifting in and out of consciousness, hoping his life was not lived in vain. Everybody had tried to tell him that he shouldn't go head-to-head against agribusiness, those large farm corporations, and the rural way of life. I didn't think he understood the tight economics of farming and how much these planters were invested in that. It was a battle between the efficient family farm and the big corporate farm. He'd lost the battle before really even starting.

"Clint, you better sleep with one eye open until everything is done," Addie had said on the phone the day before. "Anything can happen. Everybody's trying to say it was a romance gone wrong. Nobody wants it to be a race murder. The planters want to be free of blame."

"My conscience is killing me," I'd told her. "I hate that they will get away with this. Wilks doesn't deserve this. The man has his faults, like all of us do. But beneath all that ego and bravado, he was trying to stand up for the little guy. I saw the look on the faces of the farmers and the drivers. He gave them a sense of pride and strength. He made them feel that they could get a grip on their lives. That's when I came around to his side. The Lord saw good in every man. I admit I was wrong about him. Wilks fought the good fight, and still, everybody turned their back on him when he needed their support most."

Addie had been very direct. "Are you going to do what they ask?"

I'd been honest. "I must. If we leave him there, they'll kill him. The sheriff and the planters leave us no other choice. We must get him out of there. Also, the reverend is scared that the crackers will burn his church down. He'll do anything to prevent that from happening."

"I'm going with you," she'd said. "You can't stop me."

Without catching a breath, Addie told me about this lavish dream of us being together in New York City, walking through Times Square, sightseeing, standing there beneath the Empire State Building, and watching the crystal ball drop on New Year's Eve. She also said she wanted to run the New York City Marathon. It was a pretty picture.

But I also couldn't shake the sad image of the badly injured Wilks's quest to help the poor black farmers. The planters didn't play around. He had often said the white folk wanted the blacks to be a landless people. His credo was that land was fundamental, that all things came from the land.

"We got to get Wilks out of there," I'd said. "I'll call the reverend and say I'll do it. If you want to come, it's all right. But we have to move fast, before these folks change their minds."

Following our call, I had packed my clothes hurriedly into my two suitcases, shaved quickly, and said a little prayer. I had then phoned the reverend and had told him my decision. He was quite pleased about it. He kept saying that he would make it up to me. I hated talking to him.

"Do you know what the sheriff said to me?" the reverend had asked me. "He said my wife did all kinds of foul things to Wilks for money. He was her sugar daddy. He got her attention with cash and gifts. That's not my wife! She would never do anything like that."

"Are you sure?" I'd asked him, a slip of the tongue.

"Maybe Wilks should die," the reverend had insisted. "It wouldn't be a great loss. A lot of people around here would be happy with that. Probably even the Lord would like it."

I didn't let him get away with that remark. "Since when do you speak for the Lord? These white people know you for what you are, and soon the rest of the community will know too."

There was a long silence on the phone.

"You owe me, Clint," the reverend said with an icy edge.

"For what?" I was getting a little fed up.

"You owe me for helping you through that crazi-
ness after your wife killed the kids and you were out
of sorts," he replied. "You didn't know what to do. You
were going crazy. I helped you out. You owe me something for that."

Friendship, I thought, was something where two
people were supportive and cared for each other without thinking that one good turn required payback. Yes,
he had helped me out, but good friends did things like
that. I didn't like that he was throwing back in my face
the fact that he had been there for me. It stank.

He could tell he had gotten under my skin. "I don't
take orders from you, Peck, or nobody else," I told him.
"I was here because of our friendship. I appreciated
how you helped me through that stuff in New York, but
I don't like this one bit."

"Clint, I didn't mean for you to take it this way," he
said, switching gears. "I'm desperate. I've got to do everything right. My life depends on it. If you walk out on
me, it will all fall apart."

I was quiet, letting him ramble from point to point.

"Are you talking Addie up North?" he asked.

"Yes, I am."

"We need her down here," the reverend said harshly.

"I need her up there," I replied. "She needs to get out
of here."

Satisfied that I'd signed on for the sheriff's scheme,
the reverend had asked if I was packed, had told me to
meet him at the hospital in two hours, and then had
said his farewells. I'd hung up, thinking I was walking
into a trap.

The rain continued coming down as I went to the
hospital, checked in, and were shown to the private

room where Wilks was being prepared for the journey. Everything went like clockwork. Two nurses dressed the injured man in street clothes and plopped him in a wheelchair, and then the group headed down to a secluded section of the parking lot, where Wilks was loaded onto a stretcher and placed in a van.

"He ain't so high and mighty no more," the sheriff said, gloating over the unconscious man while he was being strapped down for the trip to the airfield.

I looked at the reverend, who was so pleased that his problems were about to come to an end. He avoided my stare. One of the medical attendants got into the rear of the van with Wilks. The sheriff shook hands with the hospital staff, talked with a nurse about what was needed for the trip, and got back in his patrol car.

This didn't feel right. I sat in the rear of the van with Wilks and the attendant, because I couldn't stomach what was being done. I glanced at Wilks, whose head was thickly bandaged. The bandages were immaculately wrapped, pristine white. One side of his face had been ravaged by shoddy hospital care.

"I see they took good care of him," the reverend said to the attendant from his seat up front. He said that for my benefit, which meant that the planters were keeping their part of the bargain.

"Yes, they want him healthy for the flight north," the attendant replied.

I frowned. "I don't think he looks that good. Maybe he should have stayed in the hospital until he was better. Germs. Aren't you worried about germs?"

"Not really." The attendant smiled weakly at me.

The van pulled out of the lot, moved north, and got on the highway. Smiling, the reverend kept looking back at Wilks and the hospital attendant, but his eyes shifted whenever I returned his gaze. The visibility was horrible. The windshield wipers couldn't keep up with the downpour. Cars whizzed past without any thought of safety.

"Where are we going?" I yelled to the driver. "I thought we were going to pick up Addie? She's waiting for me."

Annoyed, the driver looked at the reverend, who said nothing. He continued to watch Wilks, who was becoming agitated and was muttering short, incoherent phrases. There was no doubt that in this condition he should be in a hospital room.

I knew my part of the deal, and that included Addie coming along. "Reverend, this was not a part of the deal. We were supposed to pick up Addie, and she was going with me. We agreed on that."

Finally, the reverend rubbed his weary eyes and spoke in a way I didn't like. "There's been a change in plans. Addie is in Boss Chapin's car, because the planters thought something might go wrong. They knew you wouldn't leave without her."

"You're right," I agreed. "I will not leave without her. Is Boss Chapin going to be at the airfield? This scheme is starting to go sideways."

"Yes, he's going to be there," the reverend said.

"Who else will be there?" I realized it was a trap, but who was the mouse? Now was not the time to go on autopilot.

A truck pulling a bulldozer slid in front of us, and we slowed down, letting it adjust itself in the passing lane. The rain was making the road slick.

The medical attendant was holding one of Wilks's hands as he muttered nonstop. He seemed to be in a lot of pain. I wondered if there were enough painkillers to prevent him from suffering.

I thought about Wilks's trip to a local senior center on a day not much different from this one, raining heavily, bad wind, and a little chill. He had walked around the room, going to each of the aged residents, smiling and giving them a kind word. The administrators had loved him being there for the old folks. Suddenly, he'd asked them, those who were able, to kneel, and he led them solemnly in the Lord's Prayer. Some of them had cried, tears rolling down their wrinkled faces without shame. He'd stood, pulled up a chair, and spoken in earnest about the gifts of giving, kindness, compassion, and a generous nature.

How could you fault a man like this? Wilks was a complex man, somebody who instilled terror and anxiety into the hearts of those men who asked for obedience, submission, and loyalty. This was why Wilks had to die.

Moaning, Wilks lifted his head and stared at me. I knew he was blind, but it felt very eerie having him face me in that way.

"They're all pygmies when you get down to it," the holy man mumbled. He was straining against his bonds, trying to pull himself up.

"Is he in pain?" I asked the attendant.

"He shouldn't be," the man in white said. "We gave him enough drugs to numb a horse. He's just talking out of his head. He doesn't know what he's saying."

"A pair of argyle socks from Sears," Wilks rasped.

I didn't like the look of him. "He should be in the hospital, in intensive care, somewhere. Don't you think so?"

"Probably," the attendant replied. "I just do as I'm told."

I grinned solemnly. "Don't we all do that? Obey?"

"Take no prisoners. . . . Love to win," the holy man said, trembling. "Play for keeps. . . . Give no quarter. . . . Show no weakness."

The reverend grimaced and made a low sound in his throat. "Don't feel sorry for him. He brought this on himself. He didn't give a darn about anybody. Some of these white folks wanted to castrate him for causing so much trouble. People get fooled by his Jekyll-and-Hyde attitude, but he didn't have me fooled. Not one bit."

We turned down a long country road, went past fields that had been harvested, drove over muddy ruts, almost getting stuck. Nobody was around. It was just an open expanse of green, fields, trees, and bushes. Eventually, we got to the end of the road, then drove up an incline and onto another highway.

"Everybody's going to die . . . die . . . die," Wilks moaned, a red stain seeping through his bandage and dripping down his cheek. .

"Can you wipe it at least?" I asked the attendant.

"No, he'll keep," he snapped at me.

The driver shouted that we were getting close, were about ten minutes out, and then we were at the airfield. I think everybody wanted the trip to be over, however it was going to end, just to bring it to a close.

Down a small hill sat the airfield, surrounded by fruit trees. Three long black Cadillacs were parked there, their windshield wipers laboring against the driving rain. Two large men were standing under umbrellas, one carrying a sawed-off shotgun. Another car, the patrol car driven by the sheriff, was facing toward the road near the gleaming steel corporate jet on the make-shift runway.

Quickly, the sheriff covered the ground between his car and our van, hands on his gun, wearing his all-business face. I noticed one of the windows ease down on the lead Cadillac, and I saw the familiar silhouette of Boss Chapin. He was smoking a cigar and motioned to the driver to let Addie out. She stumbled into a nervous run in my direction, with her arms outstretched. The driver threw her suitcases out of the car. One bounced and spilled its contents.

I jumped out of the van, and we hugged like high school kids on a first date, touching each other like it was our last time together. She was whispering to me, but I couldn't pick up what she was saying. There were tears in her bloodshot eyes and a big bruise on her cheek.

"He kept saying he had a surprise for you," she muttered. I could finally figure out what she was saying. "He kept saying it, and then he'd laugh this crazy laugh. I think he's nuts."

"He cannot hurt us," I said. "A deal is a deal." I was actually skeptical. Getting out of here alive was a long shot, but I didn't want to tell Addie that.

Ever so jovial, the sheriff talked to the reverend with that silly salesman smile on his pasty face. He kept the reverend in check by dangling a carrot in front of him, the promise of everything going back to like it was, of none of this crisis mattering after this day.

How could the reverend make such a bad decision? The chatter between the sheriff and the reverend sounded scripted, as if it had been rehearsed. I felt a twinge of worry, but I kept my mouth shut.

"Riding in that little plane will give me the creeps," Addie said. "I hate being cramped in a tiny space. It's almost like a coffin."

I touched her arm and nodded. "Claustrophobic, eh?"

"Heck yeah." She glanced nervously at the Cadillacs.

We moved a little away from the others and continued talking under our breath. The bottom line of all this was to get out of here alive.

"Are you going to kill us?" Addie asked the sheriff directly.

Annoyed, the sheriff, with the planters looking on, flashed that loony smile again, then walked up to Addie and whispered something in her ear. She jerked away from him. She took offense at whatever he had said. I heard him curse before he stepped up to her again, raised a ham-like hand, and slapped her violently, sending her body against me. She didn't cry.

"Don't you do that again." I grabbed the lawman. I thought of how many countless black women had endured such cruelty and rage and had never whimpered.

"I can do whatever I want to this darkie slut," he snarled. "Mr. Uppity Northern Cullud Boy, know your place and stay in it. Come heah, girl. Come!"

Addie stood there, rooted to the ground.

"Bring her heah, Jethro," the sheriff said, putting his hands in his pockets. "I want her next to me. I don't want her to get any ideas."

One of his deputies snatched Addie by the arm and dragged her over to the lawman. That ticked me off. I reached out, turned him around, and decked him. Furious, I stood over him, wanting to hit him again. All these nutty ideas went up in smoke when I sensed a gun barrel aimed at the base of my neck.

"Is everybody going crazy?" the sheriff asked. "We should kill all of y'all. Except the boss figger it would be messy."

The sheriff made me kneel down in the mud, and then he steadied the gun and put it to my forehead this time. I was scared to death. None of these white folks liked me, anyway, an uppity Northern nigger who had come down here to cause trouble, just like Wilks. The driving rain blended with my sweat on my bare face. I remembered him slamming the gun against my head with a loud thud, metal against flesh, setting off a bright flash behind my eyes. I knew my life was over right then. I waited for the gunshot while I was down in the mud.

"Please, please don't kill him, Sheriff." The frantic voice of Addie came from above me.

Everything was coming undone. Going all to pieces. I tried to talk, tried to tell the reverend he was a fool to trust them, these darn crackers, but the words got all tangled up, and the big boy slapped him down with the butt of a shotgun. The big boy, who snatched Adele by the arm, liked violence. The reverend was motionless, barely conscious, his face shattered and bloody by the savage blow.

"We had a plan, everything was worked out, but no, you darkies had to go and spoil it," the lawman barked. "You'll be lucky if any of y'all get out of here alive."

Hearing Addie's voice far off, almost as if she was underwater, I tried to move, but my legs didn't obey. I couldn't even crawl. I didn't understand why the reverend hadn't run, especially when he saw everything was going to ruin. He should have run for his life. His head was as hard as a pine nut. He still thought he hadn't made a colossal mistake, trusting that these people would restore life to the way it had been before.

Addie was hysterical. She was shouting and screaming like she had been stabbed or worse. The sheriff was talking with Boss Chapin, who had never left the car, and she knew what that meant. Maybe their sinister intentions were to kill all of us. I knew what the boss planter had in store when the big boy loaded a sawed-off shotgun, the rain dripping off the double barrels. He started for the van to dispose of Wilks. Addie screamed and screamed and screamed.

The big boy dragged the attendant out of the van, shoved him down on the ground, and put the shotgun in his chest. The attendant crawled away. Growling, the big boy hopped into the back of the vehicle. The deadly sound overwhelmed Addie's screams. *Boom! Boom!* Jumping back out of the van, the killer ran to the sheriff like a dog dropping a bone before his master. He was shouting in an excited voice that nobody would ever be able to identify Wilks, not with his face blown off.

The Cadillacs left one by one, driving down the rutty road, moving toward the highway. Their work was done. Those inside had given orders to the sheriff to get rid of us. For some reason, as I pulled myself up, I thought about the message on the card that Dr. Smart had sent to my apartment after Terry killed herself. *If you're right and know it, speak your mind. Even if you are a minority of one, the truth is still the truth.* The quote was from the pen of Mahatma Gandhi, the Indian visionary. Dr. Martin Luther King swore by the wisdom of Gandhi. If I got out of here alive, I'd make sure that the truth would be known.

Just then, the big boy pounded me in the chest for good measure and gave me a solid lick to the cheek. I fell again. Addie was shouting again, shrill shrieks that penetrated the heart. God, I didn't want to die like this. I felt strong hands drag me to the jet as it revved up, and they hoisted me through the door and passed me to a seat near the wing. Through the window, I saw them help the battered reverend to the patrol car, and the van followed it while the jet taxied down the runway. Then I passed out.

When I awoke in a fog, Addie was holding my hand tenderly, lovingly. She smiled at me in the kindest way, whispering that the worst part was behind us, that she loved me, that all that mattered was that we were together and were going home. I thought this love thing might work better than expected. Addie was a low-maintenance gal. I wanted a love where I loved a woman more than myself. I didn't have that with Terry, but maybe it could be possible with Addie.

Then the jet shuddered from the turbulence. We were going home, finally.

DISCUSSION QUESTIONS

1. In this second novel of the "Gift" series, how do you feel Clint is coping with his overwhelming grief over the loss of his family?
2. Has the church responded to Clint's spiritual and emotional needs?
3. Why is Clint so loyal to Reverend Hickory Peck and so willing to go south to support him in his campaign to win back his church?
4. Why does Reverend Peck feel that "the prophet" Wilks is such a threat?
5. Do you believe that Reverend Wilks is a good minister or a false prophet trying to get all he can?
6. Do you believe Reverend Wilks is sincerely supportive of the poor black farmers?
7. Can Addie, the down-home schoolteacher, be a positive force in Clint's life?
8. Is Reverend Peck a willing partner in the powerful planters' sinister plan to get rid of Reverend Wilks?
9. At the end of the novel, why does Clint approve of Addie's journey to New York? Is love about to bloom between them?

UC HIS GLORY BOOK CLUB!
www.uchisglorybookclub.net

UC His Glory Book Club is the spirit-inspired brain-child of Joylynn Ross, an author and the acquisitions editor at Urban Christian, and Kendra Norman-Bellamy, an author for Urban Christian. It is an online book club that hosts authors of Urban Christian. We welcome as members all men and women who have a passion for reading Christian-based fiction.

UC His Glory Book Club pledges its commitment to providing support, positive feedback, encouragement, and a forum whereby members can openly discuss and review the literary works of Urban Christian authors.

There is no membership fee associated with UC His Glory Book Club; however, we do ask that you support the authors by purchasing their works, encouraging them, providing book reviews, and, of course, offering your prayers. We also ask that you respect our beliefs and follow the guidelines of the book club. We hope to receive your valuable input, opinions, and reviews that build up, rather than tear down, our authors.

WHAT WE BELIEVE:

—We believe that Jesus is the Christ, Son of the Living God.

—We believe that the Bible is the true, living Word of God.

—We believe that all Urban Christian authors should use their God-given writing abilities to honor God and to share the message of the written word that God has given to each of them uniquely.

—We believe in supporting Urban Christian authors in their literary endeavors by reading their titles, purchasing them, and sharing them with our online community.

—We believe that everything we do in our literary arena should be done in a manner that will lead to God being glorified and honored.

We look forward to online fellowship with you. Please visit us often at www.uchisglorybookclub.net.

Many Blessing to You!
Shelia E. Lipsey,
President, UC His Glory Book Club

ORDER FORM
URBAN BOOKS, LLC
97 N18th Street
Wyandanch, NY 11798

Name (please print):_____

Address: _____

City/State: _____

Zip: _____

QTY	TITLES	PRICE
	3:57 A.M Timing Is Everything	$14.95
	A Man's Worth	$14.95
	A Woman's Worth	$14.95
	Abundant Rain	$14.95
	After The Feeling	$14.95
	Amaryllis	$14.95
	Anointed	$14.95
	Battle of Jericho	$14.95
	Be Careful What You Pray For	$14.95
	Beautiful Ugly	$14.95
	Been There Prayed That:	$14.95
	Betrayed	$14.95

Shipping and handling-add $3.50 for 1st book, then $1.75 for each additional book.

Please send a check payable to:

Urban Books, LLC

Please allow 4-6 weeks for delivery

ORDER FORM
URBAN BOOKS, LLC
97 N18th Street
Wyandanch, NY 11798

Name(please print):_____

Address: _____

City/State: _____

Zip: _____

QTY	TITLES	PRICE
	By the Grace of God	$14.95
	Confessions Of A Preachers Wife	$14.95
	Dance Into Destiny	$14.95
	Deliver Me From My Enemies	$14.95
	Desperate Decisions	$14.95
	Divorcing the Devil	$14.95
	Faith	$14.95
	First Comes Love	$14.95
	Flaws and All	$14.95
	Forgiven	$14.95
	Former Rain	$14.95
	Forsaken	$14.95

Shipping and handling-add $3.50 for 1st book, then $1.75 for each additional book.
Please send a check payable to:
Urban Books, LLC
Please allow 4-6 weeks for delivery

ORDER FORM
URBAN BOOKS, LLC
97 N18th Street
Wyandanch, NY 11798

Name (please print):_____

Address: _____

City/State: _____

Zip: _____

QTY	TITLES	PRICE
	From Sinner To Saint	$14.95
	From The Extreme	$14.95
	God Is In Love With You	$14.95
	God Speaks To Me	$14.95
	Grace And Mercy	$14.95
	Guilty Of Love	$14.95
	Happily Ever Now	$14.95
	Heaven Bound	$14.95
	His Grace His Mercy	$14.95
	His Woman His Wife His Widow	$14.95
	Illusions	$14.95
	In Green Pastures	$14.95

Shipping and handling-add $3.50 for 1st book, then $1.75 for each additional book.
Please send a check payable to:
Urban Books, LLC
Please allow 4-6 weeks for delivery